A Lady of Embers

Fires of the Fae
Book One

Erin O'Kane

A Lady of Embers

Fires of the Fae

Book One

By

Erin O'Kane

Copyright © 2021 Erin O'Kane
A Lady of Embers, Fires of the Fae, Book One
First publication: 2021
Editing by Elemental Editing & Proofreading
Proofreading by Norma's Nook Proofreading, LLC
Cover by Jodielocks Designs
Formatting by Kaila Duff
All rights reserved. Except for use in any review, the reproduction or utilisation of this work, in whole or in part, in any form by any electronic, mechanical, or other means now known or hereafter invented, is forbidden without the written permission of the publisher.
This is a work of fiction. Any resemblance to places, events or real people are entirely coincidental.
Published by Erin O'Kane
erin.okaneauthor@gmail.com

CONTENTS

Prologue	1
Chapter 1	3
Chapter 2	16
Chapter 3	33
Chapter 4	46
Chapter 5	61
Chapter 6	81
Chapter 7	99
Chapter 8	113
Chapter 9	131
Chapter 10	154
Chapter 11	172
Chapter 12	189
Chapter 13	206
Chapter 14	221
Chapter 15	239
Chapter 16	255
Chapter 17	276
Chapter 18	288
Epilogue	301
Afterword	303
Acknowledgments	305
Also by Erin O'Kane	307
About the Author	309

*To everyone who needs an escape from reality.
This one is for you.*

Prologue

Deep in the south, in the foothills of Morrowmer, the earth quakes, and a corridor to a strange new land appears.

In the fae domain, a monstrous being that has been sleeping for centuries awakens. His bloodlust, despite the long slumber, has not been sated. He has been waiting for his time, and as the mountains separating it from Morrowmer are cleaved in half, the being smiles cruelly. The prophecy is in motion, and soon, he will be free.

Nothing is ever going to be the same again.

Chapter 1

The smoke from the fire stings my nose and burns my eyes, my keen fae senses both a blessing and a curse. Thanks to my heritage, I can hear much farther than humans, but in this crowded refugee camp, a myriad of sounds constantly fills my mind, making it difficult to discern one noise from another.

Queuing with the other refugees, I patiently wait for my food. I don't mind waiting, I get to stand near the fire and warm my chilled hands. It's freezing here, the frigid air finding every bit of my exposed skin. I can't even imagine how they survive in the northern camps. Pulling my thin cloak tighter around my body, I ensure my hood is still in place, and most importantly, that it's covering my ears. It's not good to stand out in places like this, and I know my looks and elvish ears will draw attention.

I'm not the only elf in the camp, but I specifically travelled north, away from the elves in the south. Any who made their way here have a reason—most likely chased by the demons of their past—and want to be left alone as much as I do. Tensions between elves and humans are still high despite the peaceful outcome of the war, so I keep my head down and avoid trouble to remain unnoticed.

The humans I stand with ignore me, which is exactly as I prefer it. Glancing around and using my hood as a buffer, I take in the camp. Like the previous camps I visited, they are noisy, smelly, and full of desperate people. The large bonfire in the middle of the site is a hub of activity, the tents surrounding it occupied by the leaders and the healers. Ahead, the food tent beckons, but I wait my turn in the seemingly endless line. Everything here is grey, even the mud beneath my boots, like all the colour and happiness has been sucked from this place. There isn't much to be joyful about in these camps. Desperation can make monsters of men, and even the most upstanding citizens can do awful things if it will protect their families.

The line moves slowly, taking me from the warmth of the bonfire, but the prospect of food, of filling my cramping, empty stomach keeps me moving. Reaching the front of the queue, I accept the bowl handed to me and approach today's chef. He's big in every sense of the word with an attitude just as large. As I lift my head, holding out my bowl to receive my food, he sneers at me, noticing my fae-like features despite the hood I'm wearing. He empties his ladle into my bowl before scowling at me. I wait for another second, since he's only given me a third of the daily rations, but I don't say anything as he continues to stare me down. Biting back my retort, I simply turn and exit the tent.

I'm used to this behaviour. Most of the refugees keep their distance once they realise what I am, but some glare, snarl, and spit as I pass. The worst of them sling verbal abuse my way and occasionally throw items, hoping to injure me. After a close encounter in my first camp, I learned that I needed to have a shield around me at all times. It's exhausting to constantly use my power in this way, but it keeps me safe. No one here has been outwardly hostile yet, and I've managed to avoid the gangs of males who prowl about, looking for their next victim to torment. I think they fear me.

Taking my meagre meal, I leave the main area of the camp and enter the woods that flank us. It's calmer out here, and the humans tend to avoid the forest. I've heard their tales, which are merely scary stories used to make children behave, but they seem to believe them, thinking the woods are full of foul beasts who will tear them limb from limb if they leave the safety of camp.

I don't believe their stories, but even so, I don't venture far, just enough so the noise of the camp fades to a low din. Finding a felled tree, I sit and grimace at the food that's supposed to sustain me until this evening. The grey gruel looks as unappealing as it smells, but I'm used to the humans' bland cooking by now, and I'm not stupid enough to refuse it. I need to maintain my strength and keep my wits about me. Eating slowly to stretch out the food, I attempt to trick my stomach into thinking I'm eating a full meal. I scrape the bottom of the bowl clean with a sigh before resting it on my knee.

A strange, unnatural screech fills the air, causing me to jump up and scan the forest behind me. I've heard that sound before, causing memories to flood my mind.

The ground rolls and bucks beneath me. I'm near the edge of the forest by the mountains. I've heard of earthquakes, but only in the north of Morrowmer, not in the south where I currently am. Crouching low, I grab onto the nearest tree trunk as the ground continues to rumble. With an almighty roar, everything shakes, and I'm thrown to the dirt.

The world falls silent, so I hesitantly stand and slowly creep forward, my gaze flicking around, looking for any threats. When I reach the edge of the forest, my breath leaves me in a rush. The mountains still stand before me, but they look like they have been severed in two, and between the two halves of the mountain is a pathway.

This shouldn't be here. Yet, somehow, just when I needed an escape, one appeared. Do I take it?

I've heard stories that the mountains were the only barrier keeping the foul creatures of the fae lands from Morrowmer. Were those stories true? With a shudder I step back from the mysterious chasm. I go to return to the forest when a piercing shriek rents the air. My head whips around, and I narrow my eyes on the crack in the mountains, backing away slowly. I don't observe anything coming through it, but I don't want to wait around to see if it does.

Once in the safety of the trees, I finally turn my back on the mountains and start running once more.

Blinking, I emerge from the memory, my stomach twisting and threatening to expel the meal I just consumed. Taking deep breaths, I scan the area for danger. I can't see anything, and the noise was far away, only able to be heard by those with enhanced hearing.

Suddenly, I remember overhearing one of the camp leaders saying they received a message from a southern camp disclosing they had been attacked, leaving many dead or taken. They mentioned beasts with claws and fangs. I hadn't taken it seriously, since humans are superstitious beings, but now I'm not so sure.

Mountains that once acted as a barrier from fae lands were cleaved in half. By what, I have no idea, but when I saw the magical corridor connecting the two lands, a fear like no other filled me. I've known my fair share of terror and pain under the hands of my last master, so I've learned to trust my instincts.

Legends of what lies beyond the mountains are enough to scare anyone, the tales detailing creatures that were once distantly related to us but have turned into beasts over time.

Shuddering, I turn from the forest and walk back to camp, trying to keep my footsteps steady and even. If I hurry into camp looking like I'm running away from something, then people will start asking questions, and I want to avoid that sort of attention. Reaching the line of tents marking the boundary of the camp, I release a quiet sigh of relief.

I deposit my empty bowl with the others before I begin the trek to my tent. Keeping my head down, I walk silently, my cloak billowing around me from the icy wind whistling through the encampment. I'm almost back at my tent when I hear it—a muffled scream.

Freezing, I bite my lip as I debate what to do. I should walk on, not draw attention to myself. After all, no one would help me if the situation was reversed. Steeling myself, I erect the wall that kept me going through years of torture and kidnapping, and then I start to move away.

The scream sounds again, this time ending with a sob. This is what breaks me. Closing my eyes, I extend my senses, listening for the quiet noises that most in the camp wouldn't hear. The muffled cry, the hissing of her attackers, the tear of cloth. My eyes snap open, and like an avenging angel, I stalk through the camp, my resolve making me strong. Winding through the maze of tents, I ignore the onlookers' shocked expressions. They must have seen the woman being dragged away, yet they did nothing but turn a blind eye to the situation. Ever-present anger stirs to life in my gut at their lack of action, but I push it down, needing a clear head.

Before I reach them, I look within myself and reach for my power, humming as I find my shield still in place. All elves have power that resides inside them, and while mine is weak, it helps protect me against the powerless humans.

I find them at the far edge of the camp. They have not even left the clearing, their fear of the forest proving stronger than their desire for privacy—or perhaps they just don't care if they are overheard. These camps are dangerous, especially for lone women, but many of us don't have a choice, since being alone in the wild is even more risky.

There are three of them. Two of them hold down the gagged, bound woman. Although she's sobbing behind her gag, their victim is fighting like a mountain cat. She's doing everything to free herself, thrashing around on the ground and refusing to accept this fate. They really have to put their weight into it to keep her restrained. The third man leans over her, tearing at her modest dress so her pale breasts spill out. Lust gleams in the eyes of the men as disgust twists my stomach.

"Enough." Although my voice is quiet, it holds authority.

The attackers finally realise they are not alone, their gazes jumping to me. The two men pinning the woman look nervous, and I don't blame them. I've got a bit of a reputation. It's unfounded, all based on rumours, but that doesn't matter to them, and right now, it works for me. My hood casts my upper face in shadow, so although I can see them, they can only see my pale nose and lips.

The third man, the one who ripped the woman's dress, takes one look at me and sneers, dismissing me as a threat. I've met men like him before, thinking women are the weaker sex. I've enjoyed proving them wrong.

When I don't move and simply stare them down, the man spits at me. It bounces harmlessly off my shield, making him glower. "Get out of here, freak."

I don't move. The men holding the woman start shifting anxiously, glancing at each other, and I smirk at their quiet whispers.

Seeing my lips twitch, the leader finally climbs off the woman and stands, taking a menacing step towards me. His eyes rove up and down my form, not that he can see much thanks to my cloak, but I shudder anyway. Seeing the movement, he smiles, thinking he's won.

"Oh, so you want to be next?" In a move I'm sure passes for fast in the human world, he reaches out to grab me, only to come into contact with my shield. I grit my teeth against the force, adding a bit more of my power to reinforce it. The man is blown backwards, repelled by the protective shield. He lands flat on his back, staring up at the sky, stunned. My shield doesn't usually have the power to throw someone like that, but my anger fuels me.

Turning my head, I give the final two men my attention. I pull at the last of my reserves, willing a white glow to surround me so brightly they have to shield their eyes. Dimming the light enough so they can see me, I take another step forward.

"Let her go."

This time they listen, releasing the woman, scrambling to their feet, and running through the gap in the tents. The leader seems to have regained his senses and sits upright. Glancing at my figure and the soft glow that still surrounds me, he sneers once again as he gets to his feet, but I see the fear in his eyes.

"You'll regret this, freak," he snarls, glaring once at the woman on the ground. He turns and runs away, following the same path his friends used just moments ago.

The woman stares at me with fear in her eyes as she struggles to sit up. The light around me vanishes in a blink, and slowly, so as not to spook her, I walk to her side and kneel when I reach her. "Are you hurt?" My voice is soft, melodic, and after such a long time of not being able to speak, not hearing myself talk, the sound still surprises me.

She shakes her head, but I can already see the bruises forming on her arms and shoulders, and her cheek is red with a handprint. I suspect the blow to her pride hurts more than her physical injuries right now, but it aches to see her hurt like this.

Reaching forward, I untie the gag in her mouth and the bindings around her wrists. She reaches up and tries to pull the ruins of her bodice together, covering her naked chest. Without giving it a second thought, I unfasten the binding at my neck and release my cloak, pulling it from my shoulders and offering it to her. Her eyes widen as she takes in my elvish features and my pointed ears. I think she's going to reject my offer, but with shaking hands, she takes it and pulls it around her.

Nodding my head, I turn to leave, knowing she's not comfortable around me.

"Thank you." Her voice wobbles, and I know the reality of what just happened has hit her and she's thinking of all the awful things that could have occurred if I hadn't stepped in.

Meeting her gaze, I nod again, this time in acknowledgement. As I step away, I hear her ragged breaths. I glance over my shoulder, seeing her climb to her feet, her whole body shaking with adrenaline.

Leave the poor girl alone, Annalise.

The thought spins around in my head. I know that's what I should do, but there's a part of my soul that can't just leave her. Perhaps it's the part that wishes someone had done something like this for me.

You're going to get yourself in trouble, my conscience warns again, and I'm sure it's right, yet...

"Shall I escort you back to your tent?"

She seems surprised that I asked and quickly shakes her head. No, she doesn't want my help. For the third time, I nod, a habit I'm still trying to break after my years in captivity. I disappear between the tents. Only, I don't leave. I watch from afar and follow her back, ensuring she reaches her tent unharmed. I know she doesn't want my help, but I need to be certain she's safe.

When she slips inside her tent, I release a sigh. Now without a cloak, many people stare at me. The fine hair on my arms stands on end, not only from the numerous sets of eyes on me, but also the cold wind that whips around my body. Making my way to the makeshift well, I grab one of the buckets and scoop out enough water to last me for the day. To call it a well is an overstatement, but it's all we have. It's a hole in the ground with a waterproof lining, and whoever is on water duty for the day has to trudge to the nearest spring and drag back buckets of water to fill it.

I get a couple of dirty looks as I take the water, but no one stops me. Walking back to my tent with my bucket, I ignore the stares but silently wish I hadn't given away my cloak. My tent is at the opposite end of the camp from the food tent, right on the edge. Everyone is supposed to share, but it turns out people would rather sleep in an overcrowded tent than share one with an elf.

After what feels like a lifetime, I reach my tent. Pushing through the entrance, I look at my measly possessions, which are so at odds with where I lived before. I will gladly live in this paper-thin tent in the freezing land between the mountains and the forest, however, if it means I am free and don't have to live in that gilded prison.

Setting the bucket down, I remove my boots by the entrance, not wanting to tread mud into the space. Most of the tent is taken up by my thin bedroll and blankets, but I have a pack which holds the rest of my possessions. There isn't much inside save borrowed spare clothes. When I escaped and fled the elvish city of Galandell, I left with only the clothes on my back, choosing to leave anything from my past behind. Besides, in these camps, valuables tend to go missing fairly quickly.

Lowering onto my bedding, I roll my neck and rub at the gooseflesh on my arms, trying to warm myself. I'm starting to really regret giving my cloak away, but I couldn't just leave the poor girl exposed like that. Humming in the back of my throat, I reach for the bucket to scoop some water into my hand, but I stop as I catch sight of my reflection.

I barely recognise myself. When I was in captivity, the elf I was forced to work for liked us to look a certain way. Most high elves have the palest blonde or white hair, so I stood out with my long, brown locks. She cast magic over me to make me more 'aesthetically pleasing,' causing me to look the same as the others. As soon as the spell broke, my hair returned to its natural state.

My blue eyes and pale skin look the same. I reach up and brush my fingers over my rose-pink lips. They are delicate, and the skin is unmarred, perfect even.

I scream as I'm dragged away. I didn't choose this, didn't want this, yet I've been chosen anyway. It's because I heard something I shouldn't have. I was in the wrong place at the wrong time.

"It's an honour to serve me, you should be proud." Her cultured voice rolls over me, making me want to vomit at the prospect of serving her for eternity.

I've seen what happens to her ladies-in-waiting, and now it's about to happen to me. Struggling against the two guards holding me, I throw my weight against them, but they barely budge an inch. "No, please!" I'm not too proud to beg, and as I look up into her serene face, I feel a flash of hope. "I won't tell anyone, I swear it."

Her nose wrinkles like she just saw something displeasing. "I won't miss that voice of yours," is her only reply, her tone light as if she's discussing the weather. She turns her attention to the guards, the corners of her lips curling up into a cruel smile. "Hold her down, this one's going to fight."

"No!" I scream, struggling all the more against the tightening grips as I'm dragged back. Suddenly, my lips are sealed shut, cutting off my cries. Only muffled noises escape me as tears roll down my face. Next to me, I see another elf heating a needle over a fire until it's red hot. He turns and walks closer, a grim smile on his face as he leans forward.

"This may hurt."

Yanking myself out of the memory, I fall back onto my bedding, my heart pounding and chest heaving with my panicked breaths.

You're safe. You escaped, you're safe, I repeat over and over until my heart rate and breathing return to normal. I can't stop myself from reaching up and touching my lips again, reassuring myself they are whole.

That was the first day of my captivity, and they took away my voice, crudely sewing my mouth together with thread and magic.

Pushing away the thoughts that threaten to consume me once more, I lean forward and splash cold water on my face, refusing to let them have that power over me any longer. Despite that, a familiar feeling flows through my veins, knotting my stomach—the need to flee, to pick up my pack and run. I try to sort through my thoughts.

Maybe it is time to move on. I've been here for at least six weeks now, far longer than I've stayed in the other camps, and after my little stunt with those men who attacked the woman... That little piece of me that always seems to know when I'm in danger throbs in my chest. Yes, it's time to leave, but I don't think I'm in any immediate danger and the sun will be setting soon. It would be foolish to depart in the dark, as there are far worse things prowling the forests at night than those men. I'll leave in the morning. I don't know where I'll go yet, but I've heard people talk of another camp not too far from here.

Sure, I'm just an unknown elf refugee, and I look different due to my hair returning to its natural colour, but I can't risk them finding me. I can't ever return home, not that it feels that way now thanks to the atrocities committed by my captor. Nowhere is safe for me anymore, which is why I have to keep moving. In the beginning, I had a few narrow escapes when guards from Galandell showed up at refugee camps looking for me, but I managed to flee before anyone connected the dots. It's been a while since anyone has come for me, but I can't let my guard down. I'm sure they are still searching for me. They'll always look for me because I killed my captor.

I killed the elf queen.

Chapter 2

I spend the rest of the day in my tent. I've not been assigned any camp duties, so my time is mine to spend as I wish. Lying on my bedroll, I extend my fae senses and listen to what's going on around me. I can hear every little detail of what my neighbours are doing. Most of it is mundane chatter, but occasionally I'll pick up some useful information.

Footsteps catch my attention. The camp is full of people, so a single set of footfalls shouldn't make me wary, but there's something about them that has me sitting up and tilting my head to one side as I listen harder. They are light and tentative, like they are trying not to be seen. They come nearer, and I hold my breath, poised to run if I need to. The person hurries over to my tent, and then seems to hesitate. I hear their breathlessness and their fear fills the air. What are they doing that's causing such a reaction?

Then, as quickly as they arrive, they run away. Frowning, I wait a few seconds, allowing them plenty of time to get out of sight, and then I crawl towards the exit. I stick my head through the tent flaps, my eyes widening slightly when I see what awaits me on the ground—my cloak. Glancing around, I try to see if I can spot the deliverer, but they are gone. I grab the cloak and retreat into the tent, smiling down at the fabric. It must have been the girl I helped. She risked a lot by bringing it to me. If someone saw her, it would make life much more difficult for her.

As I unroll the cloak, something falls from the bundle and lands in my lap. Making a small noise of surprise, I reach for the item. It's half a loaf of bread. My stomach growls, reminding me that all I've eaten today is a small portion of gruel. I want to tear into it like a feral beast, but I force myself to pull off pieces and eat it slowly. She must have given me her ration. If her family finds out, she'll be in trouble, but I'm grateful for her act of gratitude.

My body has become thin and bony thanks to a life on the run and small portions of food. And my magic... it's been weakened. As a prisoner forced to work as a silent lady-in-waiting to the queen, my magic was muted by another spell, allowing me to use it for small, menial tasks. When it returned after I killed the queen, I was shocked by how frail it had become. Like a muscle, if you don't use your power regularly, it becomes weak. Other than shielding myself, which takes almost all of my energy, I haven't been able to practice, so it's stayed this way.

The sun has finally set, and I can hear people heading towards the heart of the camp. It's time for dinner.

With a small, rare smile, I pull on my returned cloak, making sure the fastenings at the neck are properly fixed in place. Pulling on my boots, I exit my tent and stand up straight, letting the fabric fall around me. The cloak covers most of the simple, pale blue dress I'm wearing—another borrowed item of clothing. Pulling up the hood, I cover most of my features, and a sense of security surrounds me.

While I was a prisoner, I was forced to wear a cloak. Its wide, large hood covered pretty much all of my face, and I was only allowed to remove it at the queen's behest, so it would be easy to assume I might never want to wear a hood again. Initially, I swore I would never touch one after I escaped, but I gathered too much attention from those in camp who were struggling to understand that the war between humans and elves was over.

Recovering from the atrocities of the elf queen and the battle that followed, Morrowmer is a nation of divided people. For centuries, the elves and humans were at war, and no one remembered why or how it started. Then, our goddess, Menishea, the Great Mother, chose her beloved to unite us. A half-human, half-elf slave girl who knew nothing of her heritage or family.

The elf queen, my captor, had been dabbling in evil, dark magic gifted to her by a forgotten god. The power turned beings into undead vessels who would follow her every order, known as the forsaken. The Great Mother guided her chosen one, and ultimately, the beloved risked her life in a battle to save us all.

Although the beloved was victorious with her mates at her side, many died, both humans and elves, but the high elves took the biggest hit, and our numbers were drastically depleted. The human king was imprisoned for his crimes and for helping the elf queen, and since then, chaos has befallen the human capital of Arhaven. The city had already been rife with crime, and the divide between rich and poor was vast. This only increased, the poor and those in the slums suffering the worst. Many fled the capital to escape it, and based on the stories I've heard survivors whisper, I don't blame them for trading a home for living in camps like this.

Walking between the tents, I make my way to the middle and join the queue outside the food tent. A huge human male catches my attention as I wait. Frowning slightly, I turn my head and try to watch him from the safety of my hood, attempting to make the action look natural. The last thing I need is to attract attention from someone like him.

I've not seen him here before. He stands taller than the others, his muscles bulging and gleaming in the firelight. He's clothed in a lot fewer layers than the rest of us, wearing a sleeveless smock, tight trousers, and a whole arsenal of weapons strapped to his back. I spy tattoos wrapping around the tops of his arms, and I recognise who he is. He's one of the tribesmen from the mountains. They are a tough, hardy people, living high up in the mountains in small travelling clans. He's certainly not someone to mess with.

The queue moves, and I look away as I step forward. What is someone from the tribes doing down here? They helped during the battle, as well as assisting with some of the rebuilding afterward, but most of them returned to their tribes. He's not a refugee, is he? He's talking to some of the camp leaders, the deep timbre of his voice reaching me. I shouldn't listen in, but I can't help myself.

"My tribe is north, at the far edge of Morrowmer. We've been hearing strange noises from the fae lands for many years. We know not to cross the mountain border." His voice deepens, and I shudder at his implication—cross the mountains and die. "However, recently, things have changed. There have been sightings of beasts. They have never come so close to the mountains before, but now they are pushing the boundaries, getting bolder. One of my scouts went missing after checking the boundary."

Beasts, and not just any, but *fae* beasts. Mothers tell scary stories of the creatures beyond the mountains to make their children behave, but I know at a soul-deep level that this warning is nothing to wave away.

"We appreciate the warning, but the fae lands are not our problem. We don't even venture into the mountains, let alone beyond them."

My stomach sinks at the camp leader's response. Surely they can't be so ignorant? If the creatures from the fae lands have found their way into the mountains, they will eventually leave the mountains. As a camp full of scattered, lost people without homes, we wouldn't stand a chance.

"A path has opened between the two lands—a strange, magical corridor. You should be on your guard," the tribesman warns.

"So it's true? We heard rumours about the mountains being cleaved in half…"

I feel a kernel of hope. Perhaps they will take this seriously and place guards around the camp, or move farther inland to put some space between us and the mountains. If they were to communicate with the other camps, they could share information about sightings.

"But that's in the south, we'll be fine here."

The hope that had been blooming inside me shrivels at the camp leader's dismissive comment. I can sense his fear from here, and instead of doing the sensible thing, he's burying that angst and replacing it with denial.

"Fools." The tribesman's voice is full of disgust, and

when I glance over, I see him sneering down at the leaders. "Have you not heard of the raids on other camps? Survivors reported that strange beasts with fangs and claws attacked them."

"It could have been something from the forest, that's not proof they were beasts from the other side."

Many different fae creatures live in forests, but they don't tend to leave their homes. For the camps to have been attacked... this wasn't a creature native to Morrowmer.

The tribesman doesn't say anything for a long moment, and even *I* start to feel awkward, so I can't imagine what it's like to be under his disapproving stare. "You're not even going to warn them, are you?" The anger in his voice makes me pause, causing those in the queue behind me to mutter under their breaths, but I pay them no mind. "I pray for mercy on you and everyone here. You're fools."

I turn to watch the mountain man, unable to look away. He strides away from the camp leaders, his face twisted in anger. Sensing my attention, his eyes flick to me. I should look away, but I can't, my gaze is trapped by his. He knows I was listening, that I heard every word. He walks right up to me, scanning my face. "If you're sensible, elf, you'll leave this place. You're not safe here."

If I needed any other excuse to leave, he just gave it to me. I remember the strange screech I heard earlier and the eerie feeling I had when I witnessed the cleaving. Staying silent, I dip my head in acknowledgment and thanks. He searches my face for a moment then turns and strides away.

The line moves forward again, and I move with it on autopilot until I finally reach the tent. Numbly, I take my bowl of stew and the small lump of bread before heading to one of the logs placed around the fire in the middle of the camp.

I eat in silence. The stew is relatively tasteless, and I don't even want to know what poor creature they used for the 'meat stew.' It's food, though, and I'm going to need all the sustenance I can get for my journey tomorrow. I'm not stupid enough to leave the camp at night, especially after what the tribesman said. He's not changed my plans, but he proved my gut feeling was right. It's time to move on.

Someone appears in the corner of my vision before sitting at the end of the log. I know who it is without having to check. As one of the only other elves in the camp, the wood elf always joins me by the fire in the evenings. We've never spoken, but as a social pariah like me, I suppose he gets some comfort from being around another elf.

"You heard?"

I freeze for a second, surprised the wood elf is speaking to me. However, I know what he means without having to ask for clarification. Turning my head, I meet his deep green eyes, which are the colour of the forest. His skin is a dark brown, and if I look carefully enough, I can see his flesh actually appears more like tree bark. Like me, he wears a cloak with the hood up, so I've never seen more of his features than brief flashes of his face, but I imagine his hair is brown or another natural colour.

While high elves look much like humans with enhanced features, the wood elves stand out much more. They worship nature and live as one with the forest, and their bodies often *become* like the plants they so dearly love. The sea elves also look different, their skin so dark it nearly looks blue in certain light. Their bodies have also adapted to their surroundings, with strong, powerful legs and webbed fingers and toes perfect for swimming in the ocean. However, I've not seen a sea elf since the battle six months ago.

With a quick glance around us, I make sure no one else is listening before bobbing my head once in response.

"Those attacks were no creatures from the forest." There's a note of anger in his voice, but I believe him. If anyone would know, it would be a wood elf. Their connection to the land and the creatures that live there is legendary.

"You're leaving?" I ask, my voice scratchy from lack of use.

"I don't know. I don't have anywhere else to go."

I've never asked why he left the Great Forest where the wood elves reside, but I've wondered. I've met some high elves in the camps, but never a wood elf before him. His people are a peaceful race who generally just want to be left alone with nature, so something must have chased him from his home.

"I'm heading north." I don't know why I'm telling him this. I'm better off alone, without any attachments to anyone. It's safer that way. Yet I can't help offering up the information when I see the pain in his eyes.

There's a pause as he considers the same issues and concerns I have, staring down at his empty bowl. "We could travel together. Safety in numbers," he suggests, finally lifting his gaze to mine. "At least until you reach your destination."

Travelling is unsafe, especially for a female elf, but over the last six months, I've learned how to fend for myself. Having a companion, at least for the journey, may make things easier. In the end, it's his hesitation and the quick, added on comment that convince me.

"I leave at first light," I tell him, not confirming or rejecting his offer, instead giving him an out if he changes his mind. He nods slowly and returns to staring at the fire.

Now that I've finished my stew, I have no reason to remain in the hub of the camp where people are watching me. Pushing up from the log, I return my bowl to the food tent and make my way back to my shelter. Away from the fire, the frigid air and freezing wind wrap around me, causing my breath to mist. I speed up my steps and thank the Great Mother that my cloak was returned to me.

Reaching my tent, I climb inside and close the entrance behind me. I glance into the bucket and notice I've got enough water to last me through the night, so I shouldn't need to leave my tent again unless it's to relieve myself. Removing my cloak and boots, I settle on my bedding and make sure my pack is ready for the trip tomorrow.

Finally, with nothing else to do, I curl up under my covers and try to force myself to sleep.

Screaming wakes me.

Jolting upright with my heart pounding in my chest, I hurriedly pull on my cloak and shuffle to the exit, yanking on my boots.

The screams continue, the sounds speaking of pure terror. An orange glow lights up the side of my tent like something's on fire. Is that what's happened? There's a fire in the camp? I should stay in my tent where it's safe, but I can't seem to help myself. Something inside of me is urging me to get out, to *run*. Pounding footsteps pass my tent, and I hear someone crying out for mercy. Then the snarling begins. It's definitely not a fire then. Remembering what the tribesman warned, I feel my blood turn cold.

Reaching for my pack, I put it on under my cloak and hurry from the tent. My eyes widen at the scene before me.

It's pandemonium.

People are running everywhere.

Tents have been set alight, and I can feel the heat from the blaze even at the edge of the camp, but that's not what fills me with fear. Huge, beastly bodies chase down those who run. Some of the creatures prowl on all fours, and others pursue with a speed that even my eyes can't track. Swallowing down the nausea, I run along the edge of the camp, peering between tents to make sure my eyes aren't playing tricks on me. I watch as a man is thrown to the ground and pounced on by one of the creatures. It rears back, opening its jaws wide, and with the fire burning behind it, I clearly see its sharp, elongated fangs before they sink into its victim. Horns protrude from its shaggy, almost mane-like hair, and I have to look away as it mauls the man on the ground. I wince as the screaming is abruptly cut off.

The tribesman was right. The beasts from the fae lands are already here. I need to flee, there's no way I can fight off those creatures. My power is weak, and I have no weapon, so my best chance is to run and not look back. Yet as I turn to leave, a hysterical sob reaches me.

Leave now, my mind urges. *They wouldn't stop to help you if the situation was reversed.*

Even as weak as I am, though, I'm better prepared to

defend against these attackers. I'm faster than the humans, and I may be able to help some of them escape...

Thoughts like that are going to get you killed, Annalise.

I hesitate, my self-preservation warring with the need to help, to do *something*. Biting down on my lip hard enough to break the skin, I make my decision.

I hurry through the ruined tents, keeping low and hiding in the shadows. In the chaos, I manage to go mostly unseen. Looking around, I pray to the Mother for wisdom and guidance. I don't even know where to begin, as someone's in trouble everywhere I look.

You were stupid to think you could help. What are you going to do against beasts like that?

A tug in my gut interrupts my thoughts. I can't quite explain it, but sometimes I know things I shouldn't, like the Mother is guiding me. Frowning, I tentatively follow the tug until I find a young man being dragged away by one of the beasts at the edge of camp. The creature's long claws are hooked into the man's shoulder, and as it walks away on two legs, its victim is pulled along behind him. The man's cries of terror and pain disperse any thoughts I had of running away. There's no way I could leave him at the mercy of that *beast*.

Moving forward, I reach the edge of camp and gather my power in my fists. The human sees me before his attacker does. His eyes widen, and I don't miss his whispered plea for help.

"Stop." My voice is quiet compared to the riot of noise surrounding us, but my suspicions that the creature would hear me are proven correct.

He turns around with a growl, and I get a glimpse of its face. At one point he might have looked like a high elf, but his bronze skin is mottled with scars, and the anger and bloodlust on his face have twisted his features so he looks more like a wild animal than anything recognisable as fae. Horns protrude from his dark shaggy hair, and fangs hang over his bottom lip.

Yanking his claws from the human's shoulder, he snarls and stalks towards me.

Fear floods my veins, but I refuse to let it debilitate me. Holding up my hands, I strengthen my barrier around me and let a little light enter my palms, hoping in vain it will scare off the beast prowling closer. My little show only seems to amuse him, his snarl twisting into a cruel smile. Without warning, he charges towards me, and I only have the time to send a pulse of power towards him. He knocks into my shield, leaping back as his skin sizzles —whether from the contact or my pulse of power, I'm unsure. I stumble from the force of his hit but manage to stay upright. However, in the process, my hood falls back, revealing my face.

"Well, well, well. We have ourselves a hero," a smooth, accented voice calls out, causing me to gasp and spin. There hadn't been anyone beside me a second ago, I would have felt their presence. Now, a tall fae stands only inches away, his arms crossed as he watches me.

He has the same tanned skin and tawny hair as the other beasts, except his hair is shorter and smoothed back. That isn't what makes him stand out however, it's the way he holds himself. He has a confident expression that borders on a smirk, but he doesn't have the cruel gleam in his eyes like the rest of his beasts. Wearing trousers and a dark tunic, he seems more refined compared to the others who are hunched over and sporting shredded trousers and not much else. Power surrounds him and almost oozes from his pores. I've never felt power like it.

Whoever this is, I'd bet everything that he's in charge of this raiding party.

The mystery fae's gaze travels up my body, but when he gets to my face, his eyes widen in shock.

The creature that bounced off my shield climbs back to his feet and starts to stalk towards me, only to come to a stop when he sees the male at my side. He dips his head in reverence, confirming my theory that the new fae is in charge. Straightening, the beast's eyes fall on me and the twisted snarl on his face disappears. "*Ma promessa.*" The words sound twisted coming from his mouth, yet the unintelligible utterance still sends a tingle through me. I look away from the expression of shocked awe etched on his face. It's making me uncomfortable.

Besides, the beast is no longer the most dangerous creature in the area. Staring up at the fae by my side, I slowly take a few measured steps backward. I have no doubt that this strange male could kill me with a snap of his fingers. Tilting his head to one side, he watches me with a calculating smile on his face. "Maybe this raid will be more fruitful than it first seemed."

Fear and dread twist in my gut. Horrific, terrifying scenarios start playing out in my mind, and all the screams, growling, and other noises from the attack disappear. I take another step back, knowing it's pointless, but I can't stop that urge, that need to flee. Like a startled rabbit, I spin on my heel, and using every ounce of supernatural strength and speed I possess, I run.

It was never going to work, not against a fae who has so much power it practically pours from him—not to mention the camp is still flooded with these foreign beasts —but I had to try.

The creature that had been about to maul the young human man pounces forward on a silent command, grabbing my shoulder in a move quicker than I can comprehend, shattering my weak shield. I'm yanked to a stop, the long claws tearing into the flesh of my upper arm. Frantically, I reach for my reserves of power, but I only have enough to make a flimsy barrier over my skin, zapping the creature in whose grasp I'm still trapped. It only seems to annoy him. Snarling, he raises his free arm and backhands me. The move rocks my whole body, twisting the claws embedded in my shoulder. Blades of agony rack my frame, the pain so fierce that starlight flashes in front of my eyes.

Don't pass out, Annalise. You can't escape if you're unconscious.

Although I know escape is futile at this point, the force of the thought is enough to make me grit my teeth and take deep breaths through my nose. The beast holding me snarls again, raising his fist, and I prepare myself for another blow.

"Stop!" Power radiates from the tall fae, and my body freezes against my will. I realise the beast holding me is also frozen, his arm elevated and hovering in the air midswing. My eyes flick to the leader, and I watch as he slowly, unhurriedly, walks towards us. My fear of him rises. He managed to freeze two fae without moving a finger. "Don't kill her, we need her."

As he reaches us, he stares down at me intently for what feels like a lifetime but is probably only a couple of seconds. He rests his hand against my stinging cheek with a surprising gentleness I hadn't expected from him.

Everything inside me is screaming to get away from him, and had I not been stuck in place, I would have recoiled from his touch.

The invisible force restraining me suddenly disappears. Although I'm grateful to have my mobility back, this also means that the beast holding me is free. Yanking his claws from my shoulder, he spins and snarls at the fae in retaliation, not taking kindly to being bound. I think they are going to fight, but even I can feel the tall fae calling more power to him, his eyes turning dark as he arches a single eyebrow. "Remember your place," he warns the beast.

Shockingly, the beast agrees, bowing his head low. "Yes, my apologies, Elijah." The disgust in his voice at having to back down is obvious, but I'm too caught on the other bit of information.

Elijah. Finally, a name for this powerful male.

My breath is taken from me as the claws are removed from my upper arm, and I want to sag to the ground from the pain, but I force myself to keep standing. Elijah continues to stare at the beast, and from the look in his eye, he appears as though he's contemplating simply killing him.

"I will not go with you."

My declaration surprises them, and frankly, I surprise myself with the steel and determination that rings from the words. Never mind that my body quakes with pain and fear, and that I get the feeling my whole world is about to implode once again. Raising my uninjured arm, I press my hand against the wound, unable to hold back the sharp intake of breath as agony radiates from my shoulder.

Of course Elijah sees right through me. His eyes flick

from my face to my shaking arms and back to my eyes. There's a slight frown between his brows, but it quickly disappears, a smirk curving his lips.

"I'm afraid, *ma promessa*, you don't have a choice." His attention returns to the creature on my left, who's still bowing his head. His hands are balled into fists at his sides, the muscles in his neck cording, and I realise he's not still bowing out of choice, but because Elijah is *making* him, his power wrapped around the beast. Is it a punishment for his actions, or a show of power to scare me? If it's the latter, he needn't have bothered. I'm fully aware of how powerful he is compared to me, and unfortunately, fear isn't something I'm lacking.

"Bind her and tell the others to clean up here," Elijah orders, and then frees the beast from the magic containing him. Elijah's attention returns to me. "It's time to go home."

The creature at my side snarls—whether at me or Elijah, I'm not sure, as I'm too busy watching the strange, powerful fae. I'm shaken from my stare as I'm roughly grabbed and my hands are pulled behind my back, causing a pained sound to leave my lips.

Before I can even blink, Elijah is suddenly in front of me, his hand wrapped around the beast's neck. "If any harm comes to her, I will hold you personally responsible." His face is twisted as he snarls the words, and then as quickly as he appeared, he vanishes. Gasping, I look around, but he disappeared without a trace. I've heard stories of strong fae that possessed the ability to travel from place to place with their minds, but I always thought they were bedtime stories for our young. Never had I thought that ability was ever possible or that I would meet someone who could wield such a power.

Jerked once again by the creature behind me, I'm snapped from my thoughts as I'm pulled towards the middle of the camp. My breathing speeds up, and despite knowing it's futile, I can't help but tug at the hands holding me captive. A snarl from the beast is the only response I receive as he tightens his grip, making me wince. I'm yanked backwards, and I desperately try to keep my footing, knowing he'll simply drag me across the ground if I fall.

Reaching the heart of the camp, the creature pushes me to my knees, pulling my arms even farther behind me. My body aches, and the rope that binds my hands is coarse and tight. Raising my head, I look around camp to see if anyone might help me. Movement catches my eye, and I turn to see the young human male I just saved from the very beast who binds me. Hope blooms in my chest. If the human stayed, perhaps he'll help me.

Just as I think the words, the human meets my gaze and turns, running in the opposite direction as fast as he can. Unfortunately for him, the fae are faster, and his movement catches their attention. When they capture him and pin him to the ground, tearing their teeth into him, I can't find it in me to feel sorry.

Perhaps that makes me just as much of a monster as the beasts mauling him.

Chapter 3

Within an hour, all the refugees are dead. All except me. I wonder what happened to the wood elf who offered to travel with me, and I hope he escaped before the killing started.

Bodies litter the ground, and I have to keep my gaze raised to hold the nausea at bay. The coppery tang of blood and torn open bowels fills the air, so I have to breathe through my mouth.

I've mostly been left alone since being bound and tied to one of the tall wooden pillars in the middle of the camp. However, I can feel eyes on me, and not just those of the passing warrior beasts. Elijah is around here somewhere, watching me, but I just can't see where.

After what feels like a lifetime, the creature that bound me, who I've learned is called Brok, strides towards me. He's smiling, and given his blood splattered appearance and gore covered claws, it's not hard to guess what he's been doing. Brok scares me, all these creatures do, but he's all action. He's got little or no power—at least I've not seen him use it—relying only on his strength and brutality. It's Elijah who truly frightens me.

Untying me from the pole, Brok heaves me up to my feet and quickly reties my hands together behind my back. My shoulder wound has stopped actively bleeding, but the rough treatment makes me grit my teeth against the pain. Other creatures are gathering here now that there's nothing left to kill, their curious looks and whispers of *'ma promessa'* filling the air. I have no idea what the words mean, but they utter them whenever they spot me, so I know it has something to do with me. It almost seems like a name or a title, but I don't have time to dwell on it, because a loud noise rips through the air, sounding much like a horn. It must be a signal they are waiting for, since they all start to move in the same direction, walking through and out of camp.

It's time to go home, Elijah said. Seeing as Brok is now pushing me towards a cart, I'm assuming I'm to go with them.

I've become a prisoner again. The brief six months of freedom awakened that spirit within me, but it wasn't nearly enough time. I'm only just starting to learn who I am after decades of being taught that my only purpose on this land was to serve. Besides, flitting from one refugee camp to another didn't help. Those places aren't the best for finding yourself. Living in a constant state of suspicion and being on your guard at all times makes it difficult to discover who you are.

And now I never will.

Screwing my eyes shut, I try to push back the onslaught of feelings and grief trying to overwhelm me.

Now is not the time to fall apart, Annalise, I chide myself.

Reaching the cart, I see it's filled with sacks of grain and other food they must have raided from the chef's tent. A few bloody weapons also lie with their haul, and I assume they have been taken from the fallen men. Brok unties my hands, but as I go to let out a sigh of relief as feeling rushes back to my abused limbs, he drags me forward and ties my wrists to the back of the cart. Snarling something at me in a deep, guttural language I don't understand, he checks the knots once more and moves away.

A huge, cat-like fae creature on four legs is led up to the front of the cart and attached to the shafts. My heart sinks with sudden realisation. Wherever we're going, I'm to be hauled along like livestock. I can choose to walk or be dragged, and I have no doubt the creatures around me would enjoy seeing the latter if their twisted smiles and sick leers tell me anything.

The cart begins to move, and given no other choice, I follow. The bodies of the dead lie where they fell, no one bothering to move them or give them a proper burial. Keeping my gaze raised, I focus on not tripping rather than the fact I'm surrounded by the dead as we disappear into the dark night.

I'm exhausted. I don't know how long we've been walking for, but I can see the pink tinge in the sky that signals the beginning of a new day. Birds tweet in the distance, but as soon as we come near, they wisely fly away.

My arms burn and scream for relief after being outstretched and raised while tied to the wagon. The wound on my shoulder throbs, and my knees sting from where I've missed a step and stumbled, only to be dragged forward. I was right in my assumption that I would find no sympathy if I fell. In fact, a low rumble of laughter followed me, making my cheeks burn. It's torture in a different way than what I've experienced before, but no less embarrassing or degrading. Obviously their idea of not causing me harm is very different to mine.

I have lots of time to think. After all, other than trying to keep my footing, I have nothing *but* time to myself. I watch those around me and try to look for weaknesses. I've only seen glimpses of Elijah, but it's obvious he isn't liked by the others in the raiding party. What's also clear is that he couldn't care less. At least, that's the impression he gives off as he strides past, ignoring the quiet insults whispered in his wake. I'm sure he can hear them, yet he doesn't react, if anything, it only makes him smirk wider. I suppose when you're that powerful, you're going to garner enemies.

The issue with having lots of time to think is that worries and paranoia start to set in. It briefly crossed my mind that these guards were sent to find me for my crimes against Galandell, but I wrote that possibility off quickly. These fae are foreign and strange, certainly not from the elf city.

I have no idea why they chose to spare me and take me prisoner. I'm no one of political worth or importance. I'm just an elf with no home and nothing to my name other than the clothes on my back. However, it doesn't take much for my thoughts to take a dark turn as to what they might do with me. I'm not stupid, I know what happens to females who are captured. From what I can tell, every one of these fae are male, and I've seen the hungry look in some of their eyes. The only thing keeping them at bay is the threat of Elijah. I would rather die than be violated like that. Perhaps it would be better to die at my own hand now, at my choosing, than be used and beaten by these unknown fae.

My eyes flick up to the weapons lying in the bed of the cart. I can't reach them like this, but if I could get up into the wagon, perhaps I could hide one of the smaller blades inside my cloak.

"You're very quiet for a female who's just been ripped from her home."

The smooth timbre catches me by surprise, and a guilty blush heats my cheeks, but I try not to flinch away. I know that voice, despite only having spoken to him once. Pulling my gaze from the cart, I look to my right where Elijah has just appeared. He speaks casually, as if he's discussing his dinner plans, his accent making his words slightly clipped.

In regard to his statement, I don't bother to tell him that I don't have a home, that the camp was merely a stopping point, a place to rest my head. I've not had a place to call home in over a century. He doesn't get to know that though. Instead, I just stay silent, watching him as he walks calmly beside me.

"I know you can speak, you did before." He raises his eyebrows, the corners of his lips pulling up into a smile, but as I examine his face, I can tell something is bothering him. I remain silent, which makes him frown. "I need to know. Why did you step in to help that human?" He's fully frowning now. All pretences are gone, and confusion takes its place. "You must have known he wouldn't help you in return. You were taken and bound in the middle of camp for all to see, yet no one stepped in to help you. I watched the human. I didn't miss the moment he saw you, and I know you saw him. He ran like a coward, just like all humans." Disgust lines his voice as he grows more animated. "So I ask again, why did you help him when you knew it would only cause you trouble?"

I think about not answering him, but as I glance over again, I see the confusion etched on his face. "It was the right thing to do." Shrugging my shoulders, I suck in a sharp breath at the sting from my wound. Hearing my pained noise, he instantly looks at my shoulder and his eyes seem to darken. He appears like he's about to go on a rampage for a reason I can't quite fathom, but I know I need to get his attention off the injury. Focusing on his question, I take a deep breath. "I couldn't just walk by and leave him."

Sure, I could have left the male, and I knew no one in the camp would help me. The relationship between elves and humans is difficult, but despite that, something in me wouldn't let me turn a blind eye. Just like the woman I helped earlier in the day.

Unaware of my internal musings, Elijah shakes his head. "Your actions were in vain, and you got captured in the process," he points out, needling me for a reaction. "Regretting your decision now?"

He watches me with interest, as if my answer is important. Holding his gaze, I keep my mouth shut, but I know he can read my answer in my eyes. No, I don't regret helping despite the outcome.

Shaking his head, he sighs and runs a hand through his slicked back hair, so different from the shaggy, unkempt hair the rest of his party possesses. Even the way he walks is different to the lumbering, lurching steps of the creatures he travels with. Elijah is by no means a slight male, even under his thick tunic I can see the muscles of his chest and arms, however compared to the others, he moves with a sense of power and ease, almost a swagger, and it riles up his companions. Perhaps that's exactly why he does it.

I turn away from my examination to pay attention to where I'm placing my feet, the cart yanking me forward as I lag behind. Exhaustion floods my body and every part of me screams out in pain, yet I don't say a word. I spent over a century silenced by a tyrannical queen and suffered torture far worse than this, so I'm not about to give them the pleasure of hearing my pain.

Elijah watches me. I can feel his gaze, and I get the distinct impression he's frustrated by my lack of responses. I guess when you can control the beasts around you, you get used to people cowering at your feet.

He finally breaks the silence, unable to hold back any longer. "Will you tell me your name?"

Do I tell him? I've been captured, so I shouldn't make any of this easier for them, yet a part of me wants to tell him. It's innocent enough information, considering no one from my past knew my real name and my family is dead, so giving it to him shouldn't backfire on me. I don't quite get his fascination with me, and perhaps if I tell him, he'll leave me be.

"Annalise." I glance at him as I speak, observing him.

"Annalise," he whispers, and I can't stop the shiver that travels down my spine. No one has said my name aloud since before I was first captured, and there's almost a power to it that I don't quite understand.

Tingles suddenly cover my skin, and the air feels thick, syrupy. All the sounds of the creatures around us disappear. The sudden absence of noise is disorienting. What in the Mother is going on? With my heart in my throat, I start to glance around, my gaze shooting to Elijah to see if he's noticed anything, but he just shakes his head, his eyes forward as he walks beside me.

"Don't look around, just keep walking as if nothing's happening." His voice sounds just as nonchalant as before, reassuring a small part of me. "They won't notice for a few moments, but if you draw attention to us, they'll realise something's wrong."

Despite not understanding what's happening, and the fact this male has captured me so I shouldn't listen to a word he says, I find myself looking away and focusing on my steps. It's obvious he put some sort of shield around us, blocking sound from entering or leaving. The only question is why. The beasts here follow his orders, so what could be so important he has to erect a shield to hide his words from them?

"When we arrive at the castle, I will do everything I can..." He trails off, regret tinging his words. "But I'll have to act in a way..."

Castle. The word strikes fear in me. Whose castle, and why is he warning me about the upcoming change in his behaviour? Why would he do that? My heart speeds up as my mind starts to spin. Just what's awaiting me at our destination? I don't understand why this male would try to protect me when he's the reason I'm here. Is he just feeling guilty and trying to alleviate some of that guilt?

Clearing my throat, I make sure to keep my gaze trained on the cart ahead. "Why not just let me go?"

His low chuckle rolls over me, and I get gooseflesh on my arms from the sound. It's the sort of sound reserved for the bedroom, low and seductive, and I'm suddenly glad I'm not supposed to be looking at him. "Nice try, *ma promessa*." That foreign term slips from his tongue again before he sighs, and from the corner of my eye, I see him shake his head. "I cannot. There are forces greater than me at work here." Genuine displeasure sounds in his voice, making me wonder just who this fae is and what could possibly be stopping a male as strong as he.

Blocking off the small, frightened part of my mind, I focus on the present, on getting through this gruelling trek. Whatever is waiting to greet me at the other end... I'll deal with it when we arrive.

"What will happen to me?" I don't mean to ask, but the question just slips from my lips. Perhaps I'm not as good at compartmentalising as I thought.

Although I'm not supposed to look at him, I can't help it. I need to see his expression, to know the truth of what I'm about to face. He keeps his gaze firmly on the path ahead, but his jaw tightens as he refuses to meet my gaze. "I will do everything I can," he repeats before striding off, dissolving the barrier around us, causing sound to hit me from all angles. I watch as he stalks away, barking at some of the beasts nearby in that strange, guttural language I've heard from the others.

Well, that's not a positive sign.

I'm not sure how much time passes, but my head hangs between my shoulders. The only reason I've not fallen is due to my fae reflexes. If I were human, I would be dragging along the ground by now. We've travelled at an excessive pace, crossing a huge distance in half the time it should take, so I know magic must be involved.

No one's touched me. Elijah's threat is still holding strong, but I can feel their gazes on me. I've not seen the tall fae since our earlier conversation, not even glimpses of him, but I'm so busy focusing on putting one foot in front of the other that I stop caring.

The cart starts to slow, and I become aware of what's transpiring around me. We're in the south now and closer to the mountains, which tower above me. The creatures chatter in their strange language, and there's an excitement in the air that puts me on alert.

Elijah said he was taking me to a castle, and we've been going in the wrong direction for either of the castles in Morrowmer, meaning we're about to cross into the fae lands. I knew as soon as I saw them that these fae aren't from this side of the mountains, but knowing it and accepting what's about to happen are two entirely different things. Once we pass the mountains, everything will be different, foreign. I won't know anyone or have any allies—not that I do here, but at least I know the lay of the land and can speak the language.

A strange feeling builds inside me as we slowly move closer to the mountain, and I realise I know this feeling. I've felt it before. It's the pathway, where the mountains have been cleaved in two and a magical corridor between the realms exists.

I feel sick as memories of the first time I saw the pathway batter me. I'd been close, had *felt* the land shake and heard the roar of the rock being pulled apart. At the time, I fled, the ominous feeling warning me of the dangers on the other side. Now, though, I'm about to cross it, whether I like it or not.

Ahead, I can see some of the raiding party entering the gap between the mountains, and a strange rippling sensation hits me as they disappear. We come to a stop as we line up before the narrow passage.

"You look pale, are you unwell?" a wry voice asks.

Elijah's sudden appearance should shock me, but I'm so overwhelmed, both in body and mind, that I merely shake my head. Later, when I look back on this, despite the dry, put out way he asked, I'll wonder why he cared. He might act like he doesn't give a damn, but he didn't have to check up on me.

"The ripples, the power..." My voice is weak, and I trail off as another wave hits me. I close my eyes as I focus on not being sick. *Don't throw up, don't throw up*, I chant to myself, hoping if I say it often enough my body will listen.

"You can feel it too?" Surprise laces his tone, and I start to realise that perhaps what I'm feeling isn't normal.

Glancing around, I notice no one else seems to be affected like this. They just seem eager to cross over. Returning my gaze to Elijah, I see the strain around his eyes, although he's trying to hide it from the others. He's waiting for my response, and I wonder if I've inadvertently given away too much information. He takes my silence as an agreement, his eyes flicking over my face and resting on my forehead as if he's looking for something. "Perhaps you really are *ma promessa* after all."

My head tilts to the side as I study him. I get the feeling he either didn't mean to say that out loud, or he didn't intend for me to hear it. Frowning down at me, he scans my body from top to bottom. I should feel annoyed, but I just don't have the energy right now.

Whatever he sees is obviously lacking as he blows out a short breath. "We're about to cross. Pull all your power and try to form a shield, it may protect you. The crossing isn't always easy for higher beings like us." His voice is cold and brisk, and any hint of kindness is gone from his eyes.

I have so many questions. Firstly, higher beings? I assume he's implying the rest of his travel companions aren't 'higher beings.' But why did he include me in that designation? I'm from a different land. You can tell we're a different species just by looking at us, yet for some reason, he considers me one of these 'higher beings.' His whispered words from earlier ring in my mind. *You can feel it too?* Perhaps I'm more similar to him than I thought.

Again, although his words give the impression he's cold and doesn't give a damn, he didn't have to tell me about forming a shield to protect myself. I don't tell him that my power is almost completely depleted, so creating a shield isn't something I can manage.

However, he seems to realise this. Growling something under his breath, he darts forward. I barely have time to register that he's holding a knife before he cuts through the rope tying me to the cart. Grabbing my bound wrists, he drags me after him, his body language changing as he marches past the creatures watching us. Whispers of *'ma promessa'* follow us, along with growls and snarls any time we pass one of them.

As we get nearer to the corridor in the mountain, the strange feeling grows stronger, and I'm suddenly glad for Elijah's tight grip on my bound wrists. I'd sink to my knees under the strength of the magic coming from it if it wasn't for him.

Striding right up to what I assume is a general, given the sash over his tattered uniform, Elijah pauses. "The girl travels through with me. I don't trust her not to try and escape." The statement doesn't leave any room for argument. Raising an eyebrow as the creature opens his mouth, Elijah calls power to himself, cutting off anything the general would say in response.

Staring at the pathway between the mountains, I'm awestruck once again. My breath catches in my throat, and my body seems to buzz with the supernatural power that rolls from it. The mountains look like a giant took a sword and sliced through the rock. There is nothing natural about this, and my body knows it, the waves of nausea almost making me double over.

A soothing shield slides over me, taking the worst of the feeling away. Able to stand up straight, I glance at Elijah, but he just shakes his head slightly. Right, don't draw attention to it. For some reason, he doesn't want them to know that he's helping me, and I'm not about to risk causing him to change his mind and remove the shield.

Elijah doesn't give me any more time to think, simply tugging me closer to him as he gives me a cold smile. "Hold on tight."

He steps over the threshold, and everything disappears into darkness.

Chapter 4

The pathway between the two lands is nothing like I expected. I imagined a physical corridor that we'd walk down with the mountains towering above us, but this is something entirely different.

All I see is darkness. I was right in my assumption that magic was involved. However, this is more like... like a portal between the lands. Elijah squeezes my hand, and that's all the warning I get before we emerge from the pathway. Bright light momentarily blinds me, and I squeeze my eyes shut, blinking against the white spots now obscuring my vision. My head feels light, and I stumble as Elijah leads me away.

Pulling me to the side, he lets me lean against a tree trunk as I gather my wits and adjust to being on solid ground, my mind spinning. Sliding down the trunk, I press my head against my knees, groaning softly. I feel like I've hit the wine too hard and someone's smashing a cymbal inside my head.

"I vomited all over myself the first time I travelled the pathway, so you did well." His tone is light, teasing.

Snorting, I look up from my feet and watch as he picks an invisible piece of lint from his tunic. That strange power ripples from the pathway again, and I know the others are passing through, yet it doesn't seem to be affecting me as badly now. Glancing over, I frown slightly as I watch as more and more creatures appear.

Elijah hums to himself as if he's just confirmed something. "You won't feel it as strongly on this side," he tells me, as if he's able to read my thoughts. Surprised, I look at him with a raised eyebrow, silently encouraging him to explain. A smile flickers across his lips. "It's our magic, so the land and sky accept it. On your side, it's foreign, abhorrent, so the land rejects it."

It takes me a few moments to process what he's saying. That's why it felt so strange to me. The magic of the pathway was not of Morrowmer, it was... abhorrent, a blight on the land. His description of the land rejecting it makes sense and explains why, on the two occasions I was close, it made me feel unwell.

His eyes meet mine. "I didn't know any of your kind could feel it. No one ever has before."

So me being able to feel the magic, the mesh of the fae lands and Morrowmer colliding, is unusual. *No one ever has before.* The words play in my mind on repeat as I work out the meaning behind them. They have come into contact with other elves. Were they captured and taken too? How many times have they done this? That sick feeling rises in me again as I contemplate how many deaths these creatures have caused.

"Why were you in Morrowmer? Why kill everyone but spare me?" I speak stronger and louder than I have in decades, my anger and fear making me bold. "Are there others like me you've taken?" This must be the most I've spoken since the death of the queen, no, even before that. Now is not the time to think about that, however, not when my kidnapper is staring down at me.

"There is much I can't tell you, *ma promessa*, but we are not like you." He emphasises the last words, his expression twisting into a sneer as he takes a step closer.

I want to back up, to put distance between us, but with the trunk behind me, there's nowhere for me to go. Instead, I stare up at him silently, letting my anger show on my face.

"Stop trying to compare me to your kind and the standards you think of as right and wrong. Everything is different here."

I've pissed him off, that much is obvious. He turns without another word and strides away. Is he just going to leave me here? Sure, my hands are bound, but my legs are free, so I could easily run away. Using the tree, I struggle into a standing position and glance around. As if knowing what I am planning, a tingle runs over my skin, and my feet suddenly feel like lead. Frowning, I try to lift my left foot, but it seems to be glued to the ground. I try the other, but the same thing happens. So much for that plan. *Bastard*, I think loudly in his direction, wishing I had the courage to say it out loud. Sighing, I lean back against the tree, but I swear I hear a low, amused chuckle floating through the air.

Bound as I am, there's nothing much for me to do except wait and watch. My throat hurts from using it so much compared to my relatively silent life. I'm parched, tired, and need to relieve myself, but there's nothing I can do about any of those, except mess myself, which is something I refuse to do—my pride is too strong to allow a weakness like that.

Instead, I finally take in this strange new world around me, and I'm shocked at what I see. Everything is brighter, the colours are more vivid, and the sounds and smells are richer. For a place where such brutish beasts hail from, I expected it to be dark and gloomy, the forest overgrown with brambles, and the land almost inhabitable. It's the complete opposite. If I crossed back over now, everything in Morrowmer would seem dull in comparison.

We seem to be in a forest, the treeline ending just before the edge of the mountains. They tower above us, the rockface so sheer it would be impossible for anyone to climb it, which is probably why we've seen nothing of these creatures until the pathway was created. As I lean against the tree, I start to notice other creatures around us. They are recognisable to their counterparts in Morrowmer, but different... The butterflies are the size of small dogs, and the birds that chirp in the trees have bright red, blue, and orange feathers. I even see a hedgehog snuffling in the undergrowth for worms, except the spikes on its back are twice the length and look lethal. Everything here is beautiful but deadly. I must never let myself forget where I am or the dangers that surround me.

I'm not sure how long I wait, lost in the savage beauty of the land around me, but I startle as a figure appears beside me. On instinct, I raise my bound hands to protect myself, although what I expect to be able to do with them, I don't know. Realising it is Elijah, and seeing his smug expression, I know he's thinking the same thing. I suppose to them I must seem relatively harmless. I don't have claws, fangs, or horns. My power is weak compared to that of beings like Elijah. All I have left is my dignity and integrity. Raising my chin, I narrow my eyes at the male, daring him to say anything.

The smirk drops away as he examines my face, the atmosphere suddenly changing. Not understanding what just happened, I shift my weight from one foot to the other, frowning slightly as I watch him. Something just transpired here, but I can't work out what. This male confuses me. He's behind my capture and kidnap, yet he protected me from being mauled in the camp and has shown me kindness on a couple of occasions now.

Shaking out of whatever deep thoughts he's sunk into, he crosses his arms over his chest, his customary smirk reappearing. "We're about to start moving again." He gestures to the group of beasts behind him, and I see that they are all through now. As I pull my attention back to Elijah, I notice his eyes are gleaming with humour. "I thought you might like a few moments alone."

I stare at him for a second until realisation hits me, and then it's hard not to nod manically. He means to relieve myself, and a huge wave of silent gratitude washes through me. He lets out a low chuckle at my eagerness, and with a wave of his hand, my feet are freed from their invisible bonds. Taking hold of my wrists, he guides me deeper into the forest, away from prying eyes. We reach a cluster of trees, and he waves towards them.

"This is far enough, no one will bother you." Letting go of my wrists, he raises an eyebrow when I don't immediately move.

He can't seriously expect me to go while he watches, I think with disbelief, but when he doesn't show any sign of moving, I huff a breath. "I can't go with you watching."

He continues to observe me, that eyebrow rising

again, and I see a flash of teeth as his lips pull up at one side. "Fine, I'll turn around, but don't even think about trying to escape." He looks amused, but I don't miss the warning in his voice, the tone telling me not to push his goodwill. "I hate running, it'll crumple my clothes, so I'll have to send one of my companions after you. They are far less gentle than I am." Although he says this lightly, conversationally, I shudder, remembering the beast's claws slicing through my shoulder.

Nodding, I walk towards the small cluster of trees, glancing over my shoulder and watching as he turns around. I didn't want to test his patience by asking to have my wrists released from their bindings, so I'm now faced with the task of trying to remove my underwear and urinate in a dress while my hands are tied together.

After lots of shuffling and quiet cursing, I stand upright, brushing down the skirts on my simple dress and readjusting my cloak as best as I can before walking over to Elijah.

"Better?"

Rolling my eyes at his amused expression, I simply hold out my wrists for him to take, not bothering to reply. He must have heard the commotion I was making, but he allowed me the privacy I desired.

Taking my arm, he leads me back through the trees. I hear the low voices and the sounds of the animals from the awaiting raiding party as we approach. I watch Elijah from the corner of my eye as we walk, and I notice the smile falling from his lips and his expression becoming harsher the closer we get. I stumble a couple of times, my energy failing me. We've walked a far greater distance than should be possible in the eight hours or so that we've been travelling. Plus, with my wounded shoulder and general lack of food over the past six months, my body is screaming at me to stop and rest.

Elijah seems to realise this as we rejoin his companions. Staring down at me as I stumble once again, he releases a breath through his teeth, his face tight. As he drags me farther up the line of wagons and beasts, he takes me to a cart full of bags of grain. Suddenly, he turns and grabs my waist, and before I can cry out or try to fight him off, he practically throws me into the wagon. Using my legs and bound hands, I shuffle into an upright position, resting back against a sack of grain. One of the beasts marches over and starts barking something in what must be their language. I can't tell what he's saying, but judging from his wild gestures and glare, he's not happy. All eyes seem to be on us, watching the drama unfold, but Elijah simply stares down at the beast, his expression bored.

The beast shouts something, and Elijah stiffens before barking back a single word. The air seems to move around me, tugging at my hair, becoming thick, and I realise that Elijah's pulling power towards himself. The beast suddenly seems to remember whom he's talking to, and he steps back, a flicker of fear in his eyes.

Elijah turns to address the rest of his companions, his expression deadly calm. "The female stays up front with me." His voice leaves no room for argument, but even so, I see several of the creatures scowl. He must see it too as his eyes narrow, a pulse of that power washing over us all. It doesn't do anything to me, but I see the beasts cower slightly at the reminder of his authority. "She's *ma promessa*, and you have injured her. How will your master react when he finds out how you've treated one of his girls?"

Low mumbling fills the air, and to my surprise, the

atmosphere is tinted with their fear—I can smell it. Don't ask me how or why, but I can just sense it. The beast that has confronted Elijah sketches a low bow and replies in his native tongue. Whatever he says must be satisfactory, because Elijah nods and barks out a command. Instantly, everyone falls into position, and we start moving.

Bracing myself against the sway of the cart, I settle down, grateful for somewhere to rest. This means I have more time to think. Several things slowly start to sink in as I go over his words.

He'd spoken in the common language so I was able to understand everything he said. I know he's able to speak the same guttural language as the others because I've heard him, so why choose that? Was it for my benefit?

Beyond that, he'd called me that word again, *ma promessa*. I've come to think it's some sort of title, and for some reason, the creatures were perturbed that I'd been injured. They hadn't cared about the others at the camp, and while most of them had been humans, I'd noticed at least one elf corpse. I was the only one to survive the slaughter. They'd been about to kill me, that I have no doubt of, but once my hood fell back, something about me convinced them not to. Is it because I'm female?

Which brings me to something else Elijah said. *How will your master react when he finds out how you've treated one of his girls?* Who is the master, especially if he's able to cause fear in beasts such as these? My chest tightens at the implication that I'm 'one of his girls,' that whoever this master is owns me, that I *belong* to him. I want to shout and scream that I belong to no one but myself, but I stay silent, saving my energy for what's to come.

One positive factor is that whatever's going on here,

there are others. Perhaps being glad that there are more females who have been taken from their homes makes me a monster, but knowing I may not be alone in this, that they may be able to help me...

You survived on your own before, Annalise. You don't need anyone else.

Images creep into my mind. Flashbacks of the dagger in my hand, the shocked gasp the queen made when I shoved the blade into her flesh, the blood that glinted on my hands, and the surprised look on the Mother's beloved's face before she returned to the matter at hand.

Screwing my eyes shut, I push away the memories, breathing in deeply as if the air in my lungs could wash away the lingering images. Slowly, my heart rate settles back to normal, and my thoughts are once again my own. Opening my eyes, I glance around and catch Elijah's frowning expression. We lock gazes before he turns away, continuing his long strides at the front of the procession.

Shaking my head, I look around, taking in the scenery and the creatures. Now that it's light, I can see the procession properly. There are three of the huge, cat-like creatures, each pulling their own cart, me being in the one nearest the front. There must be about thirty creatures. Most walk on two legs, but several seem to favour marching on four limbs, however I've seen they are capable of both. They all appear to be on alert, their hands resting over their weapons as they walk, their sharp gazes watching the forest around us.

I should be concerned, worried about their wary vigilance, but the rocking of the cart, coupled with my injuries and exhaustion, finally catches up with me. My eyelids start to feel heavy, and despite myself, I fall asleep.

"Wake up, girl."

The snarling voice jerks me from my slumber, and I surge upright, blinking as I try to get my bearings. Cruel laughter fills the air, and I glance around to see most of the creatures watching me with interest. Trying to settle my breathing, I turn to the front of the procession, searching for Elijah, except the fae is nowhere to be seen. Panic twists in my gut, but I refuse to give them any more entertainment, instead paying attention to our location.

We're still in the forest, but the trees are changing, becoming more spaced apart but far larger and older than the earlier ones we'd passed. The leaves are darker, and the canopy blocks out most of the sun. There's purpose in the way the creatures move, and I get the impression we're nearing our destination.

I'm still surprised I fell asleep. Sleep has been something that often eludes me, especially in stressful situations. Yet somehow, I did, and I'd been so tired I hadn't been plagued by the nightmares that haunt me—a small blessing. The last thing I want is to wake up screaming in front of my captors.

A light catches my attention, pulling me from my musings. As we continue, I see that we're reaching the treeline. What awaits me beyond those trees? Frightening possibilities flit through my mind once more, except this time I find the thoughts harder to banish. When we break through the treeline, I blink against the sudden brightness, only for my eyes to widen as I see the grand castle ahead.

This must be the castle Elijah had been talking about,

and despite my fear, I feel awe at the sight. Made of dark stone, the behemoth structure is intimidating yet beautiful. It's very different to the white, fluid-looking palace I lived in when I was under the queen's thumb. That had been all twisting turrets and was built over a river as it flowed into the ocean.

Great stone walls surround the fortress, and creatures observe us from the watchtower with narrowed eyes. Beyond that is the castle itself. Its style is much more angular than I'm used to. It has a tower on every corner, the turrets each containing a golden statue on top. As we get closer, I realise that the figures are actually lions on their hind legs, their heads thrown back in a mighty roar. The middle of the castle has a huge tower, its spire taller than even the oldest of trees in this ancient forest.

The huge, wooden doors in the wall open slowly, revealing a smirking figure as he strolls towards us like he's got all the time in the world.

Elijah.

How had he managed to get ahead of us? *Magic, of course,* my mind chides. *You've seen him disappear in front of you, is it really a surprise he can travel distances too?* Making sure my expression is neutral, I watch him, not all that surprised when he comes to a stop at the side of the wagon.

"Welcome to my home." He smiles, but there's a tightness around his eyes that makes me think he's not all that happy to be back here. Moving to the rear of the cart, he holds out his hand and waits with a raised eyebrow. Knowing what he wants, I sigh quietly and shuffle to the edge of the wagon. Placing both hands on my waist, I brace myself as he lifts me and deposits me on the ground. Taking my bound wrists, he pulls me to the side as the mammoth cat creatures haul the carts onto castle grounds.

We remain silent as the other creatures pass us. Many of them sneer in our direction, but I can't quite decide if it's aimed at me or Elijah. The atmosphere has definitely changed now that we've arrived. The fae that we travelled with now seem more... defiant, like the power Elijah held over them doesn't matter anymore. It makes me think that whoever rules in that castle is even stronger, more powerful.

"Do you remember what I told you before?" he asks me in a low voice.

Glancing up at him, I see he's watching the gates of the castle, his hand tightening around my wrist. There are many things he could be referring to, but I know he's referencing when he said he'd be different when we reached the castle. That he'd do what he could to protect me. It should reassure me, but from the tension in his jaw, I find myself becoming more and more anxious. Another of his comments from before rises in my mind, when he warned me that everything is different here. I suppose I'm about to find out exactly what he means by that.

As I stare up at my new prison, my body stiffens. I know that as soon as we cross the threshold and those doors shut behind us, I'll be stuck here. No one will know I'm gone, and even if they did, I don't have anyone who would miss or mourn me.

When I don't answer, Elijah turns his head to look at me with a question in his eyes. I won't say it out loud, it sounds too much like I'm giving in and accepting what's about to happen. Instead, I nod slightly, but he sees and lets out a long exhale.

"Let's go meet the master." Without giving me a

chance to think or respond, he starts to move forward, his long strides causing me to stumble and practically jog to keep up. The shadow of the looming castle falls over me, and suddenly the previously impressive building looks sinister.

My chest constricts, and adrenaline pumps through my veins as pure fear builds within me. Despite knowing I won't escape them, that I'll probably be shot or mauled if I miraculously manage to get away from Elijah, I can't control the voice in my mind screaming for me to flee. Dragging my heels in the dirt, I use all my weight to pull against Elijah's hold, jerking him to a stop. As if in slow motion, he turns his head to look at me, a cruel sneer on his face.

His gaze scans me, and he must see the pure, unrelenting fear on my face, because his eyes flicker slightly, but he simply wrenches me towards him. "Don't fight it," he warns in a low voice as I stumble forward. I know I should do as he says, it will cause me less pain in the long run, as I've learned from the past, except something rises within me, and I can't just willingly walk into captivity once again. I won't.

Using my body weight, I drop to the ground, trying to make Elijah release my wrists as I thrash and twist in his hold, kicking out at him. A low, unamused chuckle is all I get for my troubles as he hauls me back up to my feet. I snarl, my feral inner fae pushing through the silent mask I usually wear. His arched eyebrow only serves to make me angry. He's looking at me as if I'm as annoying as a gnat and no real threat to him. Surging forward, I sink my teeth into his upper arm and bite down hard. His grunt of pain brings me a sense of sick satisfaction. He pulls me away and smiles at me, except it's not a kind smile. It exposes his elongated incisors and promises violence.

"You want to play it that way?" He narrows his eyes, that smile still fixed in place, and I know I've only made things worse for myself. "Fine." Without any further warning, he leaps forward and grabs my waist, throwing me over his shoulder.

A noise of surprise escapes me as he spins and starts striding towards the gates. I thrash and try to force him to release me, but his arm bands around my legs, holding me tightly against him.

"Don't even think about biting me again," Elijah comments, a hint of amusement lacing his tone, his steps unfaltering.

How he knew that was exactly what I'd been about to do, I don't know. Something deep inside me says not to push him, not here with so many eyes on us, but that doesn't mean I'm going to go willingly. I reach out for my power, any scrap of fae magic I might possess, but the small amount that has been replenished from my nap in the cart just slips away from my grasp, but I don't have time to worry about it as we pass over the threshold and into the castle grounds.

I continue to kick and try to get free, but dread and nausea rises within me as I watch the large doors on the gate close. I've lost my chance to get away.

"Master," Elijah purrs, talking to someone behind me.

Without warning, he swings me off his shoulder and practically drops me onto the ground. It's only due to my fae reflexes that I manage to get my feet under me before falling on my ass. Snarling up at Elijah, I bare my teeth, wishing my hands were free so I could wrap them around his infuriating neck.

"You've brought me a wildcat, I see."

The voice is accented like the others, but the words are said with a rumble that catches my attention. My head snaps around to find the source of the voice. As soon as I see him, I know he's the master Elijah and the others were talking about on the journey here. He's tall, and his bronze skin is smooth. He strolls towards me like he's got all the time in the world. His shoulder-length hair reminds me of a mane, the brown and golden strands framing his face. In fact, everything about him reminds me of a large cat, particularly his nose, which is wider and looks like the snout of a lion. I look closer, and I'm pretty sure I can see whiskers jutting from his face. His eyes are also feline, with the classic almond shape and piercing golden irises. My gaze travels down his body and takes in his muscular frame barely hidden by his dark blue tunic, which is accented with golden detail and buttons. I have no doubt he could run me down if I tried to escape. Looking at his hands and feet, expecting to see paws, I'm surprised they look much like mine, only he has long claws protruding from his fingertips.

"I live to serve," Elijah drawls, as I pull my gaze from the creature to glance over and see that smarmy smirk in place as he sketches an elaborate bow.

Not taking his eyes off me, the master smiles, only there's nothing kind about it as he exposes his long incisors. Opening his arms wide, his possessive gaze watches me carefully. "Welcome to your new home, *ma promessa*."

Chapter 5

This can't be happening. Not again.

The words ring in my ears as my brain tries to take in all the new information I've learned in the last couple of minutes. *Welcome to your new home.*

Firstly, the master appears to be more beast than fae. He may walk and talk like a high fae from Morrowmer, but I have no doubt that his instincts are animalistic. While he's currently acting civil, there's a reason everyone here is afraid of him, and I don't think that's wholly due to the power that rolls from him. It suddenly makes sense why all his followers look as they do. All except Elijah that is.

Welcome to your new home.

Secondly, I'm aware of dozens of eyes on me. I quickly assess the area, not wanting to take my gaze off the master for more than a few seconds, however, I notice several weapons pointed my way, some of which look a lot like crossbows. Even if I managed to get away from them

—I've seen their powerful limbs, and they would catch me in a second—I can't outrun a crossbow.

Welcome to your new home.

Those words finally sink in. Home. This will never be my home, just another gilded prison. Yet again, I've been captured by another being who thinks they have the right to rule me, to *own* me.

Baring my teeth and swallowing down the fear inside me, I embrace my inner fae, the part of me that's been silent for too long, and step forward, narrowing my eyes on the master. "This will never be my home." Truth rings from my declaration, and a tingling sensation settles over my skin, but I don't look away from the threat in front of me.

The master glares, and a low growl emits from his chest. I want to back down, I should, but something within me won't allow it. To show any weakness to him would feel like a failure. So, despite the fact my bound hands tremble, I keep my chin high and hold my ground.

The master closes the remaining distance between us, towering above me as he scowls down at me. I feel the vibration from his growl in my chest, making my heart skip a beat. "Take her to the cells," he instructs, not once looking away from me, simply expecting someone to obey his orders. "After a few days, she might start feeling more gracious towards her new master." Without another word, he spins on his heel and stalks towards the large castle doors.

"Well, that went well." Elijah reaches for my wrist, his sarcastic drawl breaking my glare at the castle entrance where the master disappeared. I half expect him to come bursting back out and punish me for my words, his thin temper snapping. Elijah begins to walk, pulling me along behind him. I follow, picking up my pace so I'm walking at his side. I still have some pride left in me, so the idea of being dragged across the castle grounds in front of everyone is abhorrent. Glancing at him, I notice he's frowning, his jaw tight. He's angry, but I don't have the energy to try and decode why.

He surprises me by ignoring the main entrance and walking to the left, following the castle wall. There's more activity down here, and I see a stable, except the large cat-like creatures being led towards it are definitely not horses. The wagons have been brought down here, and several of the creatures are unloading them, carrying the sacks of grain and other pilfered items into a castle side door. The sound of swords clashing together puts me on edge, and as we round a corner, I perceive what's causing the noise. A large training ring and several low buildings positioned against the curtain wall fill the space. Soldiers' barracks, I realise, flicking my eyes from the buildings to the training ring where two of the creatures spar. I'm not sure why they bother to use their swords, which look cumbersome in their large hands. Their claws and sharp teeth would be sure to tear up their opponent.

Many of the soldiers pause as they see us passing, aiming looks of disgust at Elijah and then stilling when they see me. Many of them seem to sniff the air as I pass. I try to supress my shudder, but I'm not successful if the deep, amused chuckles that follow us are anything to go by. Elijah ignores them all, his steps never faltering as he leads me away.

Reaching the back of the castle, I see two armed guards standing vigil by a set of stone stairs which descend below the castle. Biting my tongue to hold back the many questions circling in my mind, I attempt to take long, deep breaths to calm my racing heart. When the guards see us, they step to the side, allowing us access, but I don't miss the looks they throw at Elijah. Again, he ignores them and leads me down the short staircase, under an archway, and to a door I hadn't seen from above. Knocking once against the thick wooden door, Elijah looks down at me, and for a second, I think I see his expression soften, his mouth opening to say something, but sounds from the other side of the door interrupt us.

A slot slides open, revealing a pair of narrowed amber eyes. With a grunt, the eyehole is swiftly covered, and a loud metallic clunk is the only warning we get before the door is hauled open. A horned fae greets us, and this time his disgusted look is aimed not just at Elijah, but at both of us.

"The master's newest resident." Once again ignoring the looks of loathing, Elijah's voice remains smooth, the corner of his mouth turned up as if he finds his own comment amusing. When the guard huffs and begins to move towards me, Elijah waves him off. "I'll settle her in. We wouldn't want you to have to do any *actual* work, would we?"

I have to admit, although I wish I were anywhere else, I'd much rather Elijah take me to my cell—better the devil you know. He confuses me, but I don't think he'd hurt me, at least not in the way the guard might if the looks he's giving me are anything to go by.

"Filth," the beast growls, spitting on the ground by Elijah's feet, obviously not amused by the tall fae's comment.

Something flashes in Elijah's eyes, and before I've even registered what's happening, he spins to face the creature. I stagger back against the wall as he suddenly lets go of me, using it to stay upright. I should probably use this opportunity to free myself, but instead I can't take my eyes off Elijah, his hands glowing with the supernatural power he's gathering.

The air seems to pulse around us as he backs the guard into a corner. "That's no way to speak in front of a lady," he drawls. "Apologise." A dangerous note enters his tone at the demand, and only a fool would disobey someone as powerful as Elijah.

I don't know if the beast is brave or stupid, because he spits out something, and despite not knowing their language, even I know he's cursing Elijah.

A dark smile crosses Elijah's face, like he was hoping the creature would disagree. Raising both his hands, he makes a strange twisting gesture and the guard's eyes widen. The air becomes thicker, and I watch, horrified, as the guard clutches his throat, gurgling noises escaping his mouth. His eyes become bloodshot, and he falls back against the wall as if his legs aren't strong enough to hold him up.

"I said, apologise," Elijah demands, his voice threatening as he bears down on his victim.

The guard's mouth opens as if trying to speak, but no sound comes out, like his airway has been completely constricted. Elijah makes a gesture, and the guard gasps for air, breathing hard as he glares at the fae. His body trembles with rage, but slowly, he turns his twisted face towards me. "I'm sorry."

It's the least genuine apology I've ever heard, but it's the best I'm going to get. Watching with wary eyes, I stay away from both of them, shocked by what I just saw.

Elijah huffs, running his hands through his hair as he flashes a smile. "See, that wasn't so hard, was it?"

Turning, he reaches for my wrists, but I flinch away, appalled by his brutal display of dominance. I swear I see regret flicker across his face, but it's gone so quickly I could have imagined it. Raising an eyebrow, he simply gestures for me to walk, not trying to reach for me again. Slowly, with my gut twisting, I cross to the other side of the room where a grilled metal door awaits. With a flick of his hand, the door unlocks and swings open.

Fearing the consequences if I don't comply, I pass through the door without waiting to be told what to do. We make our way down the poorly lit corridor, cells lining the length. Around half of them have an occupant. My feet feel like lead, and my heart pounds in my chest.

What's going to happen to me here? Elijah just used his power to humiliate one of the guards. While the creature can't get his revenge on Elijah, I'm going to be down here, defenceless. He just made the situation a hundred times worse for me. I've experienced what happens to prisoners before, and I swore I'd never let it happen to me again. Yet here I am.

"Breathe."

Elijah's voice makes me jump despite the fact that he whispers, his hand coming to rest gently on the small of my back. I realise he's right, I've been holding my breath, and my head is spinning from the lack of oxygen. Taking a gasping inhale, I shake my head.

Pull yourself together, Annalise, I chide myself. *Now is not the time to fall apart, not in front of Elijah.* Chanting it like a mantra, I try to steel myself, my steps becoming surer as I'm led towards my cell.

We reach the second to last cell when the door swings open without being touched. With a quick glance at Elijah, I swallow against the rising nausea and step inside at his nod. As soon as I cross into the cell, my skin tingles with magic embedded into the metal bars around me. The slam of the door makes me flinch, but when I turn around to face Elijah, my expression is neutral.

"The guards won't touch you," he promises quietly, his expression dark.

Something in my chest loosens. Despite what I just saw him doing, and the fact that he stole me from Morrowmer and brought me here as a prisoner, I trust him on this.

He examines my face carefully, although what he's looking for, I have no idea. Whatever it is, he must have found it, because he nods to himself and takes a step back from the cell. He opens his mouth, and I think he's going to say something, but one of the cell occupants farther down starts groaning, and Elijah seems to remember where he is. His mouth snaps shut, and his face tightens in annoyance.

"Enjoy your stay." He performs an elaborate bow, sarcasm obvious in his tone, but he's smirking again when he straightens to his full height. "I hear the gruel is to die for." Without another word, he spins on his heel and strides towards the exit. As he leaves, the bonds around my hands magically release, dissolving as if they were never there. Only the raised, red marks on my wrists are proof of their tight presence.

The screech of the outer door opening and closing makes me acutely aware that for the first time since I was captured, I'm alone. I'm aware there are other prisoners down here, but they have no impact on me and seem to be happy enough to ignore me, trapped in their own thoughts. Although Elijah scares me, and his mood swings are impossible to predict, there was some sort of stability when he was around. For one reason or another, he protected me from the others in the raiding party and demanded I be left alone down here. I believed him, but now that he's gone, the fears regarding the guards start worming their way into my mind.

Focus on something else, Annalise. Taking a deep breath, I nod to myself. If I can concentrate on a task or find something else to keep me busy, then my mind won't wander to the dark thoughts looming at the back of my mind. Glancing around my cell, I finally take in my accommodations.

The square space is wide enough to fit a simple cot, which sits against the back stone wall. The rest of the walls are simply made up of metal bars, which will give me zero privacy. How am I supposed to wash or relieve myself? Swallowing against the lump in the back of my throat, I push that thought away and continue with my appraisal of the cell. It's five strides from the back wall to the cell door, and the same in width. In addition to the cot and simple brown blanket, there's a bucket in the far corner. Walking over, I find it empty, but from the smell that seems to have permeated the wood, I work out that this is where I'll be relieving myself.

There are no windows, just several lamps which line the corridor between the cells, casting us all in a dull orange glow. Examining the other cells, I realise I was right in my earlier assessment. About half of them are being used. The occupants within all seem to be male, from what I can make out, but only one has the same beastly look as the creatures that seem to live here. The others appear more like the high elves from Morrowmer, only... different, but I don't have the best view to tell why. The cell to my left, which is the final cell in this row, has two walls made of stone, and the fae within is curled up on his cot. The blanket is wrapped around him so I can't see his features. The cell to my right is empty, as are the cells directly opposite me.

Fatigue hits me like a physical blow, and I stagger towards the cot, knowing that if I don't sit soon, I'll collapse. Half throwing myself down, I wince at the hardness of the cot beneath me and the scratchy blanket, but I know it'll be better than sleeping on the dirty floor.

My shoulder throbs, demanding my attention. I've been pushing my worries about the injury aside during our journey, prioritising what was more likely to kill me. However, now that I'm locked away and under no immediate danger, I know I need to do something about it. My right arm has become more and more difficult to use, the sharp pains making movement difficult. Reaching up, I grit my teeth as I force the limb to move, untying the cloak from around my shoulders. My arm drops uselessly onto my lap. Concern and alarm make me sit forward. I may not be a healer, but even I know that my shoulder should have started to heal by now. Instead, it seems to be getting worse. Using my left hand, I unbutton the fastenings of my dress, gently peeling it away from the injury. I have to bite my lip against the pain, as sections of the fabric have stuck to the drying blood. Spots appear behind my eyes, and dizziness makes me pause—I know it's from the mixture of pain, exhaustion, and malnourishment. Panting, I remove the rest of the fabric from my shoulder, steeling myself against the burning sensation.

I have to lean back against the wall as I wait for the nausea to pass, my chest heaving with my breaths. Closing my eyes for a few seconds, I try to ground myself. I've certainly suffered through worse pain than this, only I can't banish the anxiety of what I'm going to find when I finally gather the courage to look at the damage.

There's no point in putting it off any longer. Opening my eyes, I push away from the wall, perching on the edge of the cot. Sending a prayer to the Great Mother, I look at my shoulder, and a noise of distress escapes me as I see the mutilation. Three wide slashes cut through my skin. They start at the top of my shoulder, curve slightly over my upper arm, and then stretch down the back of my shoulder blade. Mercifully, I don't think I've broken any bones, but the open wound is a cause for concern.

High elves heal quickly, so this should be a tight, shiny pink scar by now, and although the bleeding stopped long ago, the wound is still open and oozing, the different levels of fat and muscle on display. It's not impossible for us to die of infections. It's rare, yes, but I've seen high elves die because of them before and they are usually long, drawn-out, painful deaths. The fact I'm beginning to lose function in my arm and that the skin around the marks is red and hot to the touch all point towards an infection.

Closing my eyes, I desperately search for that place within me where my power resides, only to find it slips out of my reach. I always imagine it to look like a glowing ball, but right now it's barely a spark, an ember of what I once had. There isn't much there thanks to me depleting it earlier, but now it isn't responding at all. Using power has never been easy for me, but it's never felt like this before. Calling for it to fill me and flood me with healing power, I pray it works. It doesn't.

"No," I whisper quietly, despair rocking my body. I'm aware of eyes on me, and I know I shouldn't show anyone in this place my weaknesses as they will only use them against me.

"Your power won't work here."

The voice comes from the cell to my left and is scratchy from lack of use. Heart racing in my chest, I jump up and spin to face whoever's in the cell, dropping into a defensive crouch despite the fact it jolts my shoulder. The world spins around me and my vision fades in and out from the pain, but I force myself to stay upright. My eyes flick around, assessing for threats before settling on the figure in the neighbouring cell. Before, he was lying down, covered by the blanket, so I hadn't seen what he looked like, but he's sitting up now and watching me with interest.

Shaggy grey hair frames a wrinkled, elderly face. Pointed ears poke through his hair, so I know he's fae, but even without the ears, it's easy to tell this male is something... other. Rich blue eyes watch me with a focus that seems much younger than the body they are encased in. I've never met a fae that looks old, so this male must be ancient. The oldest elf I knew back in Galandell was almost eight hundred years old, and she was only just starting to show signs of age.

"Steady," the voice calls again, reaching out as if he could stabilise me. "There's magic that surrounds the cells. As soon as you pass that threshold, it neutralises your power," he explains, gesturing towards the locked cell door.

I keep my defensive position, not wanting to pull my eyes from the male, but I remember the tingling sensation as I entered. Of course there's some sort of spell over the cells. They wouldn't want prisoners to access their power when they wanted, that would make escaping too easy.

I wonder if they have magicians in this land. In Morrowmer, magicians are humans who have been gifted with magic by the gods. We were taught that the magicians were created to even the playing field between the humans and elves, and they are the humans' greatest protectors. Their magic differs from our own, as they are able to create spells that bend magic to their will. Our power is different. We don't need spells to use our power, it simply dwells within us. I know of no elf who could create something that would sit dormant on an inanimate object, like the magic that encases this cell. However, I've seen magicians' spells do something similar. They are able to create wards which set the spell in its dormant form until it's triggered, like someone crossing a threshold.

The main question in my mind right now, though, is how the fae opposite me knew I was trying to reach for my power.

He continues to watch me, scanning me until his gaze reaches my injured shoulder. Cursing in the same language as those who brought me here, his eyes harden, and his expression turns affronted. "You're injured. Did they cause that?"

My uninjured arm automatically reaches up as if to cradle my shoulder. There's no point in denying it now, he's seen it. In fact, he probably smelled the blood before he even saw the wound. I nod hesitantly.

He's angry. Something simmers in his eyes, yet he's trying to hide it so as not to frighten me. "Will you come closer so I can take a look?" he asks softly, standing up with deliberate slowness before walking towards the bars separating us.

Instantly, my guard goes up. Why would he want to see it? What's in it for him? He doesn't know me, and there would be no benefit to him helping me. If I move closer to the bars, he could easily try to attack me. Besides, if what he says is true and we can't use our powers, then what is he really going to be able to do to help me?

As if reading my mind and my suspicions, he holds up both hands. "I know all of this is overwhelming, but I won't hurt you. I just want to see the wound."

Something in my gut tells me to trust this fae. I have absolutely no reason to believe him. After all, he's locked in a prison cell, so he must have done something to deserve it.

Yet I have a strange feeling when I look at him. I feel like I'm being pushed towards him, like the Mother is telling me he won't hurt me. I guess it's wrong of me to assume he's committed a crime just because he's imprisoned down here. I'm a prime example that the master only requires the smallest slight before sending someone to the cells.

Putting my faith in the goddess and trusting my instincts, I creep towards the fae and turn so he can see the full extent of the wound. Standing like this, I can still watch him over my shoulder. His face twists as he examines the damage, and his hands twitch at his sides, like he's desperate to reach out and touch my shoulder, but he's holding himself back for some reason.

"Was it one of the apanthe?" Seeing my confused expression, he smiles gently, his quiet, scratchy voice surprisingly soothing. "One of the feline-looking fae with mane-like hair that stands on two feet and has claws and fangs. Some of them have horns."

So that's what those creatures are, I think to myself, nodding in response. Brok, the guard who did this, fits that description perfectly. In fact, most of the fae that travelled with us did.

The fae opposite me swears again in what I assume is his native language. "I thought so." His expression is grim when I turn to face him. "They can produce poison from their claws. Your power should be fighting it, but I'm assuming that since you're here, you either have very little or you used all your power trying to escape, and now you're unable to access it."

My heart sinks as he speaks. The possibility that this wound could actually kill me strikes me hard. I've always taken my fae healing for granted, but take that away and I'm as frail as a human. He hits a little too close to the truth with his comments about my power, and I have to look away, his eyes seeming to see right into my soul.

"Even if you got your full powers back immediately, you would struggle to fight the poison now that it's established. You need healing." His tone softens as he speaks, as if he knows the effect his words are going to have on me... as if he actually gives a damn about what happens to me.

Moving away from the bars, I walk over to sit on the edge of the cot, my steps unsteady. I'm dead. Do they even know that my body isn't fighting off the poison from the apanthe's claws? I don't think the master noticed I was injured.

Elijah knows. He won't let you die.

Except Elijah isn't in charge here. He might not know that the poison has slowly been working its way through my bloodstream. If he did know, he may not be able to come down here or even care. I'm a captive here, after all, so perhaps they want me to suffer.

No, they brought you here for a reason. They would have killed you back at the camp if they wanted you dead.

We're silent for a long time, my fellow prisoner letting me digest what I've learned, but I feel his eyes on me the whole time.

"What's your name?"

I glance over at his question, once again debating if I should give my name away, but seeing as Elijah knows it, I don't see the harm in this prisoner knowing. Clearing my throat, I watch him as I answer, "Annalise."

"Annalise," he repeats, reminding me of how Elijah had whispered my name to himself. The corner of his mouth twitches up before he seems to shake himself, as if remembering where he is. "I'm… Alric." He pauses before he says his name, making me wonder what he'd been about to say. I get the impression that Alric isn't his real name, but I simply nod to show I've heard him. If he wants to keep his name to himself, then that's no business of mine. I'm not here to make friends.

Not friends, but alliances may help you get through this alive. That thought weighs heavily on me. I made it through my captivity under the queen without any 'friends.' I couldn't trust anyone there, not even the other lady-in-waiting who was going through the same experience as me. Her mind had been broken from being under the queen's rule for so long. The queen constantly required our presence, even while she slept, so it wasn't like I ever had a chance to make any alliances. Things only started to change when Clarissa, the beloved, arrived in Galandell, but I can't rely on her to help me now. She's not been seen in months. Her and her mates needed time to recover from the atrocities of the war. Besides, I'm in a whole new realm now, so I can't rely on her to save me.

My limbs feel heavy and everything aches. I close my eyes, and it takes all of my strength just to stay upright.

"Annalise, you should rest." Concern laces Alric's voice, and as I crack open my eyes, I see him watching me.

The idea of sleeping in a cell in a strange place doesn't fill me with confidence, and under other circumstances, I probably wouldn't sleep, wanting to stay on guard, but my body is screaming at me to lie down, the world spinning around me. I don't have the energy to nod at his suggestion as I recline, slowly bringing my legs up onto the cot.

I'm asleep within seconds.

The queen hovers over me, smirking down at me with that cruel twist of her lips, her hands on her hips. Dismay and horror make me queasy. This can't be happening. She's dead.

"How's freedom treating you?" she purrs, her voice sending fear surging through my veins. She was always at her most vicious when she used that tone. "You were nothing when you came to me. I gave you a position of power within Galandell. It was an honour to serve me, yet you always rebelled." Sighing as if I'd let her down, she places her hand against my cheek. She may act benevolent, like she regrets having to punish me, but she's evil through and through. No one knows that better than me.

I try to flinch away from her touch, it repulses me, but the gentle hand on my cheek turns into a tight grip as she forces me to look at her.

"Well, look where that got you—captured once again and dying of poison." Her singsong voice doesn't match the

excitement and bloodlust that shine in her eyes. Leaning in closer, she places her lips against my ear. "I guess it's a fitting way for a murderer to go," she whispers.

My body seizes, contorting in pain—

"Annalise!"

The male voice breaks through the fever dream, and I realise the pain isn't coming from the queen who haunts my dreams, but my shoulder. Agony shoots through my body, the sleep not doing anything to relieve the exhaustion weighing down my limbs. My eyelids flutter open as I glance around the cell, briefly meeting Alric's gaze before my body contorts again. I shake, going from hot to cold. My gut twists suddenly, violently, and I only just lean over the side of the bed before I vomit, spilling the paltry contents of my stomach. Flopping back onto the cot, I fall into blissful unconsciousness.

"Wake up, Annalise." The barked order breaks through the darkness and I groan, not having the energy to open my eyes.

I've never felt so unwell or pathetic. I'm going to die in a foreign realm, and there will be no one here, or in Morrowmer, who would mourn me. My chest is tight, even breathing is more difficult now. My blanket is soaked from the hot sweats that rack my body, and it's cooling against my skin, making me shiver.

"Yes, good girl. Now stay with me," the voice calls again, and I realise belatedly that it belongs to Alric. "You can't die, we all need you," he whispers so quietly I almost miss it. I don't think I was supposed to hear that last part. Banging and shouting fills the underground room as someone smashes a metallic object against the bars, the sound piercing my skull.

Thankfully the noise stops when a door slams open, then heavy, angry sounding footsteps storm our way. My eyes are shut, so I don't know who it is, and I can't find it in me to care.

"Quiet down, scum," a voice spits. They are close by, but I don't think the comment is aimed at me.

"You need to... dying... get Elijah now!" Alric demands.

I can't quite make out all of their words or understand what they are saying, but I pick up parts. I feel another set of eyes on me and manage to turn my head to the side, squinting to see who it is. I recognise the guard Elijah fought with and groan again, although not from pain this time. *He won't help me*, I think to myself. *He'll prolong my suffering to get back at Elijah.*

I must fall into a fitful sleep, as I'm startled awake by loud cursing, my body crying out in protest at the sudden jolt of surprise. Footsteps and a slamming door tell me the guard has left, but I don't hold out any hope that he's going for help. I'm going to die here.

"Why the fuck didn't you alert me sooner?" Elijah's furious voice registers in my mind, and I swim through the brain fog to try and force my eyes open. Everything is stiff, and moving is a hundred times more difficult than it was earlier.

A snarl echoes around the room. "I didn't know she was unwell," the same voice from before argues, his anger obvious, and I realise it's the guard from earlier.

The voices get closer, and I feel the presence of two beings, their heavy gazes on me, but I just don't have the energy to get up. Right now, I'm struggling to open my eyes, my breathing raspy.

"You're supposed to do hourly checks. It's been twelve hours, and you're telling me you didn't once notice?" Elijah's dark voice is filled with violence and power, the air in the room electric. "Look at her!" Elijah roars, and the air seems to tremble around us. I'm glad it's not me on the receiving end of his wrath.

The squeal of a cell door swinging open and footsteps are the only warnings I have before he is at my side. I should be terrified. He's the reason I'm here, and he's so much more powerful than me, yet some of my pain and restlessness ease as he kneels at my side. A cool hand touches my forehead, and I know it's him.

"Annalise, open your eyes." Although the tone he uses with me is gentle, there's still a command behind it. I try to obey, and when I finally manage to peel back my eyelids, he curses at whatever he sees as he scans my face. "Why didn't you tell me your power wasn't healing you?" His voice is harsh, but as he leans forward, his arms sliding underneath my limp body, he cradles me gently against his chest. I don't have the strength to reply, but thankfully he doesn't demand one from me as he moves towards the cell door.

Someone growls, the guard I think, but my eyes have slid closed once more so I can't be sure.

"You can't just take—"

"I can do whatever the fuck I like." Elijah's voice is deadly again, but he doesn't stop walking as he carries me from the cell. The magic that neutralises my power falls off me as we enter the corridor, and I sigh in relief. Not having it or being able to access it was like missing a part of myself.

We pause, and I hear another door being unlocked in front of us. Elijah shifts his weight, and I feel his attention briefly move off me. "If she dies, it'll be your head on the line."

The guard grunts in response, but I can smell the sour tang of fear permeating the air.

"Where are you taking her?" Alric calls out, and I have the urge to thank him. After all, I'm sure he was the one who got the guard's attention, who then, in turn, called on Elijah. He might have saved my life.

"Keep your mouth shut, prisoner," Elijah snaps, bustling past the guard and through the door, not giving me the chance to say anything.

Fresh air kisses my skin as we leave the dungeon, and a small smile crosses my lips as a ray of sun shines down as if it beams just for me. Elijah must notice because he curses again and holds me tighter as he starts to move faster. The last of my energy fails me, and I drop once more into the blissful darkness.

Chapter 6

A strange ticking noise works its way into my consciousness. Frowning, I claw my way through the fog of sleep. Everything aches, and I feel like I'm lying on a cloud, which only confuses me. The thin bedding I sleep on at the refugee camp definitely doesn't feel like this. It's also much warmer here than my tiny tent.

Where am I?

Just like that, the last couple of days come back to me in flashes. The attack, being captured and dragged across half of Morrowmer, and travelling into a different land. My injury and the pain that slowly spread from my shoulder to the rest of my body and being locked in a cell, then Elijah taking me away. The fever dreams confuse and muddle a lot of my memories, so I'm not sure what's real and what was just a product of the poison working its way through my body.

Alric, the elderly male fae in the neighbouring cell. Was he real? Memories of him shouting and his whispered words to me, telling me to keep going, that I couldn't die. Everything else is fuzzy, but something in my chest tells me he was real.

My eyes feel like they are full of grit, but I force them open, needing to know where I am since it's obvious I'm no longer in the dungeon. Using my good arm, I shuffle awkwardly until I'm propped up on my left elbow, able to get a better look at my new surroundings.

I've been placed on the largest bed I've ever seen. In fact, it's so large that at least four fully grown males could fit comfortably. Shifting my attention to the rest of the room, I'm surprised to see a calming, airy space. Large, arched windows fill one side of the room, allowing sunlight to stream in. There's a small table with two chairs tucked in just beyond the bed and a huge wardrobe, but otherwise, the room is bare of personal effects. The walls are cream, adding to the breezy feeling. I see two open doorways, the one opposite me clearly leading to a bathroom, but I can't tell what awaits me in the other room.

Overall, it's nothing like what I'd expect from this castle of beasts. Whose room is this?

I'm surprised I've been left alone. I am a prisoner, after all. There's got to be some sort of spell around the room like there was in the cells, but as I reach for my power, I find it responds to me immediately.

Am I feeling better because my power is back? Sure, I still feel like I've been run over several times with a cart, but compared to how I had been, I feel worlds better.

Although everything in my body aches, I am far stronger than I was before. Glancing at my shoulder, I notice it's been neatly dressed with clean, white bandages. Did Elijah do this?

As if thinking of the male summoned him, there's a shift in the air that has me looking up just in time to see him walking through the adjoining doorway with a book in his hand. He seems a little surprised to see me awake, but that look is soon replaced by a raised eyebrow and a cocky smile. "That was a rather extreme way of trying to get my attention." Placing the book on the table by the end of the bed, he grabs one of the chairs and pulls it over. Once sitting, he throws his legs up on the bed and props his arms behind his head. His actions are casual and his smile is broad, but his eyes say otherwise as he watches me intently.

I go to speak, but my throat is so dry that all that comes out is a croak. Magically, a glass of water appears in front of me, and I know it's Elijah's doing even if he's just watching me with that smirk. Nodding in thanks, I take the glass and sip the blessedly cool water. It's not until I start drinking that I realise just how thirsty I am. Tipping the glass back, I swallow great gulps of the liquid. The water tastes so clean and pure here, nothing like the boiled water we had to drink at the camps. Many of the humans fell ill from drinking dirty, unclean water, so this is like a luxury.

"Steady, you'll make yourself sick if you keep gulping it like that."

As quickly as it arrived, the glass disappears. I snarl at Elijah, my fae instincts kicking in. Realising what I've just done, I instinctively shrink back, waiting for the punishment that will inevitably follow.

The high elves pride themselves on their control and wealth of knowledge. Any show of aggression is seen as a weakness. Under the queen's rule, punishment for such a transgression was swift and brutal. As such, I raise my arm to protect my head and wait for the pain to come.

Except it doesn't.

Lowering my arm, I meet his gaze. The atmosphere between us has turned tense, and although he's obviously trying to stay calm, confusion and anger simmers in his eyes. I don't blame him. I've snarled at him and many of the other fae here, but I was being dragged across the country at the time. However, he's never raised a hand to hurt me before, yet some behaviours are harder to break than others.

Lowering his hands from behind his head, Elijah leans forward, his legs falling from the bed. An air of menace surrounds him, yet I get the impression it's not aimed at me. "What was that?" His voice is even and uncharacteristically neutral.

"I snarled... I—" Saying it out loud makes it sound trivial, and my cheeks flush with my embarrassment, but I keep my chin raised, meeting his darkening gaze.

"You're apologising for your nature?" It's phrased as a question, but it comes out more like a statement. Understanding flashes across his face before being rapidly replaced by anger. "You're fae, you protect what's yours, and you should never apologise for that." He's trying to restrain his anger and frustration, his words clipped. "Ever. Do you understand me?"

I couldn't look away even if I wanted to, his gaze holding me in place. Seconds pass, but it could have been minutes as I lose all track of time, stuck in a battle of wills. Finally, I nod sharply. As if that conversation never happened, he smiles and stretches out again, his legs swinging back up onto the bed, settling dangerously close to mine.

Shuffling in the bed, I attempt to sit up properly and rest against the headboard. It feels strange to be having a conversation with my captor while I'm lying in what I assume is his bed. I'm no longer wearing the dirty dress I arrived in, and I'm only in my undergarments. Mortified, I clutch the covers to my chest. Slowly, I manage to sit up with a lot of wincing and clenched teeth. I'm sure I could ask Elijah for help, but I want to do it by myself, especially given my state of undress.

Now that I'm more comfortable, I glance at him and see he's no longer watching me, his attention on the view outside the windows. Is something happening out there, or is he just giving me the privacy I desired?

Tilting my head to one side, I examine him. Although his skin is tanned and he has the same brown and gold hair as the creatures I've seen here, that's where the similarities end. He doesn't have claws, horns, or a tail like the other fae here. From what I've noticed of the others, they seem to have little or no power. Elijah is different.

Feeling my regard, he returns his attention to me. His dark eyes gleam as he catches me staring at him, and that smirk returns.

Clearing my throat, I run my hand through my tangled hair. "What happened?" I ask, needing to fill the gaps in my memory.

Elijah's smirk drops, and his sigh makes me realise just how tired he is. He hides it well behind the swagger, but in this moment, I can see through the façade.

"Brok, the fae that injured your shoulder, is a creature known as an apanthe. They have poison on their claws, and it must have gotten into your system when he caught you," he explains, confirming what Alric told me in the dungeon. My memories from my time in the cell are fuzzy, like dreams, so I'm not sure what was real and what were fever dreams.

"I assumed your power was fighting it off. How you

managed to travel that far without collapsing from the poison's effects..." Trailing off, Elijah looks away, shaking his head as if he still can't believe it. "I've seen people die from a wound caused by the apanthe. It's one of the master's favourite ways of killing his enemies, as it takes hours to fully kill its victim and it's excruciating. Yet you hardly made a sound." His eyes flicker over my face, and for a moment, they pause on my lips, a frown crossing his features.

The hair on my arms stands on end and paranoia makes my stomach churn. Why would he look there? And that frown... it's like he knows something I've not told him. Fighting the urge to reach up and touch my lips, to check I'm still free of the queen's magic, I take a few slow, deep breaths. *She's dead, you're free of her. She's dead.*

Unaware of my internal panic, Elijah shakes his head. "Why didn't you say anything? I should have known. I noticed you were getting weaker, I just assumed it was the trauma of being taken and the journey..." He trails off, a mixture of emotions crossing his face, but I can't quite work them out.

A quiet knock sounds from the other room, and as if flipping a switch, Elijah jumps to his feet and walks away without another word. I hear a door opening and then a quiet female voice. I can't make out what they are saying, and my chest tightens with apprehension. Pulling the covers closer around me, I automatically scan the room for possible escape routes. Realistically I know it's pointless. I'm in no state to run away, not to mention the only way out would be to jump from the window.

Two sets of footsteps sound from the other room, and my head snaps around to the doorway. Elijah enters first, scanning me with his dark eyes before stepping to the side and gesturing towards me. A female apanthe approaches me with a bowl of supplies in her hands. Jerking away from her, I look at Elijah for reassurance that she's not going to hurt me. Memories of Brok slicing my shoulder and the stress of being stolen from my land are making me doubt everyone. Except Elijah apparently. I don't seem to fear him. No, that's not true. I have a healthy respect for the fact he's the most powerful being I've ever met, and his rapid change of emotions reminds me how dangerous he is. However, out of everyone I've met, he's been constant and has never hurt me. He rescued me from the dungeon when I was dying, and although he's the bad guy in all this, I still find myself turning to him.

The apanthe stops as she sees my reaction to her presence. She's shorter than others of her kind, but still taller than me, her broad body making me feel petite. Her face looks much like mine and doesn't have any animalistic features except those mesmerising golden eyes that watch me carefully. Her coarse, golden-brown hair falls in waves around her face, and unlike the others, I don't see any horns. With a shudder, I notice she has wicked-looking claws. Movement catches my eye, and I see flashes of a tail flicking behind her.

Placing the bowl on the table by the end of the bed, she holds out both hands in a gesture that I assume is her showing me she means me no harm. "Don't fear me." The words are thick with her accent, and I get the impression she doesn't use the common tongue often. She nods towards my shoulder then points to the bowl of supplies. "I dress the wound now."

Elijah has been viewing the whole exchange silently, but now he takes a step forward, pulling my attention back to him. "Bodil is a healer. I trust her. She helped remove the poison from your system."

Raising my eyebrows, I glance back at Bodil. I assumed Elijah had dressed my wound, but if this female removed the poison from my body, then she saved my life. She was probably ordered to help me and was just doing her job, and I still don't know why I'm here or what they plan to do with me, however, I'm still grateful for her care. I don't know how much of the common tongue she understands, so I place a hand over my chest. "Thank you." I put as much of my gratitude in the words as I can, hoping it crosses the language barrier.

She simply nods her large head and gestures for me to lower the covers I'm clutching tightly. "I see the wound now."

Taking a deep breath, I let the blankets drop to my waist, revealing my upper body. I'm wearing a wrap around my breasts, so I'm not wholly exposed, but I can't look at Elijah. Seeing that I'm uncomfortable, Bodil turns to Elijah. "You leave."

The stupefaction on Elijah's face is almost enough to make me laugh out loud. He's not used to others giving him orders. "Excuse me?" His tone is surprised, but a dark look crosses his features.

Bodil doesn't seem to care. Placing her hands on her hips, she meets his stare. "Leave. You make girl uncomfortable."

I want to object to the 'girl' comment, but I'm too surprised at this whole exchange to comment. The two of them face off, and to my amazement, Elijah relents first.

His gaze slides to me, and his dark expression doesn't change. "I'll be in the next room."

To an outsider, it might sound like he's warning me not to attempt to escape, but something in my gut says he's telling me this as a comfort. If I feel unsafe, he's not far away. He saw my fear of Bodil when I realised she was an apanthe and is acting almost as a protector. My mind is flooded with confusion at all his contradictions. *He's the one I should be scared of,* I remind myself, yet even I don't believe that.

"Thank you," I whisper once he's gone. It's not like I've not been naked around males before—I am over a century old, after all—but in this situation, I feel vulnerable, and I don't want him to see that side of me.

Bodil nods again, her lips twisting up into a terrifying semblance of a smile. She reaches out and pats my leg in what I assume is a gesture of assurance. *Perhaps she could be an ally.* The thought is quick and makes me frown as I consider the possibility.

I don't have a chance to think on it any further, though, because Bodil reaches forward and begins to remove the dressing on my shoulder. Wincing, I try to keep still as she peels it away and hums as she examines what's beneath. I glance at the wound despite the healer at my side tsking her disapproval. Since most of the wound is over my shoulder and down my back, I have to twist to get a better view, but what I do see makes my stomach roil. The three slashes have been left open, the position of the wound making it impossible to stitch, but much of the redness and swelling has gone down since yesterday. I must have been close to death, the muting of my power making me as feeble as a human and unable to fight the poison.

"I clean now," Bodil informs me, gesturing for me to lean forward so she can access the whole wound.

Nodding my understanding, I manage to shuffle into a more comfortable position.

We're silent as the healer cleans and dresses my shoulder. I wonder how she would manage to do it with those long claws, but she's incredibly gentle. I grit my teeth a couple of times as she dabs at it, but otherwise, I remain quiet. I can sense Elijah's presence lingering in the other room, like he's waiting to swoop in the moment anything happens.

Bodil is just binding my shoulder in clean bandages when someone pounds on the door. For a heartbeat, we all freeze. I hear Elijah's footsteps as he strides towards the door, and I tilt my head to the side, not wanting to miss anything that's said, thanking the Great Mother for my enhanced fae hearing.

"Why, Brok, what brings you to my bedroom?" Elijah purrs, his voice sensual, and I can just imagine him leaning against the doorframe, his body language casual. I stiffen as I realise who's here—Brok. He's the reason I'm injured. He caused me pain, revelled in it, and would have continued to hurt me if Elijah hadn't intervened. I hold my breath, as if by making myself as still as possible he might not see me. There could only be one reason why he's here. Brok didn't hide his dislike of Elijah, which is putting it mildly, so I know the fae isn't here for a social visit.

"I'm here for the girl."

That deep, growling voice has my heart thumping in my chest as he confirms my suspicions. I realise I can understand them and that Elijah started the conversation in the common language, knowing I'm listening. Perhaps it's a warning too, thinking Brok's presence would distress me.

There's a pause, and although I can't see him, I can visualise Elijah's icy calm expression that hides the burning anger beneath. "The girl is under protection. In case you forget, she's *ma promessa*."

A growl fills the room, and I must flinch because Bodil places a hand on my leg, squeezing gently. I turn to look at her, and she meets my wide eyes with a small nod. She's telling me I'm safe here.

"I am well aware, mutt," the apanthe snarls, the last word spat with hatred. Heavy footsteps follow, and I picture him stepping into Elijah's space. "The master sent me. He isn't happy that you took her from the cells."

My hands grip the covers, my knuckles turning white with the force.

"She was dying from *your* poison," Elijah counters, his voice sounding dangerous now. "If I left her there, she would be dead."

"You should have taken her to the healing quarters, not hidden her away in your room." There's a pause as Brok lets his words sink in. "Remember your oath."

"You don't need to remind me," Elijah sneers, disgust saturating his reply. "I know what's expected of me."

A frown pulls at my brow. *Oath?* This is the first I've heard of an oath. He says it with anger... Is he frustrated at Brok and the insinuation that he isn't doing his duty? Or is it more than that? Elijah's tied to the master somehow, and I want to know why.

"I was protecting the female," Elijah continues, his voice back to the controlled calm that I've heard him use with the other apanthe. "When she's healed, I'll send her back to the cells."

It's a clear dismissal, but Brok either doesn't take the hint or deliberately ignores it. The apanthe's snarl echoes from the other room. "The master wants her there now. She was supposed to be punished, not waited on by you."

"She's injured, she nearly died!" The words end on a growl, and I know Elijah's struggling to stay in control. "I'd say that was punishment enough!"

"It's not up to you. The girl comes with me now."

No. Images burst through my mind, flashbacks that try to drag me into my twisted memories. Although I know what's awaiting me in the cells, I can't tell the difference between fact and fiction as my past trauma replays in my head. Those same words were used as I was ripped away from the only family I'd ever known and taken to the elf queen. The sound of their cries and snarls as they tried to stop it turned to screams and shouts of pain as the guards slaughtered them.

Squeezing my eyes shut and taking several calming breaths, I force myself into the present, feeling the bed beneath me and the sun on my skin. I breathe in the fresh scent of the room and focus on the gentle sounds of Bodil working around me, grounding myself.

I hear Bodil take a deep breath and shift closer, obviously scenting my fear. I don't know what I've done to gain her protection, but I'm grateful for it. The healer is quiet and kind, caring for me now and while I was unconscious. In the very short time I've known her, I've come to like the feline-like fae.

"No," Elijah snarls.

Opening my eyes, I glance around. I obviously missed some of the conversation during my flashbacks, and I'm unsure how the exchange has broken down between the two fae at the door. I hear a commotion followed by snarling and growling, only for Brok to appear in the doorway. He's much bigger than I remember, his golden eyes narrowed on me. Brok's top lip is pulled back, exposing his fangs as he takes a step towards me. Out of nowhere, Elijah appears, blocking his view of me, his body rippling with anger. If things don't de-escalate soon, there's going to be a fight.

I hastily cover myself at the other apanthe's entrance, jerking my shoulder in the process and letting out a hiss of pain. Bodil bristles, slamming her equipment on the small table and lurching to her feet. Reaching the two males, who are snarling and facing off against each other, she growls low in her throat to get their attention then crosses her arms. "Get out, I am working."

To my surprise, I realise she's addressing both males. Elijah gapes at her with a dumbfounded expression, as if no one's ever spoken to him like that. Brok, on the other hand, looks a little frightened as he brings his attention to the healer. I get the feeling he hadn't realised she was here and knows he's about to get a lecture.

"She's coming with me," he repeats, attempting to step around the healer.

This, apparently, is the wrong thing to do. Bodil's body seems to grow, not only in height but in bulk too, her tail flicking angrily as she stares down at Brok. She reverts to her native language, the guttural sounds making no sense to me, but I can tell from her tone and exaggerated gestures that she's not happy. Striding forward, she pokes Brok in the chest, and to my surprise, he staggers back, looking contrite. He tries to argue, but the healer cuts him off.

Watching in amazement as Brok concedes, I glance over and see Elijah grinning, obviously enjoying the spectacle. Brok follows my gaze and growls at the fae, but

Bodil just barks at him again, poking him in the chest once more.

His chest heaves, and his face twists with anger and humiliation, but after a moment of silence, he nods sharply. "If she's not in the cells by nightfall, the master will have your head," Brok sneers, glaring at me as he steps back and storms from the room. I hear the door slam loudly as he departs.

The atmosphere in the room instantly relaxes now that he's gone. Elijah stalks over and leans against the footboard, flashing me a victorious smile. However, my eyes are still on Bodil, whose body has to be almost double the size it was when she first arrived. She's staring at the door as if she expects the guard to come back, and it looks like she's attempting to shield me with her frame.

Seeing my curious regard, Elijah chuckles quietly. "Apanthe females are very protective of those they think of as theirs. They are able to increase their body size as needed to protect that person." He gestures towards her as he explains. "This makes them great healers as they fully dedicate themselves to their patients."

Bodil huffs, the snorting noise reminding me of a horse, then shakes her head as she mutters under her breath in her native language. Bustling over, she attempts to give me a smile, but with her anger, large form, and dagger-sharp fangs, she looks terrifying. However, I find I'm not scared of her anymore. Wary, yes, but she doesn't frighten me.

"Males think they rule everything," she mutters, shaking her head again as she sits next to me, picking up where she left off with dressing my shoulder. "Bustle in, demanding." From her disgusted tone and the frustration that's coursing through her body, I get the impression she and Brok have a history. "Girl healing, and Bodil working."

A smile pulls at my lips. "The males are the same where I'm from," I explain, my response earning a huff of laughter from her. I'm aware of Elijah's assessing gaze on me, but I keep my attention on Bodil. She just protected me from one of her own, yet she doesn't even know my name. This is something I want to remedy. My mouth twitches up into a smile again. "My name is Annalise."

I told her because she'd previously only referred to me as 'girl.' My name is part of my identity, and that was taken away from me under the elf queen's rule, so I intend on using it. However, I get the impression from the stilling of her body and her solemn eyes that it means much more to her. She simply bows her head before continuing to wrap my shoulder.

Elijah clears his throat, and my gaze flashes up to his as he watches us from the end of the bed. "I've bought you some time, but you'll have to return to the cells tonight."

He doesn't seem happy about this development, but I'd assumed as much. I am a prisoner here, after all. I'm still trying to wrap my head around the fact I'm in his bedroom. To be in the cells one moment and then to open my eyes and find I'm somewhere different was disorienting. Knowing that for a period of time I was unaware, that anything could have happened to me...

Movement beside me breaks me from the dangerous path my mind was wandering down, and I see Bodil standing and packing her equipment. Catching me watching her, she smiles slightly, her body slowly returning to normal. "It is healing well. Keep dry. Dressing comes off tomorrow." Her instructions are halting as she searches for the words in the common language, but I nod in understanding. Spinning and narrowing her eyes on Elijah, she barks instructions at him in their language, gesturing towards me several times. I raise my eyebrows but keep quiet, not wanting her to turn that expression on me—especially when Elijah looks serious, nodding along and replying with a respectful tone.

Assured by whatever he said, Bodil huffs out a breath, and with one last look at me, she gathers her bowl of supplies and heads to the door. Elijah follows her out, thanking her in a low voice.

As he walks back into the bedroom, I notice most of the swagger he used around the others is gone, leaving only his self-satisfied smile. I don't bother to say anything, simply levelling him with a look, the question in my expression obvious.

Laughing, he strolls towards me, taking the seat at my side once again. "She was telling me off for letting you get that sick and instructing me to let you rest. She isn't happy about you going back to the cells, knowing it will limit your healing. However, if you stay up here until nightfall, your power should be able to knit your skin together enough so it won't be an open wound any longer."

Humming, I lean back against the pillows, digesting his words. I hadn't considered that going back to the dungeon would impact my healing again. However, what Elijah said is true—if my power can work on the wound now, closing the gaping slashes in my skin, then it shouldn't matter too much once I'm returned to my cell. I still have no idea why I've been brought here, but I guess only time will tell. The master will come for me eventually.

Elijah seems content to sit at my side, his book from earlier reappearing in his hand as he leans back.

"Do the apanthe have power?" I've been wondering this since I was taken and first met the beast-like fae, and the exchange between the two apanthe has only made me more curious.

Placing the book in his lap, Elijah seems to think for a few seconds, as if trying to work out how much he can tell me. "Not in the same sense as you and me. Their power comes in combat. They *become* weapons when they fight, their bodies changing to meet the need. You've seen how the females have very strong protective instincts and adaptability." He pauses, his eyes shuttering a bit. "There have been half-breeds who have had some magical ability, but they're shunned. The apanthe take breeding and keeping their family lines strong very seriously."

Although he speaks casually, there's a coldness to him. *I am well aware, mutt.* Brok's words from earlier ring in my mind. *Mutt.* Is Elijah one of these half-breeds? He certainly shares some characteristics, such as his hair colour and tanned skin, but otherwise he stands out, especially his power. I know he's under an oath, but what brought him here and bound him to these creatures?

"Now the master, he's a whole different beast altogether," he continues, chuckling, his expression dark. "He's apanthe, but he has the power of a higher being."

My ears perk at this information. Just who is this master, and how has he managed to tie someone as powerful as Elijah to him?

As if knowing I'm about to ask another question,

Elijah simply smiles and shakes his head. "That's enough for now. You need to rest."

I open my mouth to argue, I still have so many more questions, but a wave of exhaustion rolls over me and my eyelids droop. I know he's using his power, forcing me into sleep, but I just don't have the energy to fight it. The mattress and pillows welcome me like an old friend as I sink into them.

Just before sleep pulls me under, I roll my eyes over to Elijah, catching his concerned expression. I know his expression will haunt my dreams.

"Sleep, Annalise," he murmurs, his tone gentle, and I finally give up my battle.

My eyes fall shut, and I sink into blissful oblivion.

Chapter 7

As I splash warm water over my face, I smile. It's the first time I've felt clean in months. The bubbles from the bath surround me, and the steam from the water helps clear my mind.

The joy of having fresh, clean water at the turn of a tap is a luxury I missed in the camps. Six months is a long time to go without being able to bathe, unless you classify the terrifying dip I took in a lake I found in the Great Forest back in Morrowmer. Situated away from the rest of the refugees, it seemed like a good idea to wash while I had privacy. What I hadn't realised was that a kelpie lived in the lake. I was lucky he didn't drag me to the bottom, giving me a watery death. He simply screeched an ear-piercing cry, scaring the life out of me as I was about to submerge myself. I've never moved so quickly before and hadn't wanted to risk it again, instead washing from a bucket of freezing water in my tent.

When I woke from my enchanted sleep, I found that Elijah was gone, but there was a note with my name left on the chair. The elegant script explained that he was needed elsewhere, and there were wards on this room so I couldn't escape. He suggested taking a bath or browsing his collection of books rather than wasting my time trying to flee.

Of course I still had to check that the room *was* warded. I tried all the windows and then crept to the door to confirm that they were all locked. There was no way I wasn't going to at least try to find a way out.

However, the promise of a bath pulled me away from the door, which is where I am now. I don't know how long I've been in the bath, but the water is beginning to cool and the skin on my feet is starting to resemble a prune. Sighing, I pull the plug to drain the water, being careful not to get my shoulder wet. Climbing from the bath, I catch sight of myself in the mirror, and what I see causes a lump to form in the back of my throat. As an elf, my body is more lithe than a human's, but months of living on rations and moving from camp to camp have taken their toll on me. Some days I would go without eating anything, depending on who the cook was that day, since some took their prejudice against elves out on me.

My skin is pale, and I have the pallor of someone who's been sick for a very long time. Ribs and other bony prominences stick out, and the muscle I used to have has begun to atrophy from starvation. No wonder the journey here was so hard on my body. It's a miracle I even made it, considering the poison had been crawling through my veins. The Great Mother, Menishea, must have been looking out for me. My long brown hair hangs limply, and my face is gaunt. The haunted look in my eyes disturbs me, so I quickly look away.

I had been beautiful once, full of life and excitement.

I wanted to explore the world, but that thirst for more led to me witnessing too much, something the elf queen couldn't allow to be public knowledge. When she took me, I swore I hadn't told anyone else what I'd heard. She either didn't believe me or couldn't risk that I wasn't truthful, so she had my family killed before enslaving me. *All my fault*, my mind whispers, and I have to screw my eyes shut. On really bad nights, I don't always dream of my punishment or torture, instead I hear the sounds of their screams.

Pushing those thoughts deep down, I take a breath and open my eyes. I hear footsteps in the other room, reminding me that I'm dripping wet and standing naked in another male's bathroom. Reaching towards the bundle of fabric that's waiting for me on the counter, I find a towel, a simple, well-made loose shirt, chest bindings, and a pair of trousers. I dry off quickly and pull them on. There's no underwear and I have to roll up the bottom of the trousers, but I feel so much better in clean clothes.

Opening the door, I see Elijah leaning against the window arch, a faraway look on his face. I walk over slowly, curious at what's caused his expression. He glances at me briefly, taking in my new clothes and wet hair, giving me a small smile before returning his gaze to the window. Stepping up to the glass, but keeping a healthy distance between us, I take in the view. We're high up, perhaps two or three floors, and I can see the stables from here, but mostly I just see the forest on the other side of the wall. A breeze works its way through the branches, the leaves dancing on the wind as if beckoning to us. The sun has dipped behind the trees, and my stomach flips, knowing what that means for me.

"It'll be dark soon," he mutters, almost as if to himself,

but he turns his head to look at me. Although I'd rather go anywhere but the cells again, I give him a sharp nod. If I put up a fight, I have no doubt the master will come and get me, and I fear him far more than I do the dungeon. "Are you ready?"

I hadn't realised we were going now, and anticipation courses through me. What would he do if I said no? If I asked him not to take me? I almost laugh at the notion. He may be the best of a bad bunch, but he's still one of the bad guys. He wouldn't care. In fact, based on his behaviour with the others, he would probably laugh at my request and drag me down to the cells.

No, he wouldn't, my inner thoughts argue. *He saved your life.*

Elijah watches me through my internal battle, waiting for my response. Finally, I blow out a breath, remind myself I've survived worse, and meet his eyes. "I'm ready."

His expression is grim as he nods and reaches for my hands. Cringing, I have to fight my instincts to pull away and cradle them against my chest. My wrists have only just healed from being dragged here. The bonds had cut into my skin, rubbing them raw. Now, only a slight red mark remains, which just goes to show how severe the injury to my shoulder was, considering it was still an open wound this morning.

Seeing my reaction, he pauses for a fraction of a second, a frown pulling at his brow. He gently touches my forearms, making a circular movement, and the scent of his power fills the room as a glowing, cool band encircles each wrist. Eyes wide, I try to move them and find they are fixed in position. They don't hurt, instead they soothe the raised skin from the previous restraints.

I open my mouth to thank him, but he looks away and breezes past, heading for the doorway. He pauses and turns to me, arching an eyebrow as he gestures for me to follow. Gathering my courage, I keep my face placid as I pad to his side.

We reach the dungeon quicker than I'm prepared for. Each step we descend below the castle, the colder it feels, and the hairs on my arms stand on end with the chill. We're entering from a different entrance, and as we wait on the other side of the door for one of the guards to allow us entrance, I have to take several deep breaths to stay in control.

I should have paid more attention to the castle's layout as Elijah led me through, as per my original plan, but the closer we got, the harder it was for me to concentrate. From what I saw of the interior, it was beautiful in a way I hadn't expected, except we used the servants' corridors most of our journey, which limited my observations. Now that we're here, I find my stomach flipping with tension and uncertainty.

"How long will he keep me here for?"

They are the first words I've spoken to Elijah since we left his rooms, and I seem to startle him from his thoughts. He begins to answer, but the door swings open, and a disgruntled-looking guard merely grunts at us before stepping to the side so we can enter. Elijah's mouth snaps shut, his eyes narrowing cruelly on the male. The guard seems to remember who's standing before him, and he sketches a hasty bow.

Elijah ignores him, striding past and placing a hand

on my good shoulder as he pulls me into the dungeon. Although it must look like he's dragging me in, his touch is gentle. Blinking against the sudden dimness of the stone space, I realise we've entered at the other end of the cells. To the right, Alric is curled up on his cot, facing the wall, and on the other side of him is my cell, its door hanging open.

Although I know to expect it, the tingling sensation that covers me as I step over the threshold of my cell still makes me shudder. The door screeches shut behind me, and as I turn around, I see Elijah's mood has shifted again. Leaning against the bars of the opposite cell, he looks down at his nails before picking an imaginary piece of lint from his clothing, not paying any attention to me. Finally, he sighs and pushes away from the bars like being down here is a burden, but when he meets my neutral expression, his eyes flash with a warning. Everything we do or say is being watched.

Striding to my cell, he grips the bars and leans forward as far as the metal will let him. "You're being punished by the master, but don't get too comfortable. He'll be calling for you soon," he drawls with a smirk. Winking, he spins on his heel and stalks back the way he came, barking at the guards in their native language.

Glancing around the cell, I see nothing's changed since I was here last. I shuffle over to the cot and sit, thinking over Elijah's parting words. It was an answer to my earlier question and a warning. It's obvious he believes he can't talk freely down here, as there are too many listening ears to report what they hear, both from the guards and the prisoners.

I lean back against the stone wall, listening to the comings and goings of the dungeon. Something I learned in my many years of enforced silence is that people forget you're there when you say nothing and don't attract attention. Blending into the background and not being seen were skills I quickly picked up, and it's the same here. The guards relax once Elijah's gone and either forget our presence or simply don't care, moving to the guardroom at the entrance of the dungeon. They keep the door between the two spaces open, presumably so they can keep an eye on us, but they are so busy talking that I doubt they would really notice us unless we attempted to escape. They have reverted to their native tongue, so I can't understand what they are saying, but I hear Elijah's name mentioned often, and from their tones, I can tell it's nothing pleasant.

"Annalise."

The quiet, scratchy voice makes me jump, but I know who it is instantly. Glancing towards the open doorway where the guards are laughing loudly about something, I tentatively turn to my neighbour.

"Alric," I murmur in greeting just as quietly. He's sitting up and has moved towards the wall of bars separating us. For such an old fae, he's surprisingly stealthy.

"Are you okay?" He scans me from head to toe, looking like he wants to jump up and see for himself, but his hands tighten on the edge of the cot as he restrains himself. "Did he hurt you?" The quiet snarl in his voice surprises me.

I know whom he's talking about and assume Elijah wouldn't want me to tell others of his kindness towards me. From what I overheard, he should have taken me to the healers, so why didn't he? Why put himself on a limb to make sure I was healed and under his constant supervision? He keeps calling me that name, *ma promessa*, but I get the impression it's more than just that. Alric obviously expects me to be traumatised from being with Elijah. Just what did he expect the other fae to do to me?

I don't hide my shudder at the thought. There's no doubt in my mind that Elijah's done some terrible things. I've seen the darkness in his eyes, but does that mean I think he's evil? I've always believed that actions speak louder than words, and so far, everything he's done has been to help me, although he hides it. Should I play along? No, I won't lie, not about something like that.

Brushing back my clean hair, I notice my hand trembles slightly. I'm sure it's from the fact I've eaten next to nothing in the past forty-eight hours and I'm reaching the last of my energy reserves, but I notice Alric watching with a frown, clearly assuming the worst. I should correct him, tell him the real reason my body shakes and my movements are jerky, but I don't. Something in my chest twists. I may not be lying, but by not correcting what he's thinking, I'm still deceiving him. Is that any better?

"I'm healing. I was given time to let my power work," I explain. Every word is true, but as his expression shifts, I know he's taking my lack of a direct answer as confirmation of his thoughts. "No one hurt me, Alric," I add firmly.

He watches me for a few more seconds then nods, blowing out a breath as he leans back against the wall. Something has been bothering me ever since I was taken, and I'm hoping Alric can explain it to me.

Glancing around, I make sure no one is listening and the guards are still distracted. "Why does everyone keep calling me *ma promessa*?" I need to know the answer.

He stills as soon as I say the foreign words, and I think he's going to remain silent. I start to reposition myself on the cot, turning away from him when he clears his throat.

"I heard Elijah say that when he took you away, but I thought I misheard."

The way he says it puts me on edge, but I can't place a finger on why. Glancing over, I see he's watching me again, a frown pulling at his weathered brow.

"It's a name these fae give to..." He trails off and shakes his head, lost in his thoughts. "It can't be possible though." He gazes back up at me, scanning my face as if he's looking for something specific. "You're not from this land. It shouldn't be possible."

He's talking more to himself than to me, but my frustration increases. Why is getting an answer to this question so difficult? "What? What's not possible?"

"There are some fae in this land, the apanthe included, who believe there are certain females that..." His face twists as if he's in physical pain, and a groan leaves his lips. He slumps forward, taking great, gasping breaths.

"Alric?" I call, concern coursing through me. Eyes wide, I jump up and hurry to the bars, peering at the elderly fae. I have no idea what's happening or how to help him. Should I call for the guards? Would they even care?

"I'm okay. I'm okay."

A wave of relief fills me at his quiet muttering. For a moment, I thought I killed off the closest thing I have to a friend here. Heart pounding, I sink to my knees on the dirty stone floor. It's obvious he's still recovering from whatever just happened, so I simply sit quietly, offering him my silent support.

His breathing returns to normal, and with a quiet groan, he sits back, surprise flashing across his features as he sees me sitting on the floor. A strange expression crosses his face, but he looks away as he rubs his forehead. "There are some things I cannot say, otherwise this happens." He gestures to himself, phrasing his words oddly, as if unsure what to say... or what he's allowed to say.

Surely only a great and terrible magic would be able to stop him from speaking of certain subjects. A memory of Elijah comes to mind. He tried to explain something to me and was cut off. It's not just Alric, but all of them, I realise with shock. Who, or what, is powerful enough to cast something such as this?

Alric has fallen silent again, whether through choice or a magical gag, I'm not sure. Speaking still makes me uneasy beyond simple responses, however, I need answers. I'm not going to be kept in the dark any longer.

"The apanthe are searching for 'special' females?" I prompt, watching as Alric lifts his head from his hands.

He seems surprised I've instigated a conversation, but he doesn't question it. "Yes, the master collects them, hoarding them to himself..." He trails off again, and his Adam's apple works in his throat as he tries to speak. He takes a deep breath. "Until now, they have all been from this land, different territories, but from the fae lands. You are the first to be brought back from over the mountains."

So the master is creating his own harem of 'special' females and wants to add me to his collection. Why was I brought back? Are the females in this land not enough? And how did Elijah know just by looking at me that I was one of these females? There must be something that makes me stand out, considering he stopped and just *knew* in the middle of battle. That thought makes me uncomfortable and I look away, my gaze falling to my hands that rest in my lap.

I laugh once, but it's devoid of humour. "He will be disappointed, for there is nothing special about me." My own self-loathing taints my words.

Alric shifts, once again moving so fast it startles me. One moment he's seated on the cot, and the next, he's kneeling at the bars before me. "I disagree." His voice may be cracked with age, but I hear the firmness in his tone. My gaze flashes up to meet his, and I'm surprised again by the clarity in those crystal-clear eyes.

He opens his mouth as if to speak again, but his eyes shift to something behind me and his face shuts down. With a flash, he is once again curled up on his cot, facing the wall. Shuffling sounds behind me, alerting me to someone entering the room. Jerking back from the bars, I get to my feet, clutching my aching shoulder as I watch one of the guards stalk in with a twisted smile on his face. Taking the sword hanging from the holster at his waist, he raises it and runs it along the bars as he strolls down the corridor, the loud metallic noise rousing my fellow prisoners.

"Wake up, scum. It's chow time."

The use of the common tongue surprises me, but there are so many fae of different shapes and sizes down here that I suppose it's necessary. Groaning and grumbling fill the air, but no one seems surprised by the guard's abrupt entrance, so this must be a regular occurrence. However, something about this guard puts me on edge. I don't know if it's the smug look on his face or the cruel glint in his eyes, but I know I need to stay away from him. I can recognise a male who enjoys violence from a mile off, and this guard is certainly one of them.

He slows as he reaches the end of the row, his eyes lighting up as they land on me. "Well, well, looks like it's supper time for all of us. I wouldn't mind a taste of you." His eyes roam over my body, and I fight the urge to cower and cover myself, knowing it will only entice him more. I will not give males like him power over me ever again.

"A little skinny for my taste," he drawls, continuing his assessment of me. "But a beauty all the same."

He takes a step towards my door, excitement emitting from him as he wraps his hands around the metal bars separating us. Holding my ground, I snarl at him, my feral fae nature rising to the surface. Usually I'd push it down, master my anger, but I'm unable to hold back at his ogling.

"Leave that one, she belongs to the master. He'll have your head."

The other voice snaps my focus to a second guard pulling a trolley laden with trays into the room. Judging he's not a threat, I return my attention to the male still leering my way.

The comment from his fellow guard doesn't seem to deter him. If anything, he looks more excited. "Only if he finds out," he whispers to me, his eyes gleaming as he steps back.

Alric is suddenly standing at the bars, his lips pulled back in a snarl as he stares at the male, but the guard only gives him a cursory glance before winking at me and walking towards his colleague.

Backing away, I silently sit on my cot, crossing my legs beneath me. Unfortunately, I've met males like him before. They always want what they can't have. I'm a challenge, and he won't stop until he gets what he wants or is forced to halt his efforts.

Numbly, I observe as the guards place the trays through a small hatch at the bottom of each cell, only half paying attention to what's happening around me. The rest of my mind is back in Morrowmer as memories try to worm their way into my consciousness despite the wall I've built around them. I may appear tranquil on the outside, but inside there's a battle waging.

Most of the prisoners have grabbed the food, desperately slurping their meals and scraping the bottom of the bowls to get every last morsel.

"Annalise."

Alric's voice is a whispered plea, and I slowly turn my head to find him watching me. "I won't let him hurt you."

His words ring with truth, but a frown pulls at my brow as I shake my head slowly. I don't understand why he's offering his loyalty. Fae are very protective of their own, but he barely knows me, not to mention he's locked up. If that guard stormed in here right now and tried to hurt me, there is nothing Alric could do without any power and a wall of metal separating us. "How are you going to stop him?" Gesturing to the bars, I start to turn away. His words are kind, but realistically, he can't help me.

"Annalise," he calls again. Sighing, I turn to face him and find him regarding me earnestly. "Trust me."

The only person I can truly trust is myself. If I need protection, then I'm going to have to be the one to do it. Before I was the queen's captive, I used to train with my friends and was decent with a blade. My power had still been developing, but I knew enough to shield myself. Then I was captured and unable to lift a finger without the queen's permission. Since being free, my power remained weak from lack of use, and I didn't push it or train. Instead, when something threatened me, I ran. I've become very good at running, but it did me no good against Elijah and the apanthe.

As if sensing my thoughts and knowing that I'm slowly rebuilding walls around myself, Alric clears his throat. "You don't have to do this alone."

Although I know there's nothing he can do to help me, at least physically, perhaps he's right. I don't answer him, I don't even nod, I just hold his gaze for another few seconds before climbing to my feet and retrieving my food. Returning to my cot, I sit and begin to eat the watery soup. I can't quite tell what flavour it's supposed to be, and the hunk of bread with it is stale, but it fills my cramping stomach, so I don't care. I feel Alric watching me as he eats, but I pay him no mind as I swig from the tumbler of water provided.

After I've eaten and returned my tray to the hatch, I curl up on my hard cot and pull the scratchy, flimsy blanket over me. As I fall asleep, I dream of beds made of clouds and a protective set of eyes watching over me.

Chapter 8

"Rise and shine, lowlifes!"

The shout jolts me from sleep. Jerking upright, I gasp as my still healing shoulder twinges, looking around as I try to get my bearings. Reality slams back into me and I don't hold back my groan. I rest my head in my hands as I swim through the sleepy fog in my head.

Somehow, miraculously, I slept through the night despite the hard cot and uncertain circumstances, but I blame the wound for that. Healing without my power is exhausting. I don't know how humans do it.

Seeing the guards come in with trays, I stand, roll my neck, and stretch out my limbs. I'm aware of several sets of eyes on me, but I ignore them. The other prisoners have started to watch me with interest ever since I was brought back in last night. I imagine when you're stuck in the dungeon, anything new would be entertaining, especially a fae female who's obviously not from around here. My stomach growls at the smell of food. I'm sure it's just as tasteless as last night's meal, but as long as it fills me, I don't care.

The guard approaches my cell and reaches for a tray.

"Not her," one of the senior guards calls from the open doorway to the guardroom. "She's wanted upstairs."

My gut twists, and my mind spins with this new revelation. I assume this means the master has called for me. A slightly hysterical laugh leaves me as I realise I'd prefer to stay in the dungeon rather than face that beast again. *You need to get your priorities straight*, my mind chides. Taking in a deep breath through my nose, I hold it for a few seconds before releasing it slowly through my mouth, trying to calm my convoluted thoughts. Hunger gnaws at me, but I've gone without before, so I can manage without now. Pushing the hunger pangs away, I focus on the most pressing issues.

Returning to my cot, I sit down and try to ignore the sounds of everyone eating around me as I wait.

I feel his presence before I see him. Something in my chest loosens as Elijah strolls through the door, looking wicked in a black tunic and leather trousers, weapons gleaming at his waist. His hair is slicked back as usual, and his sharp gaze takes in everything. Catching me staring, he winks at me as he saunters past like he's got all the time in the world. Although I'd just been casually observing him, his wink makes my cheeks heat like I'd been caught ogling. Reaching the guardroom, he greets those on duty in their native tongue, his tone oozing confidence. This is a male who expects to be obeyed and not have to repeat himself.

I know he's here for me, so I stand and wait by the door to my cell. One of the guards walks down the row with a scowl as he leads Elijah to me. When the guard turns around to address the taller fae, the expression drops from his face as he gestures towards me.

Nodding, Elijah dismisses the guard with a single word, not even bothering to take his eyes from me. The guard looks at his back with disgust, his hatred of Elijah palpable in the air. Just what has he done to deserve that much fear and loathing?

Opening the cell, he smirks and motions for me to exit. He grasps my shoulder and scans me as if considering something, then he raises an eyebrow. "If you promise to behave, I won't bind your wrists."

Even the mention of bindings makes my wrists ache despite being almost fully healed, the memory of the discomfort still fresh in my mind. "I promise." I nod my agreement, watching as he snorts. My reply was a little too eager.

Guiding me with a hand on the small of my back, he leads me towards the door closest to us, which will take us directly into the castle. Alric's watching me intently as I walk away, and I know I shouldn't, but I can't stop my eyes from flicking over to meet his. Of course Elijah notices, and his grip on my shoulder suddenly tightens. Without another word, we leave the dungeon, climbing the stone steps into the castle proper. Once we get to the top, Elijah directs me to the right, and I recognise the servants' corridors we took yesterday. Is he taking me to his room again? My stomach flips at the idea. Being alone with him in his bedroom when I was recovering from the poison was one thing, but now...

Swallowing the lump in the back of my throat, I instinctively reach for my power, needing to check it's still there in case I need it. Yes, there isn't much, thanks to my body directing it towards healing the remainder of the wound in my shoulder, but I've got enough to form a basic shield. I don't think I'll need it against Elijah, since he's never tried to hurt me before, but trust isn't something I give away freely.

If Elijah can sense me reaching for my power, he doesn't say anything, instead he stays uncharacteristically quiet.

I glance up at him. "Where are we going?"

His jaw tightens as I speak, his gaze remaining on the narrow passageways ahead. Have I done something? Wait, am I really asking that? They kidnapped me, and I'm wondering if I've offended one of my captors?

"The master wants to meet you again now that you've had time to 'cool off,'" Elijah finally responds, his voice cold. "He wants you to meet the other females, see how they live, and show you what you could have if you agree to be his." His jaw clenches again, and he won't look at me as we walk through the passages.

I don't know why it bothers me so much that he's not looking at me as he speaks. He seems different today, and I can't figure out why. I tell myself I'm only ruminating over it because I can't tell if he's speaking the truth when he won't meet my eyes, and I need to know for my safety. While that is something I'm genuinely worried about, a part of me knows that's not the only reason I'm feeling on edge.

I'm sure he can feel my glowering gaze on him, but he continues to look away, leading me forward with the hand on my back.

"Before he'll meet you, he requires that you bathe and dress in something more appropriate." Disgust colours his words as he's forced to say them, his oath to the master overriding his will.

I freeze, coming to a stumbling standstill. He stops with me, as if he knew I would react this way. The ringing in my ears blocks out all other sounds as my panic tries to overwhelm me. Feeling like the walls are closing in around me, I move away from Elijah, unable to abide his touch. I jolt to a halt as my back hits the wall and I slide to the floor, my eyes wide but unseeing. I shouldn't let him see me like this, but it's beyond my control. The master terrifies me, that much I can admit. I've only ever met him once, but seeing the tight grip he has over everyone here, I know he's someone to fear. Now he wants to see me, only I have to dress up for his pleasure. What does he want with me? Alric's words from last night echo in my mind. Was he right? Am I here to be part of the master's collection of females?

Elijah's face appears in my narrow field of vision as he kneels before me. He looks like he wants to reach out and touch me, but he keeps his hands to himself, and for that I'm grateful. I can't cope with physical touch right now. His mouth moves as he says something to me, his expression carefully neutral, and slowly, the ringing in my ears fades.

"Annalise, breathe," he instructs, the softness of his voice betraying his cold act. "I won't let him hurt you." His promise is said in earnest, but we both know that if the master ordered him to stand back and not to intervene, then he wouldn't be able to disobey.

Taking steady breaths, I remind myself that I survived the elf queen, so I can survive this too. The queen took so much of my life, and I won't let her haunt me any longer. Something settles over me, like a warm blanket of power wrapping around me as I make this promise to myself. Feeling stronger, both physically and mentally, I let out a long breath and push to my feet. Elijah watches me with a careful expression, standing to his full height and moving back to give me space.

"Can you tell me why I'm here?" Meeting his eyes, I go for the direct approach. Is this a case of he *won't* or *can't* tell me?

His jaw works, and I see his face tighten with concentration. Letting out a noise of frustration, he shakes his head. "No, I can't. The master will explain everything."

I want to demand for him to give me an explanation, but I remember Alric's face as he tried to explain something to me, his voice taken from him. This is the same. If the master's going to explain everything, does that mean he's behind it all, and that he somehow cast a spell over everyone that doesn't allow them to speak of certain topics? I guess I'll find out when I meet him.

Pushing aside my confusion and frustration, I gesture for Elijah to start walking. "Let's go."

He doesn't say anything, simply watching me for a second before nodding and walking down the corridor. He doesn't wait to see if I'll follow, but we both know I wouldn't get far if I tried to escape. These corridors are like a maze, and if I entered the main castle, I'd be caught almost immediately.

Following behind Elijah, I try to keep calm, making sure to focus only on the immediate future and getting through the next few hours. After several minutes of silence and climbing numerous flights of stairs, he leads me to a plain-looking door. Coming to a stop, he places his hand on my lower back once more, and I know we're about to enter the main castle. I hold my chin high and straighten my spine. I will play the role and feign confidence, even if I don't feel it inside. I won't let them know my weaknesses, and I will keep playing that role until it comes naturally and I don't have to pretend anymore.

Sensing the change in me, Elijah's lips twitch up. It's not enough to be called a smile, but it settles something inside me all the same. I nod to show I'm ready, and he throws open the door. I have to blink against the bright light filling the room. Thankfully my eyes adjust quickly, and I'm able to gather my bearings enough to see we've entered a large hallway with arched ceilings. Wooden units line the walls, adorned with large vases full of dazzling flower arrangements. Paintings of stunning landscapes and mystical woodlands grace the walls, their gilded frames ostentatious. A lush, deep blue carpet absorbs the sound of our footsteps as we walk through the corridor. It's an effort not to stare at my surroundings. This is *nothing* like I thought it would be. Who knew a beast like the master enjoyed fine artwork?

At my side, Elijah seems to have rediscovered his swagger as he saunters down the hall, smirking at the few fae we pass. Most of them seem to be apanthe, wearing the master's symbol of a roaring lion, but I see glimpses of fae who look more like me. The one thing they all have in common? They are all female. It's quiet here, peaceful, until the corridor splits into two and a menacing female apanthe steps out and blocks our path.

"What do you want? You know only females are allowed in this wing," the apanthe snarls, her body shaking slightly as if she's fighting against the protective instincts her kind possesses.

"Tarren, this is the master's new *promessa*. I'm showing her the rooms," he replies smoothly, and I can practically hear the smirk in his voice. However, I don't take my eyes from the apanthe in front of me.

The apanthe's eyes light up with realisation and interest as she runs her gaze over me, like she's only just noticed I'm there. "This is the one from the other land?" Humming, she leans forward and sniffs, her nose scrunching up in distaste. "You can go through. No funny business." Waving us forward, she dismisses us immediately.

Elijah pushes gently on the small of my back and I start to move, following his directions. I'm not really paying attention, still caught on our interaction with Tarren. Discreetly, I lower my nose to my shoulder, trying to see what caused her disgusted expression. I can't smell that bad. Sure, I slept in my clothes, but I only bathed yesterday. Elijah catches the movement and chuckles low in his throat, and I jerk my head back up, scowling at him.

We stop outside a door and my gut clenches, but I mould my expression into one of neutrality. Flinging the door open, he motions for me to enter the room with a grand flourish. I raise my brows at his behaviour then walk in suspiciously. This definitely isn't Elijah's room, and it clearly belongs to a female. A huge, airy canopy bed fills most of the back wall, and light streams in from the large, arched windows on either end of the room. A beautiful wooden dresser is teeming with lotions and bottles of perfumes. There is a mirror attached to the wall behind it and a stool just waiting for someone to use. The biggest wardrobe I've ever seen, with its doors propped open, holds a menagerie of dresses and bright fabrics. Flowers sit on every available surface, giving the room a gentle floral scent. There's an open doorway to my right, and another room waiting beyond, but I turn to face Elijah who's watching me with an odd expression.

Looking around the room again, I glance at the doorway, expecting someone to come barging through any moment. "Whose room is this? Why are we here?" I keep my voice low, not wanting to disturb anyone who may be staying here. Elijah said I needed to 'prepare myself' for the master, so I assume whomever this room belongs to is expected to help me.

"This is your room." There's a flicker of amusement in his eyes, but his voice is casual like he's discussing the weather.

My expression morphs into one of shock as I turn to look at the space again. I've gone from the dungeon to having a room of my own, and not just one room, but several, if what I can see through the open doorway is to be believed. This can't be real. I've never had something so luxurious before. Prior to the queen, I had my own room, but it was *nothing* like this. Then, I went to sleeping on a hard bed in the queen's study, close enough so she knew where I was at all times. I preferred the rocky ground beneath my tent in the camps, since I was alone and free, so sleeping arrangements in the cell beneath this castle weren't too much of a shock to the system. But this... this feels like a bribe. Nothing comes for free.

Elijah moves behind me, so close I can feel his warmth against my back. "At least it could be if you do as the master bids," he whispers. I think he's supposed to sound seductive, but all I hear is the question in his voice. That, and something that sounds like dread, as though he doesn't want me to accept but knows I have to.

I should move and put some space between us, but I don't. Instead, I let the heat of his body sink into my skin as I look at him over my shoulder. "I won't be bought."

"He'll send you back to the dungeon," he warns with

a voice as dark as the expression he wears. Elijah scans my face, looking for signs of weakness.

Narrowing my eyes, I stand my ground. "Then so be it." I'm angry that he thinks that will sway me. I know what awaits me in the dungeon, and the looks that one guard has been shooting my way fill me with disgust, but at least I know where I stand in the cells. This room is a gilded prison, a reward for good behaviour, like I'm a pet to be trained. "I am not some feeble female who can be bought with pretty clothes," I snarl, baring my teeth.

For a second, excitement flashes in his eyes, but it disappears so quickly that I almost think I imagined it. "Some of the others said that too, but they caved. They all do eventually."

We face off against each other, neither of us willing to back down. Finally, he chuckles and stalks past me, throwing himself onto a large couch laden with pillows. "You should get ready. The bathroom is just off the study."

This is ridiculous. He expects me to dress up like a prize after he took me from my home, dragged me across the lands, and locked me up. I nearly died from being poisoned by one of his henchmen. *Morrowmer never felt like a home to you.* The wayward thought makes me pause, the realisation tightening my chest. No, that's not true. I had a home once, but that has long since been destroyed. However, Morrowmer stopped being a place where I felt like I belonged many decades ago. That doesn't mean I'm happy to be abducted and stolen away to a different land. Everything's different here, and I seem to be part of something far bigger than I first thought.

Taking a deep breath, I leave it alone for now and walk into the other room. My jaw drops as I step into the study. Mother above. I expected a small room with a desk, but I'm greeted with my own personal library. Shelves upon shelves are filled with books of all shapes and sizes. In awe, I wander over, reach up, and brush my fingers over some of the spines. It's almost like they knew books were my weakness, and this could all be mine...

No, don't be tempted. Remember who ordered for you to be brought here, I remind myself.

Reluctantly leaving the bookshelves, I discover another open doorway which leads to a bathroom. Shaking my head at the extravagance of the room, I survey the space with wonderment. The bath is huge, large enough for several fae, and is sunk into the floor. A counter and mirror take up one whole wall, with bottles of bath lotion covering much of the countertop. Staring at the bath once more, I examine the tap, trying to find a way to turn it on, before looking around for a lever or button.

The sound of running water fills the air and I turn to stare at the tub, the tell-tale tingle of magic settling over my skin. "You're welcome," Elijah calls from the other room with amusement, his words followed by a low chuckle.

For some reason, a blush warms my cheeks, and I quickly shut the bathroom door, not wanting to think about how he knew I was struggling to work the bath.

I spend the next twenty minutes or so thoroughly washing my body to remove any grime from the prison, using some of the lotions on my hair until it feels like silk. My shoulder is now healed enough that I don't have to wear a dressing, the raised, pink scar the only evidence of my capture.

Though I'd love to soak in the hot water for hours, I'm acutely aware that Elijah is in the other room. That, and the fact I have no idea how long I have until the master gets impatient and bursts into the suite. Climbing from the bath, I take one of the enormous white fluffy towels and wrap it around me, allowing myself a few moments to enjoy the feeling of being cocooned in the soft material.

A thought occurs to me. The only thing I have to wear is the dress I arrived in. My nose wrinkles at the thought of putting it back on after I've just scrubbed myself clean. Snorting, I shake my head. As a refugee, I often wore the same clothes for days in a row out of necessity, so I shouldn't snub the day-old clothes. However, I can just imagine the look on Elijah's face if I enter the room wearing it. Not to mention the master demanded I dress 'appropriately,' which, from the opulence of the dresses I saw bursting from the wardrobe, I assume wouldn't include yesterday's dress. My only other option is a fluffy dressing gown, but that would leave me naked beneath. I know clothing is waiting for me in the other room. Closing my eyes briefly, I gather my courage, this time for an entirely different reason. Calmer now that the decision is made, I reach for the dressing gown and wrap it around myself. It completely dwarfs me, designed for a different body type, but I prefer it this way as it covers more of my frame.

Opening the door, I make my way through the study and into the bedroom where Elijah is waiting. He's sprawled across the couch, his legs thrown up on the cushions as he flicks through a book. He glances up from whatever he's reading, and his lips twitch as he sees me drowning in the excess fabric of the dressing gown, but he simply gestures towards the bed where three different outfits have been lain.

"You can choose whichever you like." Raising the

book again, he goes back to reading, but I can feel him watching me as I hesitantly walk over to my preapproved outfits.

They are all gorgeous but completely ostentatious and not at all what I'd choose for myself. The three dresses share a few commonalities—they are all in delicate feminine colours with light, airy layers. Lifting the skirt of one dress, I see layers and layers of netting and petticoats. The outfits are all designed to make the female look genteel, feminine, and harmless. Did the master order these? This just feels like another way he's trying to control me. I am not a doll for him to dress up just to look pretty and do as I'm told. Anger rumbles to life within me, and I ball my hands into fists to control myself, otherwise I might start tearing the dresses to pieces.

"Is there something wrong with your choices?" Elijah raises an eyebrow, the closed book resting on his lap, and he smiles as if he knows exactly why I have a problem with these dresses.

Snorting, I pick up a dusky pink dress to show him. The bodice is fitted and designed to enhance the wearer's breasts and cinch in her waist. The skirt balloons out in a mass of layered fabrics, and tiny pink roses have been embroidered onto the gown. It's beautiful in its own way, but completely ridiculous. There would be no way to run or fight, which is probably exactly why it was chosen.

Throwing the dress back onto the bed in disgust, I place my hands on my hips, displaying more confidence than I feel. "I'm not wearing these."

Elijah's half-smile is now a full-blown grin, his eyes sparkling with mischief. "Then what do you propose you wear? The robe you're clinging to?"

He's right, and I *hate* that. I stay silent as I stride over to the wardrobe, flinging open the doors with frustration. Anger isn't an emotion I feel often, as it was one of the first emotions to be beaten from me under the elf queen's rule. I was supposed to be emotionless—all except fear. That was one of the few emotions I was allowed to keep. After all, it's far easier to control someone who fears you.

Staring at the many dresses that greet me, I'm filled with dismay. There's nothing here that's not full skirted or remotely like what I would choose to wear. Sliding the dresses to the side, I see some slimmer gowns at the back of the wardrobe. Hope blooms as I reach for them. The colours are still bright, but nothing like the baby pinks and bright yellows of the others. Something catches my eye and I remove it so I can get a better look.

It's a beautiful black two layered A-line dress. The gown is brushed satin, and the bodice is strapless but modest, cinching in slightly at the waist before the skirt falls elegantly to the ground. It's simple, but what makes it stunning is the sheer top which is worn like a coat. The sleeves are elbow length, and it ties at the waist with a ribbon, the bottom part spreading across the skirt in a beautiful second layer. It's covered in tiny embroidered black flowers, giving it a more formal feel than the simple dress beneath it.

It's gorgeous, but it also makes a statement. Not only because I've chosen it myself, but because it's black, the colour of mourning. I won't let them forget that I didn't come here willingly, that I'm mourning the life they took from me.

"I'll wear this."

My back is to Elijah as I hold up the dress, but I know he heard me despite the pregnant pause. Pivoting to face him, I see him sitting up in the chair with a frown. Is he going to refuse? I'm not sure what I'll do if he says I have to wear one of the other dresses. I suppose we'll be at an impasse, as I won't be dressed up like a gift for the master to unwrap.

"The master won't like it. In fact, he'll hate it. It makes too much of a statement," he remarks, his eyes skimming over the dress before meeting my gaze. "I love it." His grin is large and makes me want to smile and laugh at his blatant disregard at what's expected. All of a sudden, he stills, his breath catching as he stares at me. His smile slowly drops from his face, leaving an intense expression that makes my heart race. I have no idea what caused the change in him or the atmosphere between us.

Opening my mouth to ask what's caused him to look like that, he seems to snap out of his stare. Winking, he stands and strolls through the open doorway and into the study.

"I'll be in here while you change. The door is locked, so don't try and escape."

As soon as he's gone, I glance over at the mirror and check to see if there's something on my face, trying to figure out what caused that look. Seeing nothing out of the usual, I sigh softly and shake my head. Males. Once again ignoring his warning about the door being locked, I tiptoe over, using my fae grace to keep as quiet as possible, and twist the handle. My heart soars as the handle moves, only to jam. Locked. Not that I would try to flee in a dressing gown anyway, but I had to check, needing to know my exits in case I have to escape quickly. Elijah's low laugh makes me scowl and scuttle back to where the dress is now waiting for me. How did he know I'd try the door? Am I that predictable?

Needing undergarments, I search the dresser, finding

soft silk underwear and matching chest wraps. There are other much more revealing pieces I have to search through with burning cheeks until I find something more appropriate. Glancing over my shoulder to ensure I'm alone, I shed the dressing gown and slip into a pair of black silk and lace pants, and then I bind my chest with a plain black wrap. The black makes me look paler than usual, and shiny silver scars across my abdomen glisten in the light. I know I have matching ones on my back, and now the long slash marks on my shoulder and upper back. Elves have the ability to heal almost any injury, so for us to scar, it has to either be a very serious wound or repeatedly inflicted over a long period of time. Thankfully the dress will cover most of them.

I unbutton the gown and step into it, marvelling at the luxurious feel of the fabric against my skin. Pulling the gown up and around my chest, I realise my issue. The fastenings are on the back of the dress. Cursing, I hesitate for a moment and then walk over to the study, finding Elijah examining one of the bookshelves. He turns, a half-smile on his lips, only to freeze when he sees I'm partially dressed.

In the short time I've known him, I've never seen him speechless, and it ignites something within me. Pushing all my doubt, embarrassment, and confusion aside, I walk right up to him and turn, baring my back to him as I hold the dress against my front.

"Can you fasten this please?"

He doesn't reply, but I feel the gentle brush of his fingers against my back, my skin sparking with feeling everywhere he touches. Instinctively, I lean into the touch before realising what I'm doing, and then I force myself to stay still. He suddenly seems to be the only thing I can smell, his ocean scent making me dizzy. Shaking my head to dislodge the strange feelings coursing through me, I hold my breath as he works his way up the buttons. As soon as the top of the dress is fastened, I step away, needing to put some space between us and clear my head. Glancing at Elijah, I notice I wasn't the only one affected by whatever just happened. His pupils have constricted, and his hand is held out as if he's going to stop me from leaving. However, it's his stunned expression that hits me the hardest.

"Thank you," I whisper and hurry from the study in a rustle of skirts.

Back in my room with a wall between us, I can breathe freely again. Mother above, what was that? After a few minutes, I feel like I've recovered enough to continue getting dressed. Picking up the lacy over dress, I thread my arms through the sleeves, wincing slightly at the tug on my shoulder. Tying the ribbon at my waist, I run my hands along the fabric, straightening the skirt and marvelling at how beautiful it is. I look into the mirror, and my breath catches in my throat as I see my reflection. I hardly recognise myself.

Slowly, I walk over to the dresser, take a seat on the stool, and reach for the brush that's laid out. Brushing my hair is an almost euphoric experience, one I've not been able to have since I was with the queen. Working through the knots, I smile slightly as I see myself start to emerge. I'm still not used to seeing brown hair in my reflection. For the last century, I've had blonde hair—the queen's glamour making me into her vision of a 'perfect' high elf. In the last six months since the war, mirrors were a luxury they didn't have at camps, so other than the occasional glance in a river or puddle, I'd hardly seen myself.

"Are you ready? The master's going to send someone if we don't leave soon," Elijah calls from the other room, his voice getting louder as he appears in the doorway. A predatory look enters his eyes as he takes me in. I'm wearing no makeup, I've done nothing special with my hair, and I wear no other adornments. Along with my black dress, my choices make a statement. I'm here because I have no other option, and I reject all other objects put out to tempt me.

A slow grin appears on Elijah's face, and I know he sees what I've done and why I'm dressed the way I am. "You look unbelievable. He's going to be furious."

Perfect.

"Good, then I'm ready."

Chapter 9

I perceive the exact moment we enter the main body of the castle. There's a line on the ground separating one area from the other as we leave the luxurious rooms and corridors behind us. The female wing is where all of the other females are being kept. I suppose it makes sense to keep us all in one area. Examining this new part of the castle, I take in the stark differences. The vases of flowers, incredible paintings, and soft muted tones disappear. Instead, the walls have been left bare, with the occasional decorative golden crest. Male apanthe seem to be everywhere, as well as creatures that look more animal than fae, and their cruel gazes have me stepping closer to Elijah as he leads me through the castle. *This* is what I expected this castle to look like, the oppressive feeling putting me on edge.

As we round a corner, I hear a feminine laugh followed by the gentle sound of china plates being set down, clacking against each other. It's so out of place.

This doesn't seem like the type of setting for a tea party. Surely I misheard?

Frowning slightly, I glance up at Elijah, but he's confidently striding forward, his swagger firmly back in place. A large set of wooden doors stand open, with two apanthe guards who watch us closely, but my escort directs me straight past them and into the room.

I assumed I was being taken to the throne room, and while there is a huge golden throne in the middle of the space, this is more like a reception room. Lush, deep red carpet covers the floor, and the walls are painted a gentle cream colour. Large, arched windows fill the wall opposite the door, allowing plenty of bright sunlight to illuminate the area. Loungers and long couches are dotted around the room, as well as low tables laden with cakes and sweets. The contrast between the rest of the castle and this room is sudden and unanticipated.

The feminine laughter sounds again, and I finally take in the occupants of the room. Several females are sitting on the couches or standing in small groups, talking amongst themselves.

I have a sneaking suspicion that whoever designed the 'female wing' of the castle also decorated this room, as it really doesn't fit in with the master's image. But why? Why go through so much effort to decorate parts of the castle just for the females?

I'm now thoroughly confused. My initial suspicions were right, they are having a tea party in here, and although this room is beautiful, can they not see the rest of the castle? That their every move is being watched? I thought I was going to see the master, and instead I've been brought to this room of giggling females. I hoped I would have allies here, thought these females were taken from their homes like me, yet here they are, happily sitting around, drinking tea, and snacking on cake like they aren't being kept against their will.

Feeling like we've just walked into an alternate world, I turn to Elijah with wide eyes. "Why did you bring me here?" I practically snarl as I speak, images of the castle in Galandell darting through my mind. This looks exactly like the rooms the elf queen would entertain her female friends in with seemingly endless tea parties. Words are often sharper than swords, and gossip was almost a type of currency. I witnessed what happened to those who were at the wrong end of those words.

Elijah stops just inside the room, frowning as he sees the change in me. He starts to answer, but a high-pitched cry of surprise cuts him off.

"Elijah! You're back. I missed you," a husky female voice purrs.

There's movement from the corner of the room, and my body tenses out of habit, but I keep my eyes locked on him. I don't miss his wince before he spins around to face the female who's now right behind him, a flirty smile crossing his lips.

"*Ma promessa*," he greets, and the seductive tone in his voice makes my gut clench tightly.

My eyes finally move from Elijah to the female. She's obviously related to the apanthe in some way. Her features are feline but much more delicate than the female apanthe I've seen around the castle. She's around my height, and her nose is small and petite, with fine, almost invisible whiskers protruding from her cheeks. Instead of long, pointed ears on the sides of her head like mine, hers sit atop her head much like a house cat's, nestled in her luscious black hair with a fine layer of fur covering them, the tips ending in black tufts. I notice her ears moving, taking in every sound as she watches Elijah with her feline amber eyes. She wears a dusky pink dress with layers of white lace. The neckline is revealing, and the bodice shows off her tiny waist before the skirts bloom out around her. I don't miss her rolling her shoulders back, bringing more attention to her generous bust.

I hate her. The thought pops into my head out of nowhere, and I have to fight my snort. I've had experience with plenty of females like this, despite the whiskers, cat ears, and tail I see moving behind her.

Elijah seems to be loving the attention, and like he's a siren's call, the other females bustle closer as if they can't stay away.

There are six of them in total, including the cat-like female. Glancing around, I'm shocked by what I see. They are all very different looking, and the only similarities between them are the grand dresses they all wear. My eyes are immediately drawn to a female with a delicate set of wings pulled in closely to her back, covered in beautiful, golden-brown feathers. She wears a burnt umber dress that flatters the range of colours on her wings. Her limbs are thin and willowy, covered in smooth caramel skin. Her face is more like mine in proportion, her pointed ears like that of an elf's. Her brown hair matches her wings and is pulled back into a bun.

Two females approach together, one of which has tall ears like that of a rabbit. Her face is gracefully pointed, and her small nose twitches slightly. She is tall, and her upper body is slim, but her hips flare out. She watches me warily, like she's ready to bolt at any time, and I realise she reminds me of a hare.

Her companion is like a fawn, with short, beautiful

pale horns peeking through her blonde hair. Her almond-shaped eyes are framed with luscious long lashes, and I swear I see kindness shining out at me. Around my height, she has tawny skin and moves gracefully.

As the last two walk over, I have to work to keep my surprise from my face. One is completely bald with shimmering blue scales covering her body. Her face, free of scales, is a light blue which is iridescent in the light. Her pointed face and thin lips make her look intimidating, and as she smiles, I see a row of sharp, needle-like teeth. She reminds me of a cross between the sea elves of Morrowmer and some of the more dangerous fae creatures of the Great Lake. I get the feeling I should not upset her unless I want to die a watery death.

At her side is a fae with the body of a high elf, but on her face, beneath her nose, are six tentacles of various sizes. The rest of her face is beautiful, her red hair falling in luscious waves over her shoulders, but I can't seem to pull my eyes from the independently moving tentacles. Her green eyes are bright against pale, fair skin, her light blue dress complimenting her curvaceous body.

Forming a loose semi-circle in front of us as they crowd Elijah, the females watch me with curiosity.

"Elijah, we're so happy you're back."

"Is this the new girl?"

"Why's she wearing black? She looks like she's going to a funeral."

The cacophony of their voices makes it difficult for me to pinpoint who's speaking, my gaze flicking from one female to another.

"I think that's the point," another voice calls out, and I lock eyes with the female who I think spoke. It's the one who reminds me of a fawn, with her horns and kind eyes.

I see intelligence in her gaze, and I realise that perhaps I might have an ally here after all.

"*Ma promessa*! Please, there's enough of me to go around." Elijah smirks, opening his arms wide as if to embrace them. His gaze flicks to me as if I am an afterthought. "Oh, this is Annalise. I found her across the mountains."

All attention turns to me, and the assessing looks turn predatory, as if I'm suddenly someone to compete against. It makes my back straighten and my skin tingle, and I get the urge to check if my shield is still in place. Reaching for my power, I call for more and shape it, strengthening the shield around me. It still seems weak, but I feel better knowing it's there.

The feline female glares at me before dismissing me completely, her eyes widening as she bats her lashes at Elijah. "I thought he had all of us now. Why did you bring *her* back?" She emphasises 'her' like it's a dirty word, and if I hadn't instantly disliked her, then this would have done it. I've never been able to stand females who are vicious to each other and then turn into a simpering maiden as soon as a male walks into the room. Unfortunately, there had been many who surrounded the elf queen. Fighting the urge to roll my eyes, I pretend to watch the other females, but really, I'm trying to judge Elijah's reaction from the corner of my eye.

"You know I can't control the magic, Elia," he replies, his smile still in place, but his voice holds a light warning, and I have the suspicion he's trying not to snap at her. "She's *ma promessa*, just like you, and as such, she has the same chances as you do."

Elia, so that's her name. I'll need to watch this one closely. I'm struggling to keep up with the conversation, too many unfamiliar terms are being used, but this last sentence makes me pause. *I have the same chances as the others? What in the Mother is that supposed to mean? Chances at what?*

Brushing off his comment like it's nothing, Elia moves closer to Elijah. So close, in fact, I have to take a step back so her voluminous skirts don't knock me over. "Why don't you come and sit with me, Elijah? The new female will be fine." She reaches out to place her hand against his chest, like she means to pull herself flush against him.

Irrational anger rises within me, and my fae instincts make me see red. I can't seem to move my gaze from her hand, but before I do anything stupid, Elijah chuckles quietly and steps out of her reach.

"Annalise is here under... different circumstances. I've been instructed to stay with her until the master arrives," he replies smoothly, flashing her a dangerously charming smile that makes something in my chest flip.

I'm not sure if I should or shouldn't feel grateful that he hasn't revealed where I've been residing the last few days. I'm not ashamed that I refused the master, and as such, I don't feel shame at staying in the dungeon. However, with these sharp-eyed females watching me like I'm fresh meat for them to enjoy, I know that telling them I've been sleeping in a cell will only alienate me further. *Why should you care what they think of you?* my mind argues, and while I agree, I begrudgingly have to admit that I might need alliances with these females. I shouldn't burn any bridges yet.

The females turn their attention to me once again, and I get the distinct impression they are sizing me up as their competition—although for what, I don't know.

A shift in the atmosphere announces the master's

arrival before he even comes into sight, and I'm already turning to face the door half a second before he enters. From the corner of my eye, I see Elijah's surprise, but as I glance over at him, he's smirking as the master walks through the open doorway.

"Ah! My newest *promessa*," the master cries out as he bursts into the room, a predatory gleam in his amber eyes as he looks at me.

The females who were gathered around us coo their greetings, dropping into curtsies while wearing welcoming smiles on their faces, but I notice the tightness in their eyes —all except for Elia, who hurries to his side and simpers, her attention switching from Elijah to the master in seconds. He barely looks in her direction, however, his whole focus on me. Suddenly realising what I'm wearing, the master growls, the sound rumbling in his chest. His narrowed eyes shoot to Elijah, but the fae at my side just shrugs and holds up his hands as if he weren't able to stop me. I know the master sees this for what it is, my one small rebellion.

He seems frozen in the doorway with his collection of females surrounding him, and I wonder if he's going to punish me. There's an aura of violence around him, like the animal side of him is fighting for dominance.

"Come," he growls before stalking towards the throne, knowing the females will follow him. Climbing up to the dais, he sits down and leans back as he surveys us. He may call himself master, but he's acting like a tyrannical king.

Reluctantly, I follow behind the other women, but only because Elijah places a hand on the small of my back, guiding me forward. The females part to allow me through, and I pray they can't hear the pounding of my heart inside my chest. Power fizzes in my veins as if responding to my fear and anticipation, but I know it's nothing compared to what the master commands. I keep my chin up and my steps steady. The last thing I want to do is stumble and make him think I'm a weak female. When I reach the foot of the dais, I raise my eyes and meet his heavy gaze.

He seems to have settled from his initial irritation at my choice of clothing, watching me with a hungry expression. Resting his head on his fist, he remains silent, which I know is an intimidation tactic. The other females around us shift their weight awkwardly, sensing the tension, and the master seems to finally realise they are there. Either that, or he just enjoys the power he holds over them.

"Entertain yourselves." With a wave of his hand, he dismisses the others until only Elijah and I are left.

I watch as the females wander back over to the loungers, breaking off into small groups and whispering to each other as they glance at us.

I move my attention back to the master, who's observing me with a contemplative expression. "You've seen what I can offer you. You'll be looked after and given everything you could ever wish for." He gestures around as he speaks. There's no boasting, only a promise. However, I've learned the hard way that promises like that always come at a cost, and usually that's a price too steep to pay.

The master smiles slightly, and at first, I think he's trying to be reassuring, but with his animalistic features, it looks more like a snarl, his sharp incisors flashing in the sunlight. "You just have to submit." He opens his arms wide and his smile broadens, and I see the possessive gleam in his eyes.

I get the feeling that submitting to him is more binding than just agreeing to stay here, and I recall Elijah telling me about his unbreakable oath. Besides, I still have no idea *why* he brought me here.

Clearing my throat, I raise a single eyebrow, praying to the Mother that my voice stays strong, unwavering. "What I wish for is to be free."

Teeth flashing, the master leans forward on the throne, gripping the armrests so hard his knuckles turn white. Then, as quickly as his anger appeared, he relaxes back and brushes some of his mane-like golden hair from his face, looking thoughtful. "I know you were found in a refugee camp. Isn't the luxury here better than returning to that?"

His mercurial emotions are making it difficult for me to keep up, and the way he speaks of my past rouses the anger in me once again. There's a sudden lull in conversation from the other side of the room, and I know the females are listening in. They will all know I was a refugee, fleeing from one camp to the next, but I'm not ashamed of that part of my past, so instead of taking it as a slight as the master meant it, I wear it like a badge of honour. Everyone in those camps had been displaced from their homes and lost almost everything, but they survived, and there's a strength in that which is often overlooked.

Instead of answering him, I ask a question of my own. "Why am I here?"

Elijah stills at my side like he's expecting the master to lash out, but a look of surprise flashes across his feline features. "You are *ma promessa*, just like the others in this room." His arms spread wide, gesturing to the other females, as if that should have some significance to me. Arching a single eyebrow, I wait for him to continue.

Elijah hisses out a breath and I glance over at him, seeing how tense he is. Is he worried about how I'm acting? He should know by now that I'm not suddenly going to start bowing and grovelling. I have no idea what the master is talking about and no one else can tell me, so I'm going to ask questions.

The master huffs out a laugh, and I watch Elijah's shoulders relax a little before returning my attention to the fae on the throne. "I forget you know nothing of our lands, our traditions." He pauses, looking thoughtful once again. "Elijah will teach you the basics, but all you need to know for now is that you've been chosen. All the females here share something with you and as such, presented as *ma promessa*—the promised one."

The promised one, so that's what *ma promessa* means. Doubts fly through my mind, and I want to wave away his absurd comment. I am no 'promised one.' I'm not special in any way. Why would they want an elf from another land? There's obviously something bigger at work here. Elijah knew what I was as soon as he saw me, and he's made comments about the magic that commands him, but why would it choose me? And how am I the promised one when the other females in this room are as well? If there is more than one, then why do I have to be here? The others clearly seem to resent my presence. I can feel their narrowed gazes on me as they pretend not to watch us.

As if sensing where my thoughts are going, the master hums in his throat. "One of you will become the true *promessa* and take your place at my side." His smile is wide, as if he's expecting me to fall at his feet and beg him to choose me. Well, he's going to be disappointed. When I don't react as he expected, his eyes narrow, and I see his tail flicking in agitation. "That is all you need to know for now. You're expected to attend the sessions and be present at any events I hold."

I have so many questions, and I'm still not sure why I'm here. They may think I'm one of their 'promised ones,' but why? Who decided all of this? Their gods? I'm not even sure they have gods and goddesses here, and if they do, I've not seen any sign of them. And if I have been promised, what for? There must be a bigger purpose than taking a place at the master's side. I have a horrible suspicion I know exactly what he's implying, and I want nothing to do with it. Also, what are these sessions he mentioned?

"Now, I ask again..." The master stands from his throne and steps down until we're face to face. "Do you submit?"

I don't even need time to think, my answer is immediate. "No."

My face stings as his palm connects with my cheek, snapping my head to the side, the sound loud in the suddenly silent room. The force of the blow sends me jolting backwards, but Elijah is there, catching me before I can fall to the ground. The sour tang of fear permeates the air, but it's not mine, which isn't to say I'm not frightened, because I am, but I hear the quick breaths of the females on the other side of the room.

Lowering his head to mine, the master bares his teeth, his gaze flicking to my throat. I know a threat when I see one. Swallowing the terror rising inside me, I remove myself from Elijah's arms and raise my chin despite the quaking in my limbs.

The master sees this, both my defiance and the trembling, and he can smell my fear. "Then you will be spending a lot more time in the dungeon. If you think your life was hard before, you're in for an unpleasant surprise," he threatens. "All you have to do is say you submit," he adds, dropping his voice to a seductive whisper. He strokes his hand down my burning cheek, his claws gently scraping the skin. The gesture is loving, but the sting of his claws reminds me exactly who this is.

I hold his stare. I will not be cowed. He's not bluffing, that much I know—the pain in my cheek is a testament to that. What he doesn't understand is that I've been through all this before, and while my knees shake at the thought of what's in store for me, I survived then, and I'll survive now.

Seeing my answer isn't going to change, the master's head snaps around as if he's only just remembering the other females are still there. His roar of anger makes the windows rattle and the females squeal before they quickly find something far more interesting to do other than watch us.

Turning his piercing gaze on Elijah, his top lip pulls back in a snarl. "Take her back to the cells." His words are barely understandable, but Elijah nods despite the onslaught of power that's emanating from the master. Without so much as a glance at me, he storms past us, leaving the room as quickly as he arrived.

Frowning, I stare at the spot where the master had just been standing, the echo of his power lingering in the room. It's not his display of power that's bothering me, but the feel of it is… off. There's no doubt that he's powerful, however, Elijah is more so. This felt more like… like his animistic nature was pushing down on me, trying to bend me to his will. It was strong, but I was able to resist it. The full force of the power hadn't been aimed at me though, so I can't even imagine what it would feel like to have it concentrated on me.

"Annalise," Elijah calls, pulling my attention from my thoughts. Blinking slowly as if awakening from a dream, I turn to face him. An odd expression crosses his face, and he opens his mouth to say something.

"Things will be easier for you if you just agree."

The voice is harsh, but as I turn to discover who's speaking, I'm met with startling amber eyes, almost the colour of honey, filled with understanding. The female who spoke is the one who reminds me of a hare, her high ears twitching.

Considering her words, I glance at the others and see a couple of nods as they concur with her comment. She's right, it would be easier to just allow him to control me, but I'm done having someone else dictating what I can and can't do.

Meeting her gaze, I tilt my head slightly to the side. "If I agree, I'll be just as much a prisoner here as I am down in the dungeon."

Something sparks in her eyes, a fire that makes me think we may be more alike than I first thought. She's as much of a prisoner as I am—they all are. For a moment, I think she's going to snap back at me, but the fawn-like female steps forward, standing at her friend's side and placing a gentle hand on her arm.

"At least you would be in comfort though. You wouldn't be alone." The fawn smiles as she gestures to the others. "We help each other as much as we can. It makes this less lonely."

"Annalise, we have to go." Elijah's hand lands on my

shoulder, the tightness of his grip giving away his urgency. "Mia, Gail, ladies," he addresses the fawn first, then the hare-like fae, before turning a flirtatious smile on the remaining females. "It's been a pleasure, as always." He performs an elaborate bow, and the fae giggle at his theatrics. Now, with his hand on my shoulder, he guides me from the room.

Taking a deep breath, I shake my head. I don't know what I expected from the females, the other *promessa*, but giggling and tea parties certainly wasn't it.

"We're better off without her." Elia's haughty voice reaches me as we enter the hallway. "She's a troublemaker and just more competition for us."

Elijah acts like he doesn't hear them, and the smile drops from his face now that we're away from the others. He doesn't even swagger as he passes the apanthe guards, his dark mood making them think twice about giving him any grief. In fact, many flinch as we pass, their eyes dropping to avoid his attention. I've never seen him like this before, but something's put him in a foul mood, and I'm thinking that something is me. Leading me past the light and airy female wing, we continue down the main corridor. Reaching a nondescript door, he opens it and sharply gestures for me to enter.

Once inside, he shuts the door behind us with more force than necessary, the wood groaning as it slams shut. We're back in the servants' corridors, and a quick glance tells me we're alone—that *I'm* alone with a very angry fae.

Growling in frustration, Elijah spins around to face me. "That was stupid," he sneers. "Brave, but stupid."

Raising an eyebrow, I hold my ground. Did he really believe a bath and a pretty dress would change my mind and I'd agree to shackle myself to the master? Elijah's practically vibrating with energy, but after a few seconds, he lets out a weary sigh and leans against the wall, rubbing his hands over his face.

Looking away, I place my hand on my burning cheek. The fact that the master was able to break through my shield is making me uneasy. I know it wasn't the strongest shield, but he batted through it like it was a piece of paper.

Stronger, I need to get stronger if I'm going to survive here.

"Are you okay?" His question is soft, tentative, like he actually wants to know the answer.

I huff a laugh. No, I'm not okay. I'm in a strange land with a beast who thinks he can rule over me, telling me that I've been promised but somehow have to prove it, and when I refused to blindly accept him, he lost his temper and hurt me, then sent me back to the dungeon. The threat of torture was clear. So no, none of this is okay. Glancing up at Elijah, I say nothing, but he knows the answer to his question.

His eyes stray to my swollen cheek. "I'm sorry, there was nothing I could do to stop him. Sometimes I..." He trails off, his hands balling into fists as he looks around, remembering where he is.

His apology seems genuine, so I sigh and nod. Overall, the meeting with the master has only left me with more questions, and remembering that he said Elijah could fill me in, I clear my throat. "Can you tell me any more now?"

"Yes, the master gave permission, so the magical gag has been removed," he grumbles, moving away from the wall and gesturing for me to begin walking.

His comment triggers something in my mind, something that was bugging me while I was in the master's presence. "The master's power feels... strange." I don't move, ignoring his signal to walk as I try to think of a way to describe what I felt. "It's different than mine and yours." It's a poor way of defining the tingling sensation that ran over my body at his demands, making me want to obey, but I don't have any other words to describe it.

"You can feel that?" His body stills, and his eyes widen for a second. I wonder if I said something wrong.

"Am I not supposed to?" I've always been able to feel the power levels of those around me, but I didn't realise it was different from what anyone else felt. Another thing that makes me unusual.

From the expression on Elijah's face, I get the impression that this isn't a usual ability. "The apanthe generally don't have power like you and me," he explains, gesturing between us. "Instead, their animal within gives them that strength. The stronger that bond, the stronger they are. A rare few will have a little power, but it's weak."

I've never heard of this. There is nothing like the apanthe back in Morrowmer. The idea that these creatures have their own inner animal makes sense, seeing as I've witnessed how they sometimes seem to give in to the animal within. They certainly have an aura about them, some of which seemed stronger than others.

As if Elijah can hear the process of my thoughts, he nods slowly. "The master, however, is different. He has the power, as you felt, but also a huge amount of alpha strength from his animal, which means he can force those under him to obey his commands."

This would explain why the master's power feels so peculiar. It's a hybrid mix of fae power and alpha energy. Elijah's final comment makes my chest constrict. Is this what's binding him to the master? The alpha energy? No, that doesn't make sense, Elijah isn't apanthe.

"Most people can't feel power levels like you can. That you can..." He trails off in a whisper, scanning my face once again. A shudder passes over him, and his pupils dilate for a second before he screws his eyes shut and presses his hands to his face.

Concern has me stepping closer, my instincts fuelling my actions. "Elijah—"

"Don't touch me," he warns, and I yank my hand back, cradling it to my chest. How did he know what I'd been about to do? I watch cautiously as he blows out a long breath, the tension in his body seeming to ease with the air he releases. Opening his eyes, he grins at me as if nothing happened. "Sorry about that. Right, where were we?"

I jog a few steps to catch up with him. He's not going to pretend like nothing just happened, is he? I'm not even sure exactly *what* just happened, but it feels important. "Elijah—" I begin, but he cuts me off with a wave of his hand.

"After the War of the Gods, we were unable to reach your land any longer, and what was left of the fae who survived created..." Humming in thought, he glances over his shoulder at me. "I'm trying to think of the word in your language... Factions? The Master of Beasts, Ajax, rules this land with the apanthe and other feline beasts following him. There are other factions, seven in total." Turning a corner, he continues, barely looking to see if I'm keeping up. "The magic over us was in place before Ajax became the master, even before his predecessor— someone who was immensely powerful—but never underestimate Ajax. The Master of Beasts is just one of his titles. Oath Maker is another. Never promise him anything, as it will bind you to him until you either fulfil the oath or die." Bitterness coats his words, and I realise this is why Elijah can't break ties with the master despite obviously despising him.

I'm overwhelmed with the barrage of information, and there's still so much I don't know or understand. What is the magic he was speaking of? Deciding to start from the beginning, I reach out and place a hand on his arm, attempting to slow him down. "The War of the Gods?"

He glances at me in surprise. "I—" His words twist until he growls with frustration and gives up. "The master obviously doesn't deem that necessary information."

Frustration fills me, but I know it's not Elijah's choice to omit information, the binding not allowing him free rein. Moving on, I pick another topic. "Why are the other females here?"

The master called us all *promessa* and said we were promised. Apparently one of us is the true *promessa*, and somehow, we have to prove it. I still don't understand how I fit into all this and how they know we're these 'promised ones.' I want to hear Elijah's explanation to see if he can help me make better sense of what's going on.

"Elia, as I'm sure you gathered, is from this faction."

That doesn't surprise me, but not because of her feline features. She seemed the most comfortable here, like she's fully embraced her status. I overheard her calling me 'competition,' as if being tied to the master is a grand prize. If she grew up here, she would have known of the *promessa*. What does surprise me, however, is the sneer in Elijah's voice as he speaks of her. *What's the story there?* I wonder, glancing up at his face.

"The others are from the other factions. One *promessa* from each, all except Mamos. They paid dearly for their refusal. The master went to war with them over it and all but wiped them off the map. By the time he was finished with them, there were no women left, so either the *promessa* died or she was moved to a different faction." I raise my eyebrows, shock coursing through me. He destroyed an entire faction because they wouldn't let him take one of their females, and in the end it was fruitless anyway? Such a pointless waste of life.

Sensing my rising emotions, he slows down. "Don't forget that you were stolen from your land, Annalise. You think all these females came willingly?"

I remember what Gail, the hare-like fae, told me. She said it would be easier if I just accepted my fate. Perhaps this is what she meant, that there's no escaping it, or that by submitting she's protecting her people. What she doesn't know is that I don't have people to protect.

"Their factions allowed them to be taken?"

He shakes his head at my question, wearing a grim expression. "No. Many of the factions don't believe, as the master does, about there being a promised female. Against the might of the apanthe, many would fail, just like Mamos, so for the sake of one female, they grudgingly let it go."

I can't imagine the sense of betrayal they must have felt when their faction didn't put up a fight to get them back. Shaking my head, I barely take in my surroundings as we make our way through the castle. I know we're heading towards the dungeon, and I know the fate that awaits me there, but I try to keep my mind busy. I don't know how long Elijah will be allowed to explain this to me, or when I'll see him next, so I'm taking advantage of it.

"Why were they promised? For what purpose?"

He tries to speak but can't, the words getting caught in his throat.

The other factions don't support the master. If I could escape, would they help me? I have no idea if the other factions are any better than this one, and I get the feeling there is something far greater going on, I just can't see it.

We climb down a spiral staircase, and my gut clenches as a sense of foreboding increases with each step. My chest tightens and my heart speeds up.

Growling low in his throat, Elijah stops and turns to face me. Anger pulses from him, his power reacting to his heightened emotion. I've not been frightened of him for a long time, in fact, I'm not sure I've ever truly been scared of him. The situation and the uncertainty surrounding me, yes, and I'm wary of his power, but Elijah has always tried to help me to the best of his ability. Now, however, as he stalks towards me with a predatory look, I back up until I hit the wall. This doesn't stop him though, he keeps walking until we're almost touching, his arms penning me in. My pulse flutters under my skin like a startled bird, and his eyes are drawn to it, but I'm not afraid, not of him.

"You rejected the master again, and in front of the other females. He's not going to make this easy for you, and I'm forbidden from interfering," he bites out. He's angry with me, that much is clear. To my surprise, my own frustration and irritation surface in response to his words. Yes, I've not made this easy on myself, but I don't regret my actions.

Raising my chin, I meet his glare with narrowed eyes.

"Would you have preferred if I agreed? If I bound myself to him?"

"No!" he roars, pounding his hands into the wall behind me. Dust rains down around us, but I don't take my gaze from his blazing stare. "I just—I *hate* this! I hate *him,* and most of all, I hate that I know you're about to be hurt and I can't do anything to stop it." The anger abruptly leaves him, leaving only a ragged-looking male standing before me, his pain clear on his face. "Why did you have to be at the camp the night we raided it? Why did you stop to assist that human who had no intention of helping you? As soon as I saw you, the power that binds me made me take you. I couldn't stop it." His voice is almost pleading. He wants me to understand that he didn't choose this. Elijah's face is so close to mine that if I took half a step forward, we'd be touching. "Why you?"

The need to comfort him rises within me. *He's your captor, he's the reason you're here*, the rational part of my brain screams. *Why are you comforting him?* Yet I can't shake the part of me that *needs* to do something, to wipe that look from his face.

"I'll be okay," I whisper.

"No, you won't." His searing gaze almost seems to look through me. He searches my face, but what he's looking for, I don't know. Breaking eye contact, he steps away as if he's unable to look at me anymore. "They won't kill you." His tone is firm. "And I'll make sure the guards know what will happen if they even try anything..." He trails off, but I know what he's hinting at, remembering the guard who wanted a piece of me.

I can't even think of the word without feeling like I'm going to vomit, but the thought of anyone trying to touch me in that way... Shuddering, I keep my back straight despite wanting to rage, cry, and scream.

It finally hits me that there's no way out of this. Whether I accept the master or am kept in the dungeon, I'm not getting away from here alive. I will never see Morrowmer again.

As we descend deeper into the bowels of the castle, the scent of my fear and desperation fills the narrow staircase. Without thinking, I reach out and take Elijah's hand. At this moment, I don't care whom he works for, only that I need comfort, and as he looks over his shoulder at me in shock, he doesn't push me away.

Instead, he squeezes it tightly, his expression filled with sadness.

Chapter 10

I don't bother to plead with him. We both know the magic that binds him to the master is forcing his actions. No amount of crying or begging would change the outcome, it would only make it worse for both of us. As the door to the dungeon opens, the apanthe guard grinning cruelly at me, I start to withdraw. As they lead me to my cell, I block out all sounds around me, letting it become unidentifiable background noise. Keeping my head down, I allow a curtain of my long brown hair to separate me from the rest of the dungeon, focusing only on putting one foot before the other.

One of the things I learned from my captivity and torture under the elf queen was that the anticipation of pain is almost worse than the actual act itself. In the early days, they would place a clock in my cell, telling me the exact time they'd be coming for me. I'd spend hours watching that clock, my mind getting more and more worked up with each tick of the second hand.

Stepping into my cell, I stare at the back wall, aware

of all the eyes on me. There's one set of eyes in particular that I can feel like a physical touch—Elijah's. I sense his concern for me, his fear and hatred for this entire damn castle. A thought briefly flickers through my mind that I shouldn't be able to know how he's feeling, not in this much detail, but I push it away, keeping my mind blank.

I don't know how long I stand there. There's movement in the cells around me, and I'm aware of the exact moment Elijah left the dungeon, but it's been a while now, and my body is shivering from the cold as it seeps into my bones. I'm still wearing the dress from earlier, but we're below ground level, and the air is frigid and damp.

"Annalise!"

The whisper-shout breaks through my haze, and I tilt my head to the side. My neck protests the small movement and my body is stiff, which tells me I've been standing and staring longer than I thought.

"Thank the gods," the voice mutters, although I think he's speaking more to himself than me. A shuffling noise sounds, and from the corner of my eye, I see movement. "What happened to you?"

Turning around, I finally connect the voice to Alric. He's kneeling by the bars that separate our cells, his rich blue eyes flashing with anger as he takes in my blank face.

"If that bastard Ajax laid a finger on you..." He trails off, a low growl rumbling in his chest. We both know there's nothing he can do about the master, not while he's locked up down here and his magic is blocked. Even if he could, Alric is one of the oldest fae I've ever met, so what could he do against someone like Ajax? Alric wouldn't get anywhere near him, not with an army of beasts at Ajax's disposal.

However, something about his expression and the

anger emanating from him awakens me. As I rise to the surface, the sounds of the rest of the dungeon reach me, and the fear and hopelessness of my situation hits me once again. Alric curses the moment he sees my eyes widen, as if my fear causes him physical pain, his hands tightening around the bars.

"Alric—" The word breaks on my lips, and I take a small step towards him. I don't know what I'm going to say or how to explain the despair and desperation I'm feeling. I'm so terrified I can't even begin to think of the words. I can't see my future anymore or a way out of this.

Several heavy footsteps stop outside my cell door, saving me from having to answer. Like someone has bound my chest, my breaths come in quick, startled gasps. I know they can scent my fear, and their deep inhales and sadistic chuckles confirm it. Spinning in a whirl of pale limbs and black fabric, I face the guards who let themselves into my small cell. There are three of them, although from a quick glance, I can't see the one who fills me with terror, so that's a small blessing. Their bodies are so big that I have to back up for them to fit, my calves hitting the edge of my cot. Their claws, fangs, and tails identify them as apanthe, but I can't tell their features apart. In my panicked mind, they all just look like beasts, and their expressions promise pain.

They don't bother to close the cell door behind them, so either they plan to take me somewhere else, or they know that after whatever they have planned for me, I'm not going to be able to run anywhere.

The one closest to me slides his eyes over me, a purr of excitement rumbling in his chest. My pulse pounds in my ears, and I notice their gazes catching on my exposed neck. Huffing a laugh, the apparent leader steps closer, dwarfing me in size. "Don't damage her face, she's still expected to attend the events with the others."

Extending a huge paw-like hand, the guard swipes at me. The blow throws me from my feet, slamming me into the metal bars. My head smashes against them so hard that I momentarily lose my vision. I blink as the world spins around me. I see the three guards shouting at each other, but all I can hear is a loud ringing in my ears. Something warm runs down my cheek and drops onto my arm. With numb detachment, I glance down to see blood dripping onto my skin. The bright red blood and the black fabric of my dress make my skin look even paler than usual. I don't know if I make a noise or if the apanthe just smell the blood, but as one, they turn to me, expressions of need covering their faces.

I'm yanked up, my feet dangling above the floor as a hand wraps around my neck. I uselessly claw at their grip, my mouth opening desperately to try to draw oxygen into my lungs. Something seems to have taken over the guards, a bloodlust, as the one holding me pulls me close and buries his nose against the side of my head. Pain zings through my skull, and as he pulls away, I see my blood smeared across his muzzle. Over the ringing in my ears, I become aware of another one of the guards growling.

Pain bursts from my newly healed shoulder as I'm pried from the guard's grip. As soon as his hold on my neck loosens, I'm gasping for air, greedily gulping down as much of it as I can before I'm held in another tight grasp. They are fighting over my blood. As I'm ripped from each guard's grip, my body starts to break under their rough, jarring actions. So far I've not made a sound, falling back into my silent, withdrawn shell. It's the only way I know how to protect myself without access to my power.

However, as the bone in my upper arm snaps under their tug-of-war over my body, a scream of pain rips from my throat. Razor-sharp teeth bite into my shoulder, drawing out another scream as a gush of hot blood rolls down my chest and arm.

I'm dropped to the ground. Agony consumes me as my legs receive the same treatment. Fangs tear into my skin, except I'm too engulfed in pain to react. As my head rolls on the stone ground, my eyes lock with Alric's furious gaze, the bars almost seeming to bend under his clenched fists.

Taking a deep, painfilled breath, I detach from my body, my consciousness pulling away. I'm sure it's just my agony laced body's way of coping with the pain, but it's almost like I'm looking down at what's happening. Moving my gaze from the guards, who are fighting over my still form, I glance at Alric. I've never seen the fae like this before. He looks almost feral as he pounds on the bars and roars at the guards. They don't pay him any mind, even as his hands split open and his blood drips onto the floor.

Blessed numbness surrounds me, and my ethereal form starts to float away, my attachment to this world fading. A small part of me twists, not wanting to leave Alric in that state, but the farther I'm pulled away, the more my worldly emotions disperse.

That's when I realise I'm dying.

Hovering above the castle, I impassively stare down at the place that's been my prison for the last... How much time has passed? I don't remember anymore, and it doesn't seem to matter as much as it once did. Gradually, I become aware of another presence, but I'm not afraid. There's a choice before me, one only I can make. I could go back to the pain, humiliation, and uncertainty, or I could choose to leave and accept the Great Mother's warm embrace.

They need you, a woman whispers. Her voice is beautiful, and I've never heard anything like it, the melodic lilt filling me with love from those three simple words. Although I currently have no physical form, I smile at the love surrounding me. The Mother herself has come for me. Even in this strange land, she's here.

A strange chuckle sounds in my mind, and I almost feel her caress my cheek. I know none of this is possible, but I embrace it, and something settles deep within me.

I will always be with you, my child, even when you are far away and can't feel me. However, it is you who has come to me. Your soul has ascended. I cannot enter the realm your body has been taken to.

I feel her regret and sadness throughout my entire being. Her words don't quite make sense to me, but I push aside my confusion, happy she's here with me as I bask in her peace.

I become aware of a tugging on my essence, on my very soul. Although it's not painful, it's urgent and mournful and full of promise and regret. It's the strangest sensation, like I'm being pulled back into my physical body. Something is tethering me to the world below. I could choose to break those ties or follow them back, like a lighthouse in the distance guiding me home.

There's a shift, and my attention moves back to the Mother. *Your path is not easy, child. You've already suffered so much.* I can almost feel her tears against my cheeks, which is impossible, of course, but her anguish is so tangible it seems to thicken the air around me. Her love for me is overwhelming, and I know I don't deserve it, but even so, she pours it upon me, anointing me with it.

I won't force this on you. You have to choose for yourself. You can come with me now, or you can return to the realm of the living—to them.

My thoughts instantly go to the insistent tugging on my soul once more. I don't know who 'they' are, but I know she's right. If I leave, if I go with the Great Mother, I'd never meet whomever I'm connected to. The thought of returning to my body, of the pain, almost makes me recoil, but that *need* to return to whoever's feeling so much anguish…

They need you, she repeats, and my decision is made. I feel her smile like a beam of sunlight. *You made the right decision, my child.*

Without any warning, I'm falling, the castle below me getting closer and closer. Bracing for impact, I slam into my body, my muscles spasming as I gasp for breath. Pain radiates through my entire being, and each movement, each breath, is agonising.

A roar fills the dungeon, the sound bouncing off the stone walls, and I manage to roll my eyes to the side. What I see sends shock coursing through me. Elijah stands on the other side of my open cell door, trembling, and he's covered head to toe in blood. Even as injured as I am, I try to reach out to him, needing to know he's okay. I'm so weak I can barely twitch my fingers, the pain from the simple movement making me gasp in agony.

"Annalise!" Alric shouts, his voice tortured. He sounds awful, like something terrible has happened to him.

Elijah seems to react to my fellow prisoner's call, slowly turning to face me, and that's when I comprehend the blood covering him isn't his. My vision fades in and out, and I know unconsciousness will soon consume me, but my eyes drop to the dark masses surrounding Elijah—bodies. He's surrounded by the guards' bodies. He killed them. No. He butchered them, their limbs and innards scattered around like confetti.

I'm not sure if it's the gruesome scene before me or the head injury, but I barely manage to roll to the side in time to vomit. I've not had anything to eat today, so it's all stomach acid, which burns my damaged throat on the way up.

This seems to snap Elijah from his trance, his eyes widening as he hurries into the cell before kneeling at my side. "Annalise, you're alive." The relief in his voice confuses me, but I'm in so much pain I can't even begin to process it. His hands hover over my body as if he's unsure where to touch me without causing pain. His head snaps up, and he bares his teeth, biting out something I don't understand. He's talking to Alric, the two of them conversing in their native language. Finally, he looks back down at me, pain flashing across his face. "I'm going to pick you up and it's going to hurt, but I need to get you out of this cell so I can start to heal you."

I can't answer him, my tongue swollen from where I must have bitten it, but I manage to meet his eyes and blink once to tell him I understand. He nods solemnly, sliding his arms under my shoulders and knees as he cradles me close to his body.

The pain causes stars to appear in my vision, and a noise of pain that doesn't even sound human escapes my throat. My eyelids slide shut as I cling to consciousness. Elijah curses, my body rocking against his the only indication I have that we're moving. As soon as we step from the cell, I feel my limited power return. It swims through my veins as it tries desperately to heal the extensive damage.

Although I'm in agony, a part of me settles from being this close to Elijah. I'm not sure when I became so comfortable around him, but I'm not going to question it. The strange noises emanating from my throat have quieted, and Elijah releases a tense breath. "I've got you, *ma promessa*. Sleep now."

The darkness beckons me. Not the unending void of death, but the blissful state of unconsciousness. I begin to submit to it, needing the pain to end, but something tugs in my chest. Without thinking, I open my eyes and glance over at the male the sensation is coming from. The last thing I see before unconsciousness takes me is Alric's agonised expression.

I pace the small space of my cell, my heart raw in my chest as I recall what just happened.

As the apanthe scum beat and tore into Annalise's body, a rage like nothing I've ever felt rose within me. When Mauku, the head guard, hit her so hard she cut open her scalp, I knew they wouldn't be able to control their bloodlust, their feral natures breaking through. I'm not controlled by blood, but even I could appreciate how good hers smelled.

Dread filled me, knowing what would happen next. My screams for them to back off hadn't worked, and I was so consumed by need that I was tearing at the bars between us.

Then she died. It felt like the world paused as her soul

left her body. She didn't go far, I could feel her lingering above, and in that moment, I realised what she was to me. The gods have a sense of humour to place her here of all places. I thought I was going to rip through those bars and tear the scum to pieces for daring to touch her, my feral fae nature demanding I help her, hurt them, just do something. As her soul departed, I felt like mine was tearing in two, the pain unlike anything I've ever felt, but mostly, I was grieving for lost opportunities.

The asshole Elijah turned up then, his power slamming into all of us before he even set foot in the dungeon. The expression on his face was one of pure rage and death, and that's exactly what happened next. He reached into the cell and ripped one of the guards out. Without even touching him, the guard just... tore in half. I've never seen a display of power like that before. I knew Elijah was formidable, but as blood rained down on him, I gained a true sense of how dangerous he is. The other guards realised what was happening then, surfacing from their bloodlust and snarling at the fae. More guards ran from their breakroom, but they met the same fate as the ones in Annalise's cell.

Feeling her connection begin to fade, I panicked and turned from the gory scene beyond the bars. I tugged on that thin connection between us, the one I hadn't noticed until she was about to be taken from me. Then, miraculously, she returned.

Of course Elijah took her away as soon as he realised she was back, and the look on his face when I called her name was... not expected. I've never seen so much emotion from him before. He's one of the most powerful fae in the whole realm, and he delights in causing pain and misery, both to his enemies and his own people, just as this display of power demonstrated. The bastard is cold and calculating. However, that's not what I saw on his face when he realised Annalise wasn't dead.

Growling low in my throat, I glance over at the empty cell to my right, her blood still glistening on the stone floor. Moving my heavy, old body over to the small cot, I lower myself down.

I'd nearly given myself away and almost ruined everything. Once he took her, I noticed the bars I'd been pulling at and the gap between them. It was barely big enough to fit my fist through, but a fae like me shouldn't have been able to bend the bars. No one should be able to do that, not with the magical shield around the cells that removes our power. If they knew what I could do... I nearly fucked everything up.

Now she's upstairs with Elijah, the worst of them all. I have to remember why I'm here, who these fae are, and pray she lives until I can devise a way to get us both out of this mess. One thing is for certain though...

I will burn this faction to the ground.

The strange dream pulls at my mind, and it takes me a moment to remember who I am. My body feels strange, like I'd been in another form and only just returned to my natural state of being. Memories suddenly slam into me, and I jerk against the hands holding me down. My face feels swollen, and my eyelids are glued shut.

"Steady, your body was badly damaged," a thickly accented voice soothes, and while I recognise it, I can't quite place it. Blind panic rises in my chest as I remember teeth biting into me, powerful hands tearing at my broken body, and booted feet kicking my limp form.

"Annalise?" a male voice calls as he moves towards me, soothing me.

Elijah.

His cool hand rests on my cheek. "You're safe, open your eyes." His tone holds a promise, and I believe him. If he says I'm safe, then I must be.

I manage to peel back my eyelids, squinting against the light in the room. A breath that sounds like a sob escapes me as his blurry form comes into focus beside me. My tongue feels thick, and I ache everywhere. My right arm is in a sling, and one of my legs is bound in thick bandages from foot to hip. Glancing around, I see we're in a clean, airy room. There are rows of beds, a couple of which have sleeping fae in them, but most of them are empty. *The healers' quarters*, I realise when I see Bodil, the apanthe healer, at my side.

A hand gently squeezes mine, and my attention returns to Elijah. He looks awful. He's still beautiful in an otherworldly way, but black shadows circle his eyes, like he's not slept in a month, and his body is tense like he's carrying a heavy burden.

Sensing there's much the two of us need to say, Bodil gently pats my free hand and pushes to her feet. "I have to make a poultice for your injuries. I'll leave you two to talk. I'll be back shortly."

Elijah nods, but neither of us take our eyes from the other. As the healer leaves, I feel a slight buzzing, the sensation of someone using their power, and I realise Elijah's erected a shield of some sort around us.

I want to sit up, but I know without even trying it would be impossible, my body already crying out in pain from the simple act of breathing. Clearing my throat, I try to speak, but only a scratchy whisper comes out. Elijah passes me a glass of water with a straw, holding it to my lips so I can drink. The cool liquid soothes my burning throat and dry, swollen tongue. Taking a deep breath, I try again. "You were covered in blood, are you hurt?"

He looks like I've just punched him in the gut, despair and disgust flashing across his face. "You almost died, and the first thing you ask is if *I'm* okay?" He laughs bitterly, running his hand through his usually neat hair.

I've obviously said something to upset him, but I don't understand his reaction. Frowning as much as I'm able, I search for something to say.

"I thought..." He trails off, and something flickers in his eyes, but he looks away before I can tell what it is. He pulls his hand from mine, and I instantly feel the loss, but I remain silent, letting him work through whatever this is. With a shuddering breath, he turns his gaze back to me, running his eyes over my face as if he's trying to memorise every detail. "If you'd died, I don't think that even the master himself could have stopped me," he growls, his hands balling into fists in his lap.

Fear surges through me, but it's not fear of him or his words, it's *for* him. What he's saying... The bond sealing him to the master would tear him apart if he went against orders. If anyone overhears what he's saying, it'll be treason, and I don't even want to think about what the master would do to him.

"Annalise, I fear I've only just made your life more difficult."

"But you saved me," I croak, confused. There's more going on than what he's telling me. Did something else happen after I passed out?

"Yes, but I killed the guards, every single one that was down there. And I didn't just kill them, I massacred them. I used my power to tear them limb from limb." He's stiff, tense, like he's waiting for me to reject him. "Why aren't you looking at me with fear and disgust?"

"I don't know," I reply honestly. After seeing his display of power, I *should* be afraid of him. No, I should be horrified at how effortlessly he killed those guards, all of them, not just the ones hurting me. But if anything, knowing how strong he is and seeing how gentle he's been with me only shows me the kindness he's capable of. "But I know you won't hurt me."

Sighing, he takes my hand once again. "You're too pure for this world."

Part of me purrs at the contact, my skin tingling where he touches me. I should be in agony, and while pain zips through me when I move, the moment he touches me, it's like everything else fades to the background. His words finally register, and I snort. Too pure. If only he knew my past and the things I've done.

"My actions... the master..." He trails off like he's searching for the right words, suddenly unable to meet my eyes.

The master can't honestly punish Elijah for what happened, can he? Sure, he killed those guards, but they were tearing me apart. Shuddering at the shattered fragments of memory, I swallow against the lump in the back of my throat.

"You were protecting me. Those guards were going to kill me, and you saved me. If I am this *promessa* he keeps talking about, the master shouldn't punish you for that." I have to stop several times as I speak to catch my breath, and although Elijah is vibrating with energy, he lets me finish.

Tilting his head back, he stares at the ceiling, muttering something in his language that sounds like a prayer for strength. He shakes his head and finally meets my gaze. "Annalise, you don't understand!" His eyes beg me to understand as he leans in, lowering his voice. "I acted like a male protecting his mate."

Shock knocks me speechless, the word bouncing around my mind. *Mate*. Is that why I feel comfortable around him despite my circumstances? Why I gain comfort from his touch? No, this can't be right. In Morrowmer, some elves are lucky enough to discover their true mate. It's rare, but once the bond is accepted, it's unbreakable save for death. I don't deserve to find my mate, it was never something I thought was meant for me, especially in a different land. I want to reject his claims and tell him it's not possible, but I remember what the Mother said. *They need you*. I assumed she meant the females here, that they needed my help, not my mate.

Mates, my mind corrects. *The Mother said they, as in multiple.*

"The master suspects," he continues, his eyes turning flinty as if he's fighting his protective nature. "If he works it out, he'll have power over both of us. I'll be bound to him even more tightly than I am now." His hand tightens around mine, and his body tenses. "All he would have to do is threaten to harm you, and I'd do whatever he wanted."

Everything he's saying is true. The master would use us against each other and lord his hold on me over Elijah. Except, all I can think about is the implications of what he just told me, needing to hear him speak the words. "Are you saying I'm your mate?"

"Yes, I've suspected it for a while, but I felt your pain and fear like it was my own. When I got down there and saw them hurting you... that's when I knew, when something clicked inside me. I thought you were dead." His voice cracks.

Looking up at the fae, I can't quite believe what I'm hearing. The strongest fae I've ever met sits beside me, almost broken at the thought of my death. Although it's impossible to believe, that little piece inside my chest is singing, and I can't deny that he's *something* important to me. I remember when I was with the Great Mother and was leaving this world, only to be stopped. Is he one of the tethers that prevented me from leaving?

"I did die," I confess, and he goes deathly still as I speak. "My soul left my body, and I realised I had a choice. I could go peacefully into death with my goddess, or I could return. There was something that stopped me from leaving, like a cord that was tying me to life. I followed it back here, and that's when I woke up."

His eyes burn with emotion. "I—" He stops, shaking his head and taking a deep breath. "At the moment, our connection is only a promise. We're not bonded yet, and we never can be."

His words are like a knife in my heart and far more painful than any of the wounds inflicted to me by the guards. Taking a shuddering breath, I try to smooth out my expression so he can't see my hurt, but as he places a hand on his chest, wincing as if in discomfort, I realise he can *feel* my pain. Why I'm so affected by what he said, I don't know. I didn't want a mate and certainly didn't expect to find one, but now that I know the truth and he's rejecting me... *You're not good enough. He's only confirming what you already knew.* The nagging voice inside me, which I'm usually able to ignore, suddenly becomes all I can hear. *Not good enough. Not good enough.*

He leans back, removing his hand as if severing our physical contact will help him keep his resolve. "Being my mate is only going to put you in danger. You would never be safe."

"Elijah." I try to sit up, hating how weak I seem as he makes these decisions for the both of us.

Pushing away from the bed, he stands and balls his hands at his sides as if to stop himself from reaching out to me. "No, we *cannot* act on this. We just continue as we did before, but I promise you, Annalise, I will find a way to free you."

Anger finally rears its ugly head, burning brightly in my chest. "Free me from the master, or free me from the bond between us?"

Something breaks within him as he realises he's hurting me in the process of trying to protect me. He opens his mouth to reply, but at that moment, the doors of the healing quarters slam open. Brok, the apanthe guard who was in the raiding party, strides in, his face twisted into a sneer of disgust as he looks from Elijah to me then back at the tall fae. "The master wants to see you."

Animosity oozes from him, his hatred for Elijah obvious, and it snaps something inside me. Baring my teeth, I hiss at the apanthe, my fae nature ruling my actions. Elijah glances back at me, pain and pride flashing across his features before he dons that confident smirk he uses around others. When I return my attention to Brok, he's wearing a satisfied smile, and I know my reaction will be reported to the master.

Bodil walks over, standing at my shoulder, and she shares a look with Elijah before nodding deeply. She'll protect me in here, no one will harm me, but as Elijah strides away without another backwards glance, I can't help but wonder who's going to protect him.

Chapter 11

I'm in the healers' quarters for another two days, and I don't see Elijah once. It makes me anxious. I want to know he's okay after his meeting with the master, but when I ask Bodil, she just makes a noise in the back of her throat before returning to whatever task she's performing.

For a fae, I'm healing slowly. The apanthe guards didn't use their poisonous claws on me, thank the Mother, but apparently recovering from death takes time. My power seems sluggish, and it's not responding to me in the same way it did before, but I feel stronger today. Bodil has been watching me eat, cursing the guards for under feeding me and tutting at my thin, frail body. Her mothering has been surprisingly nice, despite the brisk manner she uses. I know it's her job, but I've never been looked after like this before.

The whole time I'm in the healers' quarters, my mind spins over what Elijah told me. I can't deny that I feel a pull towards him, but I've never really looked at him in that light—not that circumstances have allowed for it.

While I'm worrying about Elijah and his absence, I also can't help but think of Alric. The devastation on his face as I was taken away was heartbreaking. There is so much I don't understand about my fellow prisoner, and I know there's more to him than he lets on.

Glancing at the clock on the far wall, I see it is just past noon. Time passes strangely here, and with nothing to do but sleep or eat, I've fallen into a bit of a pattern. Wake, eat breakfast, watch the healers do their rounds, then sleep until lunch time. Once I've eaten, I usually stay awake for a few hours before inevitably falling asleep again. I wake for dinner, have a stilted conversation with Bodil as she changes my dressings, sleep again, and repeat. Who knew that healing was so tiring? It's been three days since I was beaten, and I'm finally feeling like myself. All of my dressings were removed this morning, although I'll need to wear the cast on my arm for a few more days.

Bodil appears in the corner of my vision, and I glance over, giving the healer a slight smile.

Her eyes pass over me, her expression grim. "Your presence has been requested. There's a ball you're being ordered to attend, but the master wants to see you first."

I like that Bodil doesn't mince her words, however this revelation comes like a punch to the stomach. I knew it was only a matter of time before I was forced to see him and attend his ridiculous balls. However, while most of my wounds have healed, I'm not back to full strength. "Oh..." The word is barely more than a whisper, but the healer winces.

"I tried to put it off. I've denied him access until now, but he won't take no for an answer any longer."

I suspected someone was keeping the apanthe guards

away while I was healing, but I had no idea Bodil had gone up against the master to give me more time. Gratitude swells within me at the gesture. She denied her leader to protect me.

My smile is shaky, but I hope it portrays my deep appreciation. "Thank you."

Her eyes warm, and I swear she's about to smile, but then she seems to remember herself. Glancing around to check no one is listening, she steps closer to the bed and places a large hand on my shoulder. "Be prepared." Without another word, she turns and walks back to her workstation.

Be prepared, what's that supposed to mean? Does she know something? Is the ball going to be more than just a dance? Or is she trying to warn me about meeting with the master?

One of the healers' assistants walks over with a bundle of fabric in her arms, and I have to swallow back my alarm. I hadn't realised I would be leaving now. My gut clenches painfully as I watch her pull the curtains around the bed. The female looks young, her features like that of a cat, and she reminds me of Elia, the feline *promessa*. Smiling tentatively, she places the clothing on the edge of the bed and gestures for me to stand, offering me a hand to help me up.

Sliding my hand into hers, I swing my legs from the bed, wincing slightly as I jostle my arm. Once my feet touch the floor, I slowly push to standing, closing my eyes and taking a few deep breaths as dizziness tries to take over. The thought of facing the master makes me feel nauseous, and having to attend a ball tonight makes me want to groan. Shifting my weight from foot to foot, testing my stability, I open my eyes now that I'm sure I'm not going to fall. I catch the assistant watching me with curious eyes, but as soon as I glance at her, she quickly looks away, her cheeks turning pink.

Silently, she helps me dress, buttoning up the simple, royal blue gown that's been provided. When she passes me a comb, I attempt to brush the knots from my hair. Lying down for three days straight apparently plays havoc on your hair. Now that I am fully dressed and presentable, the assistant pulls back the curtains, and I instantly notice the guard at the door. My body feels weak as fear rises inside me. Just seeing the uniform reminds me of what they did to me. *No, look closer,* my mind insists, breaking through my panic. Focusing on the figure, I realise it's Tarren, the female apanthe who guards the female wing. She is speaking with the healer, and they both turn to face me as the curtains are pulled back. I know she's to be my escort.

Walking closer with surprising grace, the guard looks me over, her eyes sticking on the cast. Tarren frowns as she takes in my face, a low growl emitting from her chest. I've not yet seen my face or neck, and I assumed they healed, but from her reaction, I'm guessing I'm still showing signs of the beating. Female apanthe are very protective, and if Tarren has been assigned to protect the *promessa*, it's not a surprise she's acting this way.

"Ready?" she asks, her heavily accented voice rolling over me.

Taking a deep breath, I nod and follow her from the room. I've not been to the healers' quarters before, so I'm unsure where it's located within the castle. As we traverse the maze of corridors, I realise we're on the opposite side of the castle of where I've previously been. As we turn and enter another hallway, the space widens, and a lush, deep blue carpet runs the length of the corridor. The walls are lined with grand paintings portraying the master and who I assume is his predecessor. Ahead, I see two huge doors leading to what I assume is the throne room. The stone and pillars around the door are carved to look like thorn-covered vines twist around them.

I'm sure Tarren can hear my pounding heartbeat as we approach the two guards who stand in front of the impressive looking arched doorway. My suspicion is confirmed when she growls quietly, stepping in front of me as if to protect me from them. We both know that if the master ordered them to attack me, there's nothing she could do, but I'm grateful for the gesture nonetheless. I've felt so alone over the last century. Even once I was free, I isolated myself, not needing or trusting the company of others. When I was brought here, I thought it would be the same, yet I've found there's a little community of fae I've grown fond of. Elijah and Alric are the two biggest examples, but Healer Bodil put her neck on the line by not allowing the master to see me while I was healing. I'm still unsure about the other *promessa*, but could Tarren be an ally too? Especially if, as I suspect, Elijah sent her to protect me.

The guards at the door sneer but stay a respectful distance away, eyeing me over her shoulder. As one, they step forward and heave the doors open. If the two of them are struggling to move it, then I can't imagine how heavy it is. If they close those doors behind us once we enter, then that exit won't be an option for me if I need to leave in a hurry. Following Tarren, my eyes widen as I take in the grand ballroom. It's huge, double the size of the ballroom back at the palace in Galandell. The room is on two levels, easily capable of fitting five hundred guests. The ground level has a large, open space for dancing with tables lined against the walls. The second floor is like a mezzanine, allowing guests to look down at the dancers below. It's held aloft by the same intricately carved pillars and has a grand feel to it. Between each column is a pair of thick, blue velvet curtains which can be pulled closed to separate the dance floor from the tables beneath the mezzanine.

A dark, caressing wave of power draws my attention to the far end of the room. There, sitting on a throne of gold, is the master, with his elbow braced on the armrest and his head propped on his hand as he watches me. His body language screams smug confidence. He knows he holds all the control here.

Tarren glances at me over her shoulder and gestures for me to move ahead of her. Swallowing back my fear, I hold my head high and walk as steadily as my wounds will allow. I don't try to hide them or my slight wince as my arm twinges in pain. His guards did this to me, and he should see the results of that. He tells me I'm special, one of the promised ones, yet I nearly died under his roof, twice. Approaching him, I force myself to breathe evenly, trying to control my pounding heart. I stop a few steps away from the dais his throne is placed upon. Tarren is just behind me, and I appreciate her presence. Why has he brought me here? To show me his might and control?

"Ah, *ma promessa*, you're here," he purrs. His tone is welcoming, but his gaze is shrewd as he takes in my broken body. "Your injuries weren't exaggerated." A low growl enters his voice, and the guards positioned behind his throne shift uneasily at the sound. We all know that for my injuries to still be obvious, I must have been gravely wounded.

Not being one for small talk, I dip my head in acknowledgement. "You requested my presence." Perhaps I should be more polite, but I've been dragged here for a reason, and I want to know why.

Thankfully, the master laughs, leaning back in the throne. "Straight to the point, I like it." Pausing, he watches me closely as if searching for something. He strokes his short beard. "You see, *ma promessa*, I have a problem."

If he's expecting me to respond to this, then he'll be disappointed. I stand as still as a statue, waiting for him to continue.

"My right-hand man, Elijah, killed all of my guards in the dungeon. I can't let that go unpunished." Although his tone is even, like he's being reasonable, I see his eyes gleaming.

"Those guards were killing me, he protected me." I gesture to my arm, which is still in a sling. I know he has all the facts regarding the attack the other day, so why am I here? If he really wanted to punish Elijah, he would have done it already, so what's with the farce?

"Even so, he shouldn't have been able to. I ordered him to do a task for me, yet somehow, he knew you were in trouble and was able to come to you. He didn't just stop them from harming you, he wiped them all out like they were nothing." He snaps his fingers. "He was able to disobey an order, which shouldn't be possible." His expression changes as he leans forward, like he's about to share an exciting secret with me, but all I feel is a sense of foreboding. "I have a theory. I think he's your mate. The only thing stronger than his bond to me is one between mates."

Dread hits me so hard that I feel like I'm about to

vomit, but I shove it back. I can't let him think he's right, and he'll take any show of weakness as confirmation. Instead, I frown slightly as if the term 'mates' means nothing to me. "I have no idea what you're talking about. I have no control over what your followers do or don't do. All I know is that he showed up and stopped *your* guards from hurting me any further." My throat burns as I speak, and my voice cracks, but I push forward. This is the most I've said in one go for a long time, especially since I was strangled, but I won't allow Elijah to be hurt because of me.

My words, however, seem to have the opposite effect than what I hoped. The master's lips twitch as if I just confirmed something before he manages to get control of himself. He gestures to one of his guards at the other side of the room, one I hadn't noticed until now. "Then watching his punishment won't be a problem for you."

"No." The whispered word escapes me before I can stop it, and from the satisfied expression on the master's face, I know he noticed my slip.

"Bring him out."

The sound of the doors opening behind me has me turning, my heart in my throat. My eyes lock on Elijah's swaggering figure, and seeing him whole and in one piece has my knees weakening with relief. His gaze flicks to me once as he approaches the throne, and he winks before turning his attention to the master, but I see through the mask. In that one look, I see his pain and rage over my injuries and his fear for me, but mostly, there's an overriding need to protect me from the master.

"Master, you have need of me?" He grins up at the beast on the throne, dipping his head in greeting, and I notice his hands are bound by strange cuffs. Glowing, archaic writing covers them, and in that moment, I realise what feels off about Elijah—I can't feel him. In my chest, I can still feel the slight pull, but there's no sense of his enormous power. Whatever these cuffs are, they obviously bind him more than in the physical sense.

Huffing at Elijah's theatrics, the master stares down at him. "I have a theory to put to the test." Staring down at his second-in-command, the master sits forward in his throne, watching his face closely. "I think the two of you are mates. *Ma promessa* denies it, of course, but I need to be sure."

"Mates?" Elijah glances over at me briefly, giving me a once over before turning back to the master with a snort. "While I can appreciate a pretty face, she's not my type. Too skinny for me, and certainly *not* my mate," he replies, instantly dismissing me.

Although I know he's just saying this to deter the master, his words still sting. He seems to reject the claim so easily, not once reacting to my presence. I don't even want to be mated, and I'm still not sure how I feel about *him* being the one I'm tied to, so why does his rejection hurt so much?

The master was expecting us to deny his statement, his lips pulling back in a cruel, knowing smile. "We shall see," he purrs. "Kneel." The demand is sharp, his eyes going cold. As I look upon him, the image burns itself into my brain. The beastly king waiting for his orders to be obeyed.

Elijah winces as he fights the directive. "Master—"

"I said kneel!" the master roars, the windows of the ballroom rattling as his power washes over us, his alpha command clear.

Stumbling, I force myself to stay upright against the

flood of power. I have no idea how Elijah is still standing under the full brunt of it. Growling, the master sends out another wave of power, and whatever strength Elijah had is finally spent. His knees hit the marble floor loud enough to send the sound echoing around the ballroom. Web-like cracks appear on the tiles he kneels upon, broken by the impact.

The master nods at his guards who come forward and surround the kneeling fae. Two take up position in front of Elijah, placing a heavy hand on each of his shoulders as if to hold him down, while the third steps up, pulling a whip from his belt.

Horror fills me as I realise what they are about to do. Glancing over at the master, I see he's watching me with a satisfied smirk. This isn't punishment for Elijah killing those guards, this is purely a way of forcing us to admit what he already knows. He wouldn't whip me because he needs me in one piece for his ball and other schemes, but Elijah is another matter.

"Begin."

The movement is so fast I almost miss it, the sound of the whip whistling through the air warning me of the blow. Elijah's back arches, and a grunt of pain leaves his lips, but he doesn't say anything, just accepts the strike. The guard raises his arm again and again, giving Elijah no chance to recover between hits. His shirt is in tatters now, exposing red welts and his torn open back. I'm barely able to restrain myself. Rage and sorrow rise inside me, but mostly, there's this overwhelming need to protect him, to protect what's mine. I try to suppress these strange new feelings, but the longer this goes on, the harder it becomes to just stand by and do nothing.

Elijah sags forward, the guards' grips the only thing

keeping him upright. The whip flies through the air, landing on an already open wound, and he lets out a cry of pain. He's been mostly silent, gritting his teeth and only grunting with each hit. The sound breaks something within me, and I step forward, only to be stopped by a hand on my shoulder. Spinning around, I bare my teeth, hissing at whoever's stopping me, only to see Tarren shaking her head, her eyes warning me not to get involved. I'd forgotten the female guard was still here with me, and her expression is blank, giving away none of her feelings. She's trying to help me, though, her hand is a gesture of warning rather than one of restraint.

Hearing Elijah cry out again, I feel something inside me fracture, releasing a part of me I didn't know I possessed. I'm acting before I even realise it. Later, I'll look back and marvel at the speed with which I move. A wall of muscle stops me from getting any closer to Elijah, but through the gap between the guards' bodies, I can still see his bleeding, shaking form. "Stop this!" I demand, spinning to face the master.

The whip stops as the master hums in consideration, stroking his bearded chin. "So his pain causes you pain? Much like a mate bond?"

Rage makes me see red. I want to fly forward and tear the master apart, but I push the urge down. I need to keep this façade going, or we'll both suffer the consequences.

"Anyone would hate to see this. You're brutalising him!" I throw my arm out and gesture to the wounds on Elijah's back. Dampening my sudden temper, I attempt to reason with the master, but I know from the glint in his eyes that it's not working.

"Give him another ten lashes," the master orders with a cruel grin, ignoring me completely.

"I said stop!" At my demand, something strikes me like a thunderbolt, but instead of pain, I feel energised as power tingles through my body like little electric shocks. I've never felt stronger, but I don't have time to marvel at the change, not while Elijah's in danger. I don't stop to think.

Running towards Elijah's slumped form, I cover his body with my own, turning around just as the whip comes whistling towards me. I hear people shouting for it to stop, but it's too late. Holding my uninjured arm above my head, I push my anger and fear into the action, and to my amazement, the whip freezes just inches above my arm. That's when I feel the power surrounding me. No, surrounding *us*, protecting both Elijah and me. My power seems to flare out in a burst, pushing the guards back. Cries of surprise reach me, but I'm too far gone to care, snarling at anyone who looks like they may come closer. "Don't touch him," I hiss. I've never heard my voice sound like this before, and I've certainly never felt so strongly about anything to risk everything to protect it.

"Annalise," Elijah croaks, and before I know it, I'm kneeling in front of him, cradling his head as I scan his face. "What did you do?" he whispers, and for the first time since I've known him, he sounds scared.

The reality of what I've just done hits me, but I gently stroke his cheek and shake my head. "I couldn't let them keep hurting you."

Elijah's countenance breaks at my words. He opens his mouth to say something, but he suddenly closes it, flicking his eyes to something behind me. Spinning and dropping into a defensive position, I bare my teeth as the master climbs down from the dais and steps towards us. "What she did, Elijah, was confirm my theory."

At the master's words, my power sputters, leaving me utterly spent. I have no idea where the strength came from in the first place, but when I needed it, when Elijah needed me, it appeared. However, now I'm as weak as a human and standing between two of the most powerful beings I've ever known.

The master looks us over like he just found a great treasure, a smug feline grin stretched across his lips. "To find your true mate is a privilege," he acknowledges. "However, this leaves me with a problem." He sighs like he regrets what he has to say next, but I see right through the act. "The *promessa* is mine." He steps closer as if to emphasise his claim over me, placing a hand on my shoulder. Snarling, I immediately shake off his touch, despising the feel of him, of the *wrongness* that shoots through my body.

Elijah growls as he gives into his fae nature, his face losing the cultured mask he usually wears. I know if he wasn't wearing those cuffs that suppress his power, the whole scene would have turned out differently.

Realising the same thing, the master glances down at the manacles on his wrists as if he does not trust them to keep Elijah at bay. Stepping back, the master turns and returns to his throne. We've spooked him, and while that fills me with a sense of satisfaction, I know it won't work in our favour. Spooked leaders make rash decisions—my captivity by the elf queen is a testament to that.

Now at a safe distance, he stares down at us with what I'm sure he thinks is a regal expression, but I only see the monster beneath. "Once your bond is completed, it will strengthen the two of you, making you too powerful. I will not have the mate bond interfere with the *promessa's* destiny, not when I've worked so hard. You're forbidden from completing the bond."

The command hits us both, but Elijah grunts at the force of it, his connection to the master making the order much stronger. He's fighting it, and the tug in my chest becomes painful as he struggles next to me on the ground, crying out in pain as the directive wraps around him.

Happy that Elijah is now back under his control, he seems to lose interest in me, only glancing at me once before waving me away. "Take her back to the cells."

Someone instantly appears at my side and places a hand on my shoulder as they try to lead me away. "No, wait!" Fighting against the hold, I attempt to break from their grip. Arms wrap around me, and part of my mind registers it's Tarren and not one of the other guards, but that doesn't seem to matter to my traumatised body. I kick out and thrash, my gaze locked on Elijah.

Tarren pulls me away, her grip on my body unbreakable. As I fight and struggle, I see Elijah trying to climb to his feet, stumbling and wincing as the wounds on his back tear. "Annalise!" His pained shout fills me with despair as I'm dragged farther away and out of the room, an animalistic cry ripping from his throat as the ballroom doors close, separating us.

"Do not fret. I will make sure he is safe," Tarren whispers as she continues to drag me through the corridors, her grip loosening now that we're away from the master's watchful gaze.

I fall silent, unable to converse as I sink into myself, my body no longer resisting the pull of the female apanthe. She glances back with a concerned expression, but I don't have the energy to care. I feel raw, like something inside me has been ripped out. What I just witnessed reminded me of what the master's capable of. He may dress in fine clothes and walk around like a king, but he's no better than the beasts he commands. No, he's worse than that, he's a monster, and I can never forget that. My body feels numb, and I can no longer deny that Elijah's claims are true. He's my mate. He said we couldn't complete the bond because I wouldn't be safe, but now the master knows. Having a fully formed bond would protect me, but that has been snatched from us. It seems cruel to find my mate in these circumstances and finally recognise the bond between us, only for it to be immediately taken away. It makes sense now why the master has ordered us not to complete it. If Elijah had been able to go against an order, then together, with our bond, he may be able to break the master's hold on him completely.

The journey to the dungeon passes in a blur. I feel Tarren's gaze on me as she leads me down, but I ignore her, too deep in my thoughts to interact. A constant, dull ache fills my chest, and I welcome the pain. It's the only thing keeping me from sinking completely into despair.

A gentle push on the small of my back has me entering my cell, and the tingle over my skin tells me that what little power I have left is now inaccessible. The tightness around my chest eases a little as the bond between Elijah and me becomes muted. While the feeling is abhorrent, it makes it easier for me to think, to function.

"Annalise!" Alric calls out, and from the corner of my eye, I see him gripping the bars between us. "What have you done to her?" he demands, but Tarren ignores him, her eyes on me as she shuts the cell door.

Remembering the guard's words as she led me down, I grasp the bars and stare back at her. "Please," is all I say, meeting her amber eyes. A flicker of sympathy crosses her face, but it's gone in a blink. Nodding her head once, she turns and leaves the dungeon without another word. She said she'd make sure he was safe, but what can she do against the might of the master? Elijah will heal, but with those cuffs on, his fae healing ability will be limited. I should be with him, but the master made it clear that isn't going to happen.

"Annalise? What happened?" Alric's scratchy voice breaks through my stoic state, and I turn slowly to face him. He's kneeling on his side of the bars, concern lining his wrinkled face. Taking two short steps, I kneel opposite him. I remember how I managed to create a barrier around Elijah and me, the power pushing the guards away. I've never been capable of anything like that before, and now I'm just left feeling... broken, raw, changed. Everything has changed.

"Elijah. He's my mate." Saying it out loud makes everything feel so much more real, and a pang of longing leaves me gasping.

"That can't be possible." A low growl rumbles in Alric's chest, and I lift my eyes to meet his determined blue orbs. I get that strange feeling that there's something different about him again, that Alric is not what he seems.

Shaking my head, I push those thoughts aside for another time, unable to focus on anything other than the ache in my chest. "They whipped him," I whisper, remembering the whistling of the whip before it sliced open Elijah's skin.

Alric goes deathly still as I speak, his grip on the bars loosening slightly, but he never once takes his eyes from me.

"I don't know what happened, but something

changed within me, and I ran in front of the whip. I needed to help him, and power like I've never known before rose up inside me." Glancing down at my hand, I ball it into a fist as my anger surges. "The master did it on purpose. Somehow, he knew. He commanded us not to complete the bond, and now I feel..." My voice trails off, not having the vocabulary to explain the range of emotions currently clouding my mind, but one thing stands out. I'm not the same person I was when I was taken to the ballroom. "I feel different, Alric." Placing my hands below his, I pull myself closer until our faces are almost touching. He's not moved since I started talking, holding his breath as I close the gap between us. His expression is intense, filled with an emotion I can't decipher. Fighting back the sob I so desperately want to release, I beg him with my eyes to understand. "Something has changed, and I don't know what's happening to me."

Chapter 12

Maids circle me, pulling and prodding as they get me ready for the master's ball, but I pay them no mind, allowing them to dress me as they like. I couldn't care less about how I appear for this farce.

When Tarren had come to take me from the cells, she nodded at my questioning gaze—Elijah's okay. She didn't talk to me other than to tell me it was time to get ready for the ball, not even when we were alone and walking through the corridors. From her stiff, defensive posture, I got the feeling we were being watched and she didn't feel safe telling me anything else. Depositing me at the door to the room Elijah had said was mine, she informed me that my maids were waiting for me inside. Just as I opened the door and began to step across the threshold, she placed her large hand on my shoulder and squeezed once, her eyes meeting mine. That was as much of a reassurance as I was going to get.

The maids titter around me, commenting on my thin form and complaining that they are going to have to take in the dresses. I don't comment, using my silence as a shield, but inside my mind is a mess. The brightness of the room, filled with its sweet scents and luxurious items, only stirs the anger in my gut. I want to scream at the frivolousness of the maids and their inane chatter. None of this matters. I don't care if I wear the baby blue or the royal blue gown, nor do I care if the red lipstick will wash me out. What I care about is the ache in my chest and the fact it won't heal until I know Elijah is okay. I also, for some inexplicable reason, care that Alric seemed so pained at the knowledge that I'd found my mate. So instead, I stay silent, retreating within myself.

Alric.

Why am I so drawn to the fae? I know nothing about him, yet he's been one of the only constants in my life since I arrived here. He always checks that I'm okay and looks out for me, even going so far as alerting the guards when I was dying of the apanthe's poison despite the fact it could have got him into trouble. I've witnessed what the dungeon guards do to prisoners who draw attention to themselves. There's something that always pulls me to him, yet I can't put my finger on it. His entire being is odd, as is the way he carries himself. At first I thought it was because he was so old, that it made the aura he gave off... different. Yet I shouldn't be able to feel that because of the magic in the cells. There's a sense of mystery around him, which makes it difficult for me to fully trust him. I know there's more he's not telling me, but I can't stay away.

The maids jerk me from my thoughts as they tighten the corset-like back of the dress they decided on, making my breath catch in my chest. Glancing down, I see the light, arctic blue fabric that bunches by my hips, showing a soft, sea foam white underskirt at the front before flaring out and falling to the floor. Matching blue embroidery graces the hem of the underskirt. The voluminous skirts are ridiculous, but thankfully not as big as I had feared. From what I can see of the bodice, it's the same blue and fits tightly, pushing up and displaying my small bust. White lace is stitched along the top of the low-cut neckline, giving the illusion of modesty. Off the shoulder straps finish the look, made of a delicate matching white material, but they have no practical function and are purely decorative.

The maids coo and guide me over to the dressing table, arranging my skirts as I sit on the provided stool. As they start brushing my face with potions and powders, I'm shocked at what I see in the mirror. I look gaunt. My cheekbones are prominent in a way that only starvation can cause. I knew I'd lost weight, the long journey here and lack of meals in the cells had seen to that, but the changes astound and distress me. My blue eyes appear striking against my pale skin as I assess my reflection. Most of the bruises seem to have faded, and only those around my jaw and neck are on show, but the maids quickly go to work covering them, their powders making my nose itch. My arm is still in a cast, and it's been covered by a swath of fabric that matches my dress, folded into a makeshift sling.

Glancing at my chest, I expect to see a wound there, something that shows the pain I feel inside. Only smooth skin greets me. Thanks to Alric, I understand why I feel like this, but it doesn't ease that sensation.

Shifting his weight, Alric reaches out as if to touch me, but pulls his hand back at the last moment. "What the master was trying to do was cause your bond to show itself," *he explains. I frown at him, not understanding his phrasing. Does he mean when I stepped in front of Elijah, protecting him?*

Sensing my confusion, he sighs and runs a hand through his greying hair. "Bonds between mates don't always snap into place straightaway. With some, it takes a significant event to make itself known." *Although he sounds sympathetic, I see anger burning in his eyes. The master manipulated me to get what he wanted, and Elijah was hurt because of it. I shouldn't be surprised, I know what that beast is capable of.*

"When the master ordered Elijah to be hurt in front of you, it forced your side of the bond to rise up. That's why you were able to protect both of you and why you feel different now. That is just a hint of the power you would wield if you completed the bond." *He moves back from the bars, as if to distance himself from me, but I reach out to stop him, my hand slipping between the rods.*

I can't have him pull away from me, not now. My mind reels from everything he told me, but it makes sense, and something is telling me to trust him. Trust has never been easy for me, but my options are limited.

He stills under my touch, his eyes burning with an emotion I can't place. "How do you know all of this?" *Does he have a mate he's separated from? That thought causes my stomach to twist, but I ignore it.*

His face lights up as he smiles. "I know a lot more than you think, Annalise. Not everything is as it appears." *His eyes glisten with humour.* "Don't underestimate me." *He reaches between the bars and strokes my cheek. I should pull away. My mate has just been whipped and my chest is still raw from the bond emerging. Yet when he touches me, something inside me settles and helps clear my mind.*

I'm pulled from the memory as my head is jerked to the side. My lips draw back as I hiss at the maid behind me before reaching up to rub the raw spot she just carelessly tugged. All of the maids gasp and jump back, the scent of their fear filling the air as they watch me warily. Unease stirs in my gut. This realm seems to bring out my baser fae instincts. I never would have dreamed of hissing or snarling at someone back in Morrowmer.

Sighing, I gesture for them to approach. I return to blankly staring at my reflection as they hesitantly step closer. Soon enough, they are chatting amongst themselves and continuing to get me ready, and I allow myself to lament on what Alric told me.

I felt connected to Elijah before, and that connection between us was building, but I assumed he was just protective of me since he was the one to find me. Except something changed for him, and he was convinced we were mates. I have no knowledge of what a mate connection is like, so I assumed he was right. Why else would I feel pulled to him in that way? Once my side of the bond was forced from me, what he was to me finally sunk in, and I truly believed him, but it's too late now. I understand why Elijah's expression had been one of devastation when he realised what I'd done.

I can still feel the echo of that power that flowed through my veins and allowed me to protect him. By forbidding us from completing our bond, the master is able to control us, and our power stays as it is.

A knock on the door has the maids scurrying to answer it, and I run my eyes over my reflection one last time. My hair has been left down, but they curled it, my pointed ears peeking through, reminding others of what I am. The whole look is effective, softening the sharpness of my jaw and making me look regal. This is only accentuated by the silver diadem resting atop my head. Each link is a delicate twist with tiny silver flowers adorning it, and in the middle, lying on my forehead, is a teardrop with a pale blue gem.

I glance towards the door at the sound of low voices. Tarren has entered the room, her eyes immediately finding me to ensure I'm okay. Pushing away from the dressing table, I stand and slowly make my way to her side.

"*Promessa.*" Dropping into a short bow, Tarren pays her respects, her thickly accented voice made deeper by the low grumble in her chest. Rising, she takes another look at me before opening the door and gesturing for me to step into the corridor.

I guess it's time to go. Taking a deep breath and pushing all of my confusion, pain, and anger down, I lock it away. The master doesn't get to see how he's hurt me, I won't let him have that power over me. Rolling my shoulders back as best as I can with my arm in a sling, I hold my head high and step from the room, the guard just ahead of me.

I've seen a lot of Tarren recently. In fact, ever since I was attacked, I've not had a male guard. Was that Elijah's doing? I'm not complaining, I far prefer Tarren's company to the male apanthe guards' attendances. They all seem to emit a dangerous energy, yet I know that my female guard will protect me, her fae instincts making her the perfect defender.

"I am your guard now."

I glance at her as we walk, her words proving my suspicions right. She's walking just ahead of me, guiding me, but I don't miss her glancing behind me, constantly on alert. Overall, I'm pleased with this development.

"Thank you." My voice cracks as I speak for the first time in hours, but I mean it.

She looks over me, her eyes widening in surprise at my gratitude. With a huff, she returns to studying the hallway ahead of us. We're silent for the rest of the journey, and before I know it, we're at the doors leading to the ballroom. They are already propped open so I'm able to see the lavish decorations that have been set up. I stop moving, taking in the room full of strange, unknown creatures. Anxiety and nausea war within me at the thought of walking into the crowded space. Images of what happened in this very room only hours ago flash through my mind. Elijah's torn back and his cries of pain he was desperately trying to stifle. Hatred for the master strengthens me, giving me the courage I need.

Blowing out a slow, controlled breath, I nod, and Tarren walks up to one of the guards positioned on either side of the door, whispering something to him in their guttural language. She returns to my side and gives me what I think is supposed to be a supportive smile, but with her fangs and twitching whiskers, it just makes her look terrifying.

"The master's newest *promessa* from the land across the mountains," a small, feline-looking creature shouts in a booming voice that doesn't fit with his short stature.

The ballroom seems to fall silent, and even the sounds of the musicians who had been tuning their instruments stops as all eyes turn to me. A nudge on the small of my back prompts me to walk forward, even though all I want to do is run and hide.

I've learned from past experiences that this much attention is never good, and from the hungry eyes that watch me, I know I'm right. Trying to keep my breathing even is a challenge, and the weight of expectation from these fae is nearly crippling. At the other end of the room, sitting atop his golden throne with an arrogant smile, is the master. "*Ma promessa*, come to me," he calls, and for half a second, I consider disobeying.

Don't be stupid, Annalise. They would catch you in a second, especially in this daft dress, I chide myself. *The master would like nothing better than to punish you and make you submit in front of all these people. Pick your battles.* Talking myself through it, I know I don't have much of an option. I surreptitiously glance around as I continue forward, looking for Elijah. My heart sinks when I don't see him. Is he okay?

At the base of the master's throne, sitting on the dais, are the other *promessa*. They are dressed in grand ballgowns, and I'm suddenly grateful my maids picked this dress. They look like dolls, with their cinched in waists and low-cut necklines displaying their busts. If I thought my layers upon layers of skirts were excessive, then what the others are wearing is a whole new level of superfluous.

Fae from all the different factions must be in attendance, as I only notice a handful of feline-looking creatures. The atmosphere is tense, and from some of the expressions on the faces of the males I pass, I get the impression they are just as pleased to be here as I am. It's so quiet in the ballroom that I could hear a pin drop. Arriving before the master, I raise my chin to meet his gaze.

The master does something that surprises me. He smiles widely as amusement twinkles in his eyes. "Welcome, *promessa*." The rumble of his voice is low, seductive, like we're the only two in the room. I've never seen him act this way, but perhaps that's how he's able to keep these females under his thumb. I don't trust this charming side of him.

"Master," I greet, keeping my voice even. I use all of my will to stop my anger from seeping through, and it takes me a few seconds to recognise the silence surrounding us. Those watching shuffle around anxiously, and the master just stares, raising an eyebrow. Finally, I realise what's happening. They are waiting for me to bow, to acknowledge the master's authority. I refuse to bow before him, but as I stand there, I know the master will keep us like this until I do. *Mother above*, I curse, grinding my teeth. I remember what Elijah said then, that I shouldn't keep pushing the master. He'll make things difficult for me, and now that he knows of my connection with his second-in-command... Biting back my pride, I incline my head, glancing down for several seconds before raising my gaze to meet his.

Smiling, the master leans back in his throne, appeased, and the rest of the room seems to let out a collective breath of relief. "*Promessa*, come sit with me." He gestures to his side, and I see a small wooden stool has been placed there. The last place I want to be right now is that close to the beast, but I have no idea what he's done with Elijah. Perhaps I can acquire some information from him. Stepping forward, I glance at the other females who are all sitting on the stone dais. A couple of them smile and nod in greeting, although the warmth of the greetings vary. Elia and the bird-like female practically scowl at me, jealousy burning in their eyes as I climb the dais and sit at the master's side. If only I could tell them they have nothing to worry about. They are welcome to him.

I hate having all these eyes on us, on me. I can just picture what we look like. The master, with his collection of females at his beck and call, all dressed up for his pleasure, and sitting at his right-hand side, elevated above the others, is me—the rare female from over the mountains. Disgust makes it difficult for me to be this close to him, but I swallow my pride.

With a wave of the master's hand, one of the guards stationed beside him hurries off. Watching the guard, I see him stop by the side door to the ballroom and whisper something to another guard. I hadn't even seen the apanthe by the door, but as I pay more attention, I notice they are all hiding in the shadows of the mezzanine, observing the guests closely. I'm not surprised, but I'm impressed with their ability to hide in plain sight. The apanthe are not small, yet with the brightly coloured grand outfits of the guests, it's easy to overlook them.

The side door opens, and a surge of power rolls over me, announcing who's arrived before I even see him—Elijah. His power meets mine, caressing me, and before I know it, I'm leaning forward, about to leap from the stool. A heavy hand lands on my shoulder, stopping my movements before they could give away what I was about to do. Snapping my head around to look at the master, I see him staring down at me with a frown. He shakes his head once as his own power settles over me, trying to infuse his will on me. Although I feel the urge to follow his silent order,

I'm not bound to obey him, so I'm able to push past the clinging power, and if I wanted to, I could disobey him. But as I become aware of how many eyes are watching us, I don't, instead stilling on the stool.

That was stupid, I chide myself as the reality of the situation hits me. *You almost caused a scene in front of the whole ballroom.*

Elijah finally comes into view, and the tight band that's been around my chest since this afternoon releases. He's wearing his usual mask as he swaggers into the ballroom, his smart black tunic and trousers only adding to the dark prince persona he gives off. It works. The guests closest to him back away, wearing fear and hatred on their faces. Watching the retreating fae, Elijah chuckles low in his throat, flashing his teeth as he grins at them. To anyone who didn't know him, they'd think he was enjoying this and revelling in the sense of power his reputation gives him, but I know different. My chest warms as he moves nearer, except he hasn't glanced at me once. I know the reason behind it, he's trying to protect us, but that doesn't stop the sting of rejection.

He doesn't look like the broken fae I saw earlier, his back straight as he swaggers towards us. The master obviously granted him his power back, that's the only way he'd be able to heal this fast. That power rolls over me again, and I want to sigh in relief as it wraps around me, acknowledging me in a way he can't in front of all these fae. Turning from the guests, he grins up at the master and drops into an elaborate bow. I don't miss the wince that crosses his face, but it's gone in seconds, replaced by an excited grin. He looks like an eager enforcer ready to inflict the master's will on any guests who displease him.

Standing to his full height at the master's gesture,

Elijah runs his eyes over the females at his master's feet, winking as he greets them with a nod. Irrational jealousy flares within me so strong and bright, I'm sure everyone around us will notice. Except they don't. Only Elijah, who must feel me through our incomplete bond, acknowledges it. His eyes snap to mine and his body stills as he takes me in. For those few seconds, as our eyes lock, I can barely breathe. Things feel different between us now. The bond is finally acknowledged by both parties, and it ignites between us, desperate for us to act on it.

Shaking from his stare, Elijah winks again and spins to face the waiting guests. "Welcome to Arpathe." His voice seems to carry through the room despite it not being raised. Arpathe. This is the first time I've learned what this faction is called. "The master appreciates you joining us to celebrate the discovery of a new *promessa*."

All eyes shift back to me, where I sit in pride of place at the master's side like the good little possession he wants me to be. Pushing down my discomfort, I stare out at the sea of faces.

Elijah continues to smile, but there's a hardness in his eyes that has those closest to him shuffling uncomfortably. "This is also a great opportunity to build your connections with the master and appreciate this time of peace."

Translation—remember who's in charge here and what will happen if you don't play ball. This isn't just a chance to show me off, it's a means for the master to flex his might over the other factions.

"Enjoy your evening." With a final smirk, Elijah gestures towards the band who immediately starts playing their instruments like their lives depend on it. Nervous energy fills the room, and the guests begin to mingle now that they have been dismissed. Elijah glances at me once before disappearing into the crowd.

A huff of amusement has me glancing up at the master, his focus on the fae who are trying to discreetly watch us as they talk amongst themselves. A mewling noise catches both our attention. Looking down, I see Elia has crawled closer to the master and is rubbing up against his legs like a house cat. My lip pulls back in disgust. How can this female genuinely want to be around this monster enough to act like his besotted puppet in front of everyone?

I may find it nauseating, but the master seems to love the extra attention. A suggestive smile appears on his lips as he crooks his finger, gesturing for her to come closer. This is all the encouragement Elia needs, immediately climbing up his legs to drape herself across his lap. Purring, the master only has eyes for the female writhing on his lap, and he waves us away without even lifting his head. "Enjoy the ball, remember why you're here."

His comment makes me frown, but the other *promessa* stand and weave their way into the crowd, disappearing before I've even vacated my stool. Not wanting to be near the master any longer, I quickly descend the dais and drift over to the side of the ballroom, standing by a pillar and wishing I could disappear.

Away from his control, I'm free to observe the many different types of fae who have gathered here. There's a large group of the strange scaled fae, and I notice the *promessa* from their land is already at their side. Their scales are all various shades of blue, an iridescent sheen making them glisten under the ballroom lights. They seem to be keeping to themselves, their sharp eyes watching everyone closely.

Near them are the fae with tentacle-like protrusions covering their mouths, and I see the *promessa* from their lands has also joined them. However, they seem to be more sociable, and I notice several of them around the room conversing with other fae.

The crowd appears to be mostly made up of the bird-like beings and males with large antlers, reminding me of Mia, the fawn-like *promessa*. Sure enough, I find her talking to a male with an impressive set of antlers. What surprises me, though, is that they are both watching me as they speak together quietly. Feeling uncomfortable, I push away from the pillar and weave behind a group of fae. Now that the music has started, several pairs have made their way to the dance floor, their moves graceful as they spin. I notice Gail dancing with a male with horns, her tall, hare-like ears giving her away. She doesn't appear like she's enjoying herself, but I've never seen her smile before, so perhaps this is just how she looks.

I spend the next hour or so watching from the shadows of the ballroom, picking at the trays of food and moving from pillar to pillar. I've managed to avoid too much attention, and so far no one has approached me, so all in all, it's going better than I expected. People watching has always been fascinating to me. During the years I was silenced by the elf queen, that was one of the only things I *could* do. I can learn so much about someone just from their body language alone and have a whole conversation without saying a word.

The *promessa* have been dancing with many of the guests, but it's clear from their body language that they would rather be elsewhere. Recalling the master's comment, where he said to remember why they were here, it makes me wonder if this is what he was talking about. They always seem to be surrounded by the male fae and never far from the dance floor. I even noticed Elia, obviously evicted from the master's lap, dancing with a male who had very hawk-like features.

A tingling sensation on my skin warns me that I'm being watched. On alert, I slowly scan the ballroom to find the source. Intuitively, I look over at the master and discover I was right, his eyes boring into me. Beside him is the fae I saw talking to Mia, his impressive set of antlers making him stand out. Whatever the male is saying to the master seems important, his gaze intense as he looks at me once more. I don't get a sense of danger from the stag-like fae, but I can't shake the feeling they are talking about me.

It's time to move. Shuddering, I slip around the pillar, only to walk straight into a hard chest. "Oomph!" The air is knocked from my lungs, and a set of hands instantly come up to steady me.

"Eager to see me, *promessa*?" a male says lightly, humour lacing his tone.

Mother above, I curse, quickly backing away and wincing at the pain lancing through my arm from the bump. Whoever this male is, he's built like a brick wall, and I think walking into the column would have hurt less. "I apologise, I wasn't paying attention," I blurt, fearing the consequences of smacking into one of the master's guests. When no blow or rebuke comes, I tentatively raise my gaze to see who I've walked into.

The male standing before me is gorgeous, that much is certain. The corners of his lips are turned up in amusement, his half-smile showing off his straight white teeth. I see a slight flash of fang, but I get the impression he's trying not to frighten me and is keeping them covered. His shoulder-length, wavy, golden-brown hair and stubbled jaw should make him look scruffy, but it suits him. He doesn't have any of the animalistic features most of the fae here do, only his pointed ears poking from his hair tell me he's fae. Well, that and the immense amount of power I can feel rolling off of him. His bronze skin is smooth like caramel, and I have the strangest desire to lick him to see if he's as sweet as he looks. Where in the Mother did that thought come from? Clearing my throat, I try not to blush.

He examines me as I study him, our gazes clashing as we finish our appraisals. As they meet, I have the strangest sense of déjà vu, like I've met this fae before. Something about his eyes is so familiar, the blue orbs glinting in the light. Frowning, I start to reach out, but I jerk my hand back. Was I really just about to touch a complete stranger? He doesn't feel like a stranger though. The thought takes me aback as I realise the truth behind it. "Have we met before?" I inquire, but I know I've never seen this male before. I've been locked in this castle since I arrived here and haven't met anyone outside of the apanthe. However, something about his energy is familiar, comforting.

His blue eyes crinkle and his smile widens. Closing the gap between us, he gets so close I can feel the heat from his body. I should push him away, make him back up. I dislike being touched, especially by strangers, but although my heart speeds up, it's not from fear, it's from excitement. He places his lips by my ear, and I feel his breath tickling the sensitive skin there.

"I'll see you later, Annalise," he whispers. He pulls back, his eyes softening at my shock, and caresses my cheek.

The movement is familiar, but it's his eyes that snap

everything into place as I realise who he reminds me of. "Alric?"

Whatever he's about to say dies on his lips, his eyes darting to something behind me. His expression darkens, but it crosses his face so quickly I almost miss it. Winking, he spins on his heel and disappears within a group of fae, leaving me stunned and staring after him.

Chapter 13

No. It can't be possible. Alric is locked away in the cells below, not to mention he looks nothing like this male other than his eyes. Perhaps he's just Alric's relative? That doesn't explain how he knows my name though. I was introduced as the *promessa*, not by my name. I step forward, determined to find him and demand he give me answers, but someone clears their throat behind me.

Spinning so quickly that I feel a little dizzy, I find the stag fae holding up both hands as if to steady me. How do these fae sneak up on me so easily? Usually I'm aware of who's around me, but tonight my senses seem to be overwhelmed.

"I'm sorry I startled you, *promessa*," the male starts, a gentle smile crossing his handsome features. "I was hoping you would accept a dance with me," he says, his wording formal but his accent smooth and cultured.

I'm prepared to say no, since the last thing I want to do is attract more attention by dancing in the middle of the ballroom. However, as I meet his eyes, I feel a push to accept. Taking a good look at him, I openly appraise the fae. I'm probably being rude, but I'm surrounded by fae I don't know, and I want to make sure I'm going to be safe. He's slim with broad shoulders, and he's just a little taller than me, however the huge pair of antlers on his head give him the appearance of being much taller. They are stunning, the branched structure gleaming in the light. I can't help but notice how sharp they look and have to admit he would be a formidable opponent. Yet I don't sense any aggressive sentiments from him at all. Most of the fae here are strutting around as if to prove they are the strongest, their dominance trying to push through, and although I can detect this fae's power, he seems to be attempting to hold it back. His presence is soothing, and although he's probably not doing it for my benefit, I appreciate it all the same. I examine his face. His expression is patient, and his full lips are still wearing a smile. His skin is pale, and he has a smattering of freckles on his cheeks that I find charming when coupled with his tousled brown hair, which is longer on the top than on the sides. He wears a smart red jacket with golden buttons and a royal blue sash, making me think he's someone of importance in his faction.

When his dark brown eyes meet mine, my stomach does a strange flip. The fact he's waited so patiently while I've obviously been evaluating him places him higher in my regard. Taking a deep breath, I decide to trust my gut. "I don't know any of these dances," I warn, finally placing my hand in his outstretched one.

His face lights up at my acceptance, and he nods his head. "I will guide you. I won't let you fall," he promises, his words formal once more, and strangely, I believe him.

My heart flutters at his words, but I don't reply, simply giving him a small smile. He leads me onto the dance floor, and the crowd parts to let us through. Although everyone is staring at me, they are also staring at him too. Raised eyebrows and low whispers follow us, but the closer we get to the dance floor, the less I care. Finding a space, he guides me into position, gripping my left arm and placing his other hand on my waist, avoiding my injured arm which is still strapped across my chest in a sling. A new song begins, and the stag begins to move, effortlessly leading me to the music.

In a previous life, before my captivity, I used to love to dance. Music and the beautiful fluidity of the movements was my life, and I'd spend as much time as I could dancing. It was mostly by myself, but I did have a dance partner whom I trained with. Before now, I'd forgotten about that, about the huge part of my life that I lost thanks to the actions of the elf queen. Although I don't know the steps to these dances, my body instinctively follows the stag's lead. My heart soars as we spin and glide across the floor, my partner an adept dancer. I thought I might struggle, as I've not danced in over a century, but a part of me has been awakened, and it's like I never stopped.

One dance turns into two, which turns into three, and we never once speak, just enjoying this feeling. For the first time in a century, I feel like myself. I know this won't last for long, and I'll soon be back in the cells below the castle, but I relax in his hold, trusting him to guide me. The current song builds to a crescendo, and he leads me into a low, deep dip. As we straighten, my cheeks flushed and a bright, genuine smile stretched across my lips, the music changes, and a slower waltz fills the air.

We begin to dance again, and after a few moments, I

feel his eyes on my face. I bring my gaze to his, wanting to blush at the look he's giving me, like I'm the most incredible fae he's ever seen. A tug in my chest has me looking away, a reminder that I have a mate and he's probably watching as I dance with this unknown fae.

As if sensing that last thought, my partner clears his throat. "I realised I've been rude and not asked your name. I planned to once we were on the dance floor, but you're such a beautiful dancer that I was distracted." He laughs, and the tinge of embarrassment in his tone catches my attention. As I look up, I see he's feeling sheepish at his apparent faux pas.

I've never seen a male fae act like this before, and I find him charming. "Annalise." My amusement dances across my face.

His happiness shines through his countenance as he lowers his head in acknowledgement. "I am Prince Able of the Doerallia, and it is a pleasure to meet you, Annalise."

My shock must show on my face, but I quickly try to school my expression into an interested mien. A prince! That would explain the sash he's wearing. I just assumed it was part of the formal dress the fae from his faction wore. Something else he said catches my attention. *Doerallia*. That must be the name of the faction he's from. I really need to try and get a map of this land, or at least find someone to explain it to me.

"You're new to this realm?" he inquires, his voice pulling me from my thoughts. He already knows the answer, the master has made no secret of the fact that I was found on the other side of the mountains. Despite this, I nod. "How are you being treated?" His question is carefully asked with light interest, but from the intensity in which he's watching me, I know the question is deeper than it seems.

I should lie. I should tell him the master's taking care of me, but I have the urge to tell him the truth. The smile drops from my face, and I decide once again to trust this stranger.

"I was stolen from my land and dragged here with no explanation," I answer, my voice soft so I'm not overheard. "I've spent every night since I arrived locked in a cell with no access to my power, and I almost died twice. I've been beaten and tortured, and I'm told that I should just accept how lucky I am to be here, to be one of the promised ones." My voice steadily gets louder as I speak, my anger stirring as I list the master's crimes against me, no longer caring who's listening. "I still don't really know why I'm here or what the master plans to do with me." Seeing his shocked expression, I bite my lip. I've overstepped, and I'm sure I'm going to suffer for it. "I'm sorry, I'm sure you didn't want to hear all that." Dropping my gaze, I stare at his chest, unable to look at him any longer.

A slender hand reaches out and softly lifts my chin, and I only glance up because of how gentle he's been with me so far. His face has morphed into a neutral mask, but his eyes burn bright with rage. His steps don't falter as he leads me around the dance floor, aware of a heavy gaze as we're watched. "I suspected the *promessa* weren't treated right and have been petitioning the master to release them to their home factions. Yet he refuses every time."

I'm not surprised, the master wouldn't want to risk that the *promessa* might not come back. Not to mention it gives him power over the other factions—if they step out of line, all he needs to do is threaten their female. I am astonished, however, that his faction has been trying to free us, *all* of us. From what Elijah told me, I was under the impression that the factions willingly handed over the females. One female was a small sacrifice to stop a war. It seems all is not as stable in the fae lands as it first appeared.

"The others are treated better than I am," I admit, my voice quiet. "I refuse to submit to the master, and as such, I'm being punished." I'm not sure why I feel the need to explain this, but I hate seeing the pained look on his face, like he's let us down by not being able to convince the master.

He falls silent as he digests this information, and for the rest of the song, he doesn't say a thing. The song ends and he bows to me, raising my hand to his mouth as he kisses the back of it. My skin tingles from his touch, and my body warms. As he stands to his full height, he steps in close, placing his mouth next to my ear and tilting his head slightly. "I'll find a way to get you out of this, Annalise. I won't allow him to keep hurting you this way." He moves back, bows his head once again, and walks from the dance floor.

Whoa, he's intense. Yet I believe him. The next song starts, and I realise I'm still standing in the middle of the dance floor as other couples gather around me, so I quickly make my escape back to the shadows of the mezzanine. I don't know why I felt so comfortable around Able, despite having known him for the better part of twenty minutes. Maybe I'm just so damaged now that I take any sign of kindness as a mark of trustworthiness. No, somehow I don't think that's the case.

As the night wears on, I'm left alone to watch the comings and goings of the ball, and I'm grateful for it. I use the time to mull over everything that's happened. The later it gets, the more uncomfortable I feel, knowing I'm going to be taken back to the cells again. I hadn't realised how much I needed this small bit of freedom, although I'm sure that was part of the master's plan. He's showing me what he can offer me if I just do as he commands.

I've seen flashes of Elijah throughout the evening, but he's never come close enough for me to talk to, and it's making me feel sick. There's been the occasional tug in my chest, making me want to abandon everything and track him down, but we have appearances to keep up. Is he mad at me for my actions earlier when our bond was revealed? He told me not to allow the master to discover our bond, yet I hadn't been able to just stand by and watch him be tortured. My mate. I don't regret my actions, but I'm filled with fear at the repercussions.

"Annalise," a low, soothing voice calls, and my heart leaps. I know that voice.

Turning in a whirl of skirts, I see my mate leaning against a pillar, as if just thinking about him had been enough to summon him to my side. Closing the gap between us, I suddenly come to an abrupt stop as a thought strikes me. I have no idea how to greet him. My instincts are urging me to throw myself into his arms, to be as close to him as possible, but the bond is so new between us that I just feel a little awkward.

His dark eyes watch my every move like a predator stalking its prey. Anger practically ripples from him, and being this close, his power surrounds me.

"Elijah! Are you okay? I'm sorry I let—" My whispered apology is cut off by his growl.

"No. Stop." He pushes off of the column and gazes down at me, and I realise he's fighting his fae nature. There's always been a darkness within Elijah, but I've never feared him, and I don't plan on starting now. He continues to stare, unmoving. "None of that was your fault. It was going to happen sooner or later," he grumbles, his voice as low and animalistic as I've ever heard it.

I don't understand what's happening. Is he trying to resist the bond between us? It's been pulling at me all evening like two magnets, and the need to touch him is growing with each second. "I thought you were mad at me. I've hardly seen you." My admission is quiet but not tentative, like it might have once been. Giving in, I reach out, and our fingers brush. Despite the small touch, the feeling of electricity flashes up my arm until it fills my entire body. My skin warms and my power awakens, twinging with his. This is the first time we've touched since the bond emerged for both of us, and the feeling is like nothing I've ever experienced.

Elijah sighs, his pupils dilating as our joint powers flood our bodies, and the tension drains from his shoulders. Raising his free hand, he pushes back his hair, which has fallen across his face. He looks wrecked, whether from the strain of healing his earlier wounds or the stress of the evening, I don't know, but seeing him like this makes my chest ache.

Observing my concerned expression, he sighs again, caressing my cheek gently with his hand, his eyes tracking the movement. "I'm fine," he assures me. "After you were taken away, they took me back to my room to recover. The bastards left the cuffs on for a couple of hours to let me suffer, but they had to release me if they wanted me here for the ball." He rolls his eyes, speaking like all this was a minor inconvenience to him, and it makes me wonder how often this happens. "I'm weaker than usual thanks to those cuffs, but I'm mostly healed. My back just twinges occasionally." He waves this off as if it's no big deal. Like his back wasn't in tatters and he wasn't slumped against the guards, bleeding on the floor the last time I saw him.

There's a change in the bond between us as his eyes return to mine. "I wanted to come to you. I could feel you, your bond... When I walked in and saw you at his side like a prize..." He growls, and I quickly glance around to make sure no one's watching us. Thankfully, we're in a darkened part of the room, and no one appears to be paying us any attention.

Seeing me scanning the area, Elijah huffs out a breath. "The master's been watching me like a hawk, so I've had to behave," he explains, and although I thought that was probably the case, the tight band of uncertainty releases. To be so close to him all evening, to know he's part of my destiny, the other part of my soul, and to be kept apart is its own type of torture.

"I've been watching you though. Are you okay? I'm sorry for how things happened earlier, it wasn't fair to you."

From his words alone it might sound like he's apologising for what I had to witness. However, I know he's talking about the bond, about how it was ripped from me. Honestly, what I found difficult was leaving him behind while he was so badly injured. If it hadn't been for Tarren, I would have lost my mind with worry.

As I watch his face, I can tell he wants to ask about the bond and how I feel about it now that it's been forced from me. "I'm fine," I say, repeating his earlier words. I don't know what to say to him. Am I happy about our bond? In truth, I really don't know. It's so new, and while I can't deny that I'm pulled to him and he makes me feel safe, I don't really *know* him. In an ideal world, I would have had time to learn about him, to court him before the full force of the bond hit us. Our circumstances were anything but that.

"I didn't understand why I felt so strange, but one of the prisoners explained how bonds can form." I start to describe what happened after I was taken away, but he stills at my mention of Alric.

"The fae in the cell next to yours?" His eyes have turned flinty, his jaw tightening, and there is a strange feeling in my chest, yet it's not me who's feeling it. When I nod in response, that feeling only intensifies. "You need to be careful around him. There's something not right with that fae, I've just not gotten to the bottom of it yet."

Once again, I dip my head in agreement. What I don't tell him is that I'm careful around everyone and don't trust easily. He's right though, there's certainly something different about Alric, something I'm going to discover whether he likes it or not. An image of the unknown fae I met earlier with Alric's eyes flashes through my mind. Yes, I'm going to find out what's going on here.

There's a heavy pause. Elijah's gaze practically burns into me, and I can feel his power building around him, like he's getting ready to attack. A quick glance around tells me that no one has come any closer or discovered the two of us together, so I don't understand this change in him.

"I saw you dancing with the Prince of Doerallia." He looks away as he speaks, his tone scathing, but I don't miss the expression on his face—jealousy. So that's what's eating him up inside. He had to have known that someone would eventually speak to me, I couldn't avoid it forever. I get the impression that it's more than the fact I was dancing with the prince though.

"I should tell you to build the alliance, to do anything to keep the prince on the master's side. That's what I'm ordered to do, to encourage the *promessa* to... form alliances." The words are forced through clenched teeth, and his hands are balled into tight fists at his sides as he continues to look away. "But when I saw you dancing... seeing your face light up like that. You've never looked at me like that before." The anger and frustration seem to drain from him, his arms hanging loosely at his sides as he finally brings his gaze back to mine. What I see has my breath catching in my throat, my heart aching at his anguish.

"Elijah," I whisper. I wish I had some way to comfort him, but I don't know what to say. We've known each other for such a short time, and it's always been under difficult conditions. I'm a prisoner here. Had we met under different circumstances and our bond had been allowed to form naturally, things would be completely different. The prince offered me something no one else has in a long time—a chance to forget, to lose myself in dance, if only for a short time. That doesn't change how I feel about Elijah, but I'm not going to apologise for the small bit of joy I had this evening.

As if sensing my train of thought, Elijah nods slowly. "I will never be bright and noble like the prince. He's a kind male and will one day be king of his land. I am nothing, just the belonging of a tyrannical leader." He takes a step away and I feel the loss of his presence immediately, the incomplete bond tugging on my soul. "I'm not good for you. I have a darkness within me that I can't always control."

I feel him pulling away from me, burying his side of the bond as he tries to sever this link between us. We simultaneously gasp in pain, our connection not wanting to release us. Agony burns in his eyes, and I know he doesn't want to do this. He's only doing what he thinks is best for me, but I've had enough of letting others make decisions for me.

Closing the gap he created between us, I place my hand against his chest, gripping his tunic as I stare up at him. "You may hold darkness, but so do I. I have a past. I've done awful things."

This time, I don't let my voice break or quaver. Instead, I let the honesty of who I am shine through, both the good and the bad. "We've been bonded for a reason, Elijah, and I don't believe you're evil."

He's done some terrible things, that much I know, things I'm sure would horrify me. That doesn't make him evil though. He's just as much of a prisoner to the master as I am. I open my mouth to say so, but I don't get the chance because he leans forward and cradles me in his arms. Spinning me around, he presses my back against the pillar, and my gasp of surprise is muffled by his lips descending on mine. I may be startled, but my body needs no prompting. He kisses me like it's the only thing in the world that matters, our bodies pressed together as his lips glide over mine. Moaning at the fire he's lit inside me, I bite his lower lip. A growl rumbles from his chest, and I worry that he didn't like it, but if anything, it spurs him on even more. His hands are firmly planted on either side of me, never once taking advantage of the situation.

Me on the other hand, well, I can't seem to get enough of him. The noises of the ballroom fade away, and with my good arm, I grip the front of his tunic tighter, pulling him close. Kissing Elijah feels like breathing, like he is my oxygen and I need him to survive. I'm sure the bond is behind these new feelings of urgency, but now that his lips are against mine, I find I don't care. It soothes that place inside me that felt damaged from seeing him hurt so badly earlier. Power seems to build within me, causing me to feel energised.

With a groan, Elijah breaks away, his chest rising and falling rapidly as he starts to withdraw from our embrace. A quiet snarl rips from me, the ache in my chest guiding my actions as I reach out and try to pull him closer again, needing the contact. He steps out of my reach and holds up both hands, wearing a rueful smile as he chuckles. The sound makes my toes curl. He must see something on my face because he groans again. "Annalise, if we continue, I won't be able to stop."

Heat fills my body as desire floods my veins. "Then don't." I step closer. My sudden confidence should make me stop and think, but I'm being ruled by a different part of me. A part of me that has been asleep for a very long time.

Elijah makes a pained noise and tips his head back as he stares at the ceiling. I'm sure I hear him praying for strength before he looks at me again. "I shouldn't have done that," he murmurs, holding up his hand again as he speaks. "No, I'm sorry. I put you at risk by kissing you here. I've been shielding us with my power as best as I can, but it's only an illusion. If someone comes looking for you, they will see through it. If the master had seen us..." Trailing off, he shakes his head, his expression turning dark.

The mention of the master and the consequences of being caught conjures an image of Elijah being whipped, and my vision turns red. Faster than a viper, I leap forward and grab his arm, pulling him towards me. A quiet snarl rips from me once again, and later, a part of me will wonder at my sudden aggressive, possessive behaviour, which is so at odds to my usual personality. "Then I will kill him." My voice no longer sounds like my own as I press against him. "You are *mine*." I ensure our eyes are locked as I speak, so he knows I'm being serious.

"Annalise." His tone is surprisingly tender as he stares down at me with a sad smile, brushing my cheek with the back of his hand. "This is just the bond talking. You're straining because it's driving you to complete it, yet we cannot. I've just made it worse for you because I kissed you. The effects will wear off in an hour or so with our distance." Seeing my sudden panic, he shakes his head, realising I've not understood what he's saying. "Not our connection, that will always be there whether the bond is completed or not."

Feeling like I can breathe again, I let out a long sigh, trying to keep all my turbulent emotions under control. We're surrounded by enemies on all sides, and we're lucky no one has seen us yet, but I can't seem to let him go.

Humming to himself, he seems to search for the words. He strokes my arm absentmindedly as he thinks. "Because your side of the bond is so fresh, it set off all of your fae instincts. Instincts you're having to go against due to the master's order. It's why you're feeling particularly... protective of me right now." He smiles, and the connection in my chest seems to swell. Scanning my face, he starts to lose his smile. "While I would usually revel in this behaviour, it's not safe here."

He suddenly stiffens, his eyes darting over my shoulder, and in a blink, he's five feet away from me. I didn't even see him move, but I can feel his power in the air. I spin at the sound of someone behind me, manoeuvring myself into a better position, and I drop into a defensive stance. I don't know how to fight, and I'm certainly going to struggle in this dress with one arm in a sling, yet my instincts seem to be ruling me tonight.

"It's okay, it's just Tarren," Elijah informs me, yet I don't move. "She won't say anything," he reassures me, but I feel his power pressing down, which makes me wonder how willing she is to help us. I knew she was assisting Elijah, but is it all under duress?

"Don't use that on me," she snarls at Elijah. "I won't say anything," she confirms, and the threatening wave of power disappears. She glares at the fae before turning her attention to me, her eyes softening. "I have to take you back now," she murmurs, but I see her taking everything in, including my defensive stance and how I've stepped in front of Elijah as if to protect him. Thankfully, she doesn't say anything, just waits for me to follow her.

Peering back at Elijah, I see he's schooled his features into a neutral expression. Inclining his head, he silently tells me to leave, that he'll be okay. I'm not sure how I know these things, I just know them to be true. With one last look, I face Tarren and let her lead me from the ballroom. Many of the guests watch me, and I feel the weight of their stares, but I don't look back, because I know if I see Elijah watching me, I'll never leave.

Chapter 14

The gruel that is my breakfast tastes blander and more unappealing than usual compared to the delights of last night. My tastebuds still remember the rich flavours of the delicate morsels of food placed on the tables around the ballroom. One of the benefits of staying away from the crowd and watching from afar was that I was able to sample at least one of everything. I've never understood why the food at those events is always served in such miniscule portions, but it benefited me last night.

My eyes keep drifting shut, exhaustion weighing heavily on me, and after the third time of almost falling asleep in my gruel, I put the bowl down with a sigh.

"Something wrong with your breakfast?" Alric asks lightly from the other side of the metal bars.

Turning my head, I pin him with my gaze, running my eyes over his dishevelled state. Alric had been fast asleep in his cell when I returned last night, and even when I whisper-shouted his name, he didn't wake. I'm still suspicious after I met the stranger at the ball, and looking at my fellow prisoner now, I see no resemblance other than his startling blue eyes. I wouldn't have even put it together if it wasn't for the comment the fae had made before he disappeared. *I'll see you later, Annalise.* The words whisper through my mind, and I continue to stare, trying to fit that voice with the decrepit male in front of me.

"How was the ball?" He tilts his head to one side, continuing on despite the fact I've not answered his first question. "Meet anyone interesting?" Although he asks the question lightly, his eyes sparkle with mischief. He knows something. Either he was involved, which seems unlikely as he was here when I was brought back, or he knew the fae stranger would be coming, which means he has some way of communicating outside of the castle.

Hope blooms inside me. If he can get messages out, perhaps he would help me send one. *What would be the point?* my pessimistic thoughts point out. *You have no one to send it to, no one that would care you've been taken.*

"I met the Prince of Doerallia." Mimicking his light tone, I run my fingers through my hair. Although I removed all the pins and the diadem last night when I was taken to undress, my hair is currently a mass of knots. "He's a very talented dancer," I continue, deliberately stretching this out. I *know* he's involved in this somehow, and he's trying to determine if I've worked it out.

"I also met a strange fae." I stare ahead as I comb through my hair, but from the corner of my eye, I see him stiffen.

"Oh?" He tries to sound politely indifferent, but I hear his heart speed up.

"It was odd, because although I'd never met him, he knew my name and I had the feeling I knew him." I drop my hand to my lap and look over my shoulder at the fae who's now kneeling by the bars. Pinning him with my knowing gaze, I arch an eyebrow. "How could that be?"

A slow smile crosses his lips. "Not everything is as it seems, Annalise," he replies, repeating his words from the other day. A tingle goes down my spine. Something's going to happen soon, the certainty sings in my blood, and somehow, Alric is involved and he is warning me.

Surging forward, I kneel opposite him, needing to know what's going on. "What—"

"Quiet!" The shout is loud enough to make me flinch as the guard strides down the corridor between the two rows of cells. "I don't want to hear your jabbering. Eat your breakfast and shut your mouths," he addresses everyone, glaring into the cells, but I know it's aimed at us when he stops outside our cells. Looking down his panther-like snout, his eyes briefly flick over me. "Your guard will be here for you soon." Turning with more grace than I would have thought possible for a creature so large, he pads back to the guardroom.

It didn't take long for the master to replace the guards down here after Elijah's loss of control. Although they are rough, they have been comparatively gentle with me, and not one of them has looked at me inappropriately, thank the Mother. I sometimes see a nervous glint in their eyes when they come to my cell, and I'm not sure if that's Elijah's doing or if they have been threatened by the master. He almost lost his prized foreign *promessa*, he's not going to risk that happening again.

Returning to my cot, I pick up the bowl of cold gruel, ignoring Alric and the rest of the inmates as I disappear into the recesses of my mind. I'd been so exhausted when I returned from the ball that after I tried to wake Alric, I just curled up on my cot and fell asleep. My dreams had been full of dancing and light, although I'd been aware of a dark pair of eyes following me as I whirled across the dance floor.

The ball had... not been what I was expecting. Although every eye had been on me when I arrived and I heard the whispers whenever I was in view, most of the guests seemed too afraid to speak to me. This suited me, as it allowed me to sink into the shadows and watch. I expected the master to parade me around and force me to spend time with him, and other than right at the beginning when I was displayed like a new toy, he'd let me have some free rein. Part of me is sure he only put me on a pedestal to remind Elijah whom I belonged to, whom we both belonged to. One of the biggest surprises from the previous evening had been the prince. Even as I think about him now, my heart flutters in my chest, but I ignore it. I already have a mate, the last thing I need is to have feelings for someone else.

My thoughts continue to replay what happened last night, analysing every encounter. I'm once again aware of Alric's eyes on me, but he doesn't speak or try to get my attention, aware of the guards who seem to be watching us closely. My breakfast has gone so cold I can barely swallow it, so I abandon the rest as I wait for Tarren. Thankfully I don't have to wait long, and as the door that leads to the main castle swings open, I smile slightly at the female apanthe as she strides in. Her eyes immediately go straight to me, checking that I'm okay as she walks past to greet the dungeon guards. They speak in low voices using their native language, and despite not understanding their words, I notice how the head guard seems to defer to her, nodding his head in respect before leading her to my cell.

Standing, I brush my hands down my simple dress as I wait for them to open the door. When I step over the threshold, I feel my power return, and I am briefly surprised at the surge that floods my body. Other than when I've been with Elijah and our energies have linked, I've not felt this strong in decades. Even before I was taken by the elf queen, I was never the most gifted, but thanks to the spell on me during my captivity, I could barely touch my power. Over the years, it faded until it was only an ember within me.

I revel in the return of my power as it energises me and lifts my spirits. I feel good, better than I've felt in a long time, strong. I glance at Tarren to see if she can feel it too, but I'm met with her usual blank expression, and the head guard behind her looks the same. Something has lit up within me, reigniting my power, and it feels so monumental that I almost expected someone else to notice. Movement in the cell next to me catches my eye, and I see Alric watching me with upturned lips and a knowing mien. Somehow, he felt it, or he's very good at reading me and knows something's changed.

Tarren starts to lead me from the dungeon, so I pull my gaze from the mysterious fae, following my guard into the main castle in silence. We walk through the back corridors side by side, her body relaxed but her eyes alert, and I can't help but recall her encounter with the guards in the dungeon. The previous guards didn't show anyone respect, so I was taken by surprise at the deference they showed her.

Clearing my throat, I decide to start a conversation. "Do you know those guards?"

Turning her attention to me, she seems wary about answering. "Some."

Tarren's never been one to initiate a discussion with me, only speaking when required, so this short answer doesn't surprise me. When we have spoken, her grasp of the common language seems good, but her replies are minimal and to the point. I'm certainly not one for pointless conversation, preferring to stay quiet and observe. However, I'm determined to get more of a response from her. I have no female friends here—the other *promessa* don't count—so my guard is the closest I've got.

"They seemed very respectful," I remark, trying again.

Tarren huffs, her shoulders shaking, and it takes me a few moments to realise she's laughing. "They are afraid of Tarren." She rolls her eyes at the statement, but a slight swagger has appeared in her step, so I get the feeling this is something she's proud of. "Female apanthe very protective of those they bond with. Is why we guard the *promessa*." Her words are thick with her accent and slightly broken, but I can understand everything she's saying. "I'm best in my class," she tells me proudly with a grin, which is slightly terrifying given the amount of fang she flashes.

Nodding, I recollect what happened before when I witnessed how protective female apanthe can get, their bodies swelling and growing until they are even larger than the huge males of their kind. The idea that she's bonded with me surprises me though. I assume it's different than the type of bond Elijah and I share, and perhaps the word is just a mistranslation, but I can't deny that my heart warms a little at the prospect of having her as my protector.

We continue the rest of the journey in silence until

we reach my room. Opening the door, she waves her hand to indicate I should step inside.

"Time for torture," she grumbles as I enter the room.

Heart pounding, I spin around, my eyes wide. Betrayal flares within me. I thought we were becoming close, yet she calmly walked me here without so much as a warning. Opening my mouth to demand answers, I finally take in her smug expression and the teasing glint in her eyes.

"You must dress up for the master. Torture, yes?" The light lilt in her voice confirms it.

She's joking with me. My serious guard pulled a prank on me. With a startled laugh, I shake my head in disbelief. "Yes. Torture," I agree with raised eyebrows, but I can't seem to wipe the smile from my face. "You almost caused my heart to stop beating!" I accuse, but she just does that huffing laugh again.

"I will be here when you are ready," she replies, turning her back to the door as she scans the empty corridor, but I don't miss her grin.

Closing the door, I snort in disbelief at the strange encounter. Perhaps we could be friends after all?

Hearing the chatter of the maids, I hold back a sigh and turn around, making my way farther into the room so they can get me ready. *Torture indeed*, I think, smiling, but it drops when I see the pile of dresses awaiting me and the eager eyes that lock on my form. Letting out a slow breath, I wait for the maids to descend.

Now dressed in a dusky pink day dress, I follow Tarren to the day room with a rustle of fabric. Healer Bodil met me in my room and checked my remaining injuries, and thankfully, she removed the cast from my arm. I flex it as we walk, needing something to focus on. Gone is the joking guard from earlier, and in her place is her usual, stoic, sneering self. I still don't know where she's taking me or what I'm dressed up for, but when I tried to ask her, she just ignored me, so we travel in silence.

Reaching the open doors to the day room, Tarren gives the two male guards a hard look before gesturing for me to enter. "I will be here." Her voice is gruff, but I take reassurance from her statement. Giving her the smallest smile, I take a steadying breath and enter the room.

Female giggling reaches me first, and I glance around to see who's here. Relief floods me when I notice the master isn't present, but I know I can't get too comfortable as he could walk in at any moment. Seeing that Elijah isn't here causes a range of emotions. I hoped to see him, our bond tugging at my chest, but at the same time, the thought of him in here with all these females makes me want to hiss and snarl as jealousy rears its ugly face. It's a strange feeling for me. I've not really experienced jealousy before our bond made itself known, and certainly not at this level with the overwhelming need to claim him as *mine*.

Mia, the fawn fae, notices my entrance first. Standing, she walks towards me with a kind smile. The others have all stood to greet me too, all except for Elia, the feline fae, and the fae who reminds me of a bird, her wings tucked in close to her back.

"Welcome," Mia greets, her pretty, delicate features open and warm. "You're Annalise, correct? Will you join us for tea?"

I'm surprised at how friendly she's being, but I detect

no falseness about her, so I nod hesitantly. Her smile widens, and her eyes sparkle as she leads me over to a semi-circle of plush armchairs. The other females take their seats, watching me with a mixture of curiosity and wariness. Elia and the bird-like fae are perched on another set of armchairs and studiously ignoring me, which suits me just fine.

Mia clears her throat, pulling my attention from Elia to her. "We haven't had a chance to introduce ourselves due to your... difficult circumstances." She almost stumbles over the last word, and I find the corners of my lips twitching up into a half-smile. Difficult circumstances... that's certainly one way of putting it.

Snorting, the hare fae raises her eyebrows, her long ears twitching as she leans back in her chair. "She's too nice to say it, but you've been locked away." Her words are blunt and cause me to reassess her, her amber eyes watching me closely. She's curious about me, but she doesn't trust easily, that much I can tell from her closed off body language.

"Gail." The fawn blushes, laughing slightly to hide her embarrassment over her friend's words. "Anyway, my name is Mia, and I'm from Doerallia."

My interest piques at the mention of Doerallia, and Mia must have noticed because she smiles and leans forward. "Do you know much about our lands?"

"No, everything is different here," I reply honestly, glancing between them. "Back in Morrowmer, I'm classed as a high elf. We have no fae that look like you." I trip over the words and come to a stop, realising I may be coming across as rude. Wincing, I go to apologise when the female with tentacles on her face catches my eye.

"I can't imagine how hard that must have been,

leaving your home to come here." She shakes her head, the tentacles moving independently of each other.

Gail, the hare, arches an eyebrow while still watching me carefully. "I doubt she was given much of a choice."

Gail perceives a lot. She's fast to talk and give her opinion, but she doesn't mince her words. I like that about her.

Mia looks flustered at the change in topic. Sitting forward, she begins to move things around on the low table between us, and I see she's making me tea. I start to say I can make my own, but she waves me off with a smile. "Our land is split into seven territories. Doerallia is my homeland. We are ruled by a king, and most of the fae there look like me." She gestures to her small horns poking through her pale blonde hair. "The males have antlers. We have very good hearing and are great foragers and plant growers."

I remember the prince from last night and can't help wondering if all the males from his land have antlers as large as his. The fae I saw with Mia shared the same features—almond-shaped eyes, blond hair, and tawny skin—other than Prince Abel, who was pale skinned and had light brown hair, making him stand out among them.

Oblivious to my internal musings, Mia continues, gesturing to Gail at her side. "Gail is from Forlin, which is the land neighbouring mine. They also have a king, and as I'm sure you've seen, share features with the hare. They are fantastic runners and very strong, so they work on building and infrastructure projects," she explains, and I see Gail nodding at her side. "The two territories on the east coast are Vipos, Marella's home, and Sidra, Rayala's home." She gestures to the two females respectively.

The scaled female, Marella, inclines her head. "It's

said that my people came from sirens and mermaids, which is why we look this way." She gestures to herself, and I have to suppress a shudder at her hissing whisper-like voice.

I can imagine her dragging helpless sailors to their deaths, drawn by her beauty. She truly is beautiful, in a cruel, wicked way. Her almost entirely black eyes watch my every move as I examine her, her bluish scales glistening in the sunlight that shines through the window.

"Unlike the last two lands, we're ruled by a lord, not a king," she adds, her eyes dropping to the floor momentarily as she remembers her homeland. "I prefer the sea, being far away is hard."

Rayala leans over and places her palm on the female's hand. They share a look of pain and understanding before turning back to me. "In Sidra, most of our land is empty, as we build our homes in the cliffs. We're ruled by a queen. I also miss the sea dearly."

I'm surprised at how beautiful and clear Rayala's voice is. I thought the tentacle-like protrusions that cover the lower half of her face would make it difficult to understand her, but I couldn't have been more wrong. The way she describes her home reminds me of the sea elves in Morrowmer, their homes beautifully carved into the white cliffs.

"Ave over there comes from Arilla. Her people all have wings and worship the birds. They live in houses built in the trees with bridges connecting them," Mia whispers as she passes me a cup of steaming tea. "As I'm sure you've already realised, Elia is from this territory, Arpathe. They are the biggest territory and take up most of the south. They share feline features and are ruled by the master."

I don't miss the tight looks the four females share when Elia is brought up in conversation. Perhaps it's just the mention of the master, but I still get the impression they don't like the feline *promessa*. From what little I know of her, I would agree with them.

There's a beat of silence as the females sip their tea and make themselves comfortable in the armchairs. This suits me as I get the chance to digest all the information I've just learned, drawing a map in my head of the different lands. Something is bothering me though.

"You said seven territories. You've only mentioned six."

All sound in the room seems to vanish, and Elia and Ave stop their conversation to glance over. Even the fire, which has been burning away in the fireplace, seems to quieten. Six sets of eyes all turn to me, the atmosphere in the room suddenly tense, and I wonder if I've made some sort of faux pas by bringing it up.

"Mamos," Rayala supplies, her sorrow palpable.

The name rings a bell, and I realise Elijah mentioned them before. The master started a war with them over the *promessa*. Did Rayala know someone from that faction?

"They lived on an island to the east. They refused to part with their *promessa*," Gail tells me, her eyebrows furrowed as she speaks. "They were destroyed. No one lives there now, it's just an island of ruins."

The matter-of-fact way she speaks tells me they are not going to say anything else. This is clearly an uncomfortable topic for them, so I'm not going to push the issue, yet I want to know more about Mamos, about the people who lived there and defied the master.

Taking a sip of my tea, I wince slightly. I never enjoyed the drink back in Morrowmer, and my trip across the mountains hasn't changed that. I still have no idea what we're doing here other than sharing small talk, and don't understand why my presence is mandatory.

"What did you think of the ball last night?" Mia inquires, breaking the silence. Her smile is bright enough to light up the room as she waits for my response. The others all watch, as if they genuinely want to know the answer.

Placing my teacup on the table, I think about how to word my response. So much happened, and the whole event was overwhelming, but I know that's not what they want to hear. "It was not what I was expecting."

They all share knowing smiles and glance at me like I'm being coy. Raising my eyebrows, I wait for them to explain their looks.

"We saw you dancing with the Doerallian prince," Marella remarks, her needle-sharp teeth glinting as she smiles wide.

Ah. So that's what they are waiting for, they want gossip. Do they think the prince and I have started a relationship? I don't understand. I thought we were the master's property now, and as much as that makes my anger boil in my gut, I would have assumed that meant we're not allowed to be with another male. I don't bother to tell them I have a true mate, keeping that information to myself.

"You looked so good with Able. You were like a princess as you danced together. You made such a natural couple!" Mia cools herself with her fan as she leans back in her chair, and the others giggle at her antics. For some reason, the fact that she's on a first name basis with the prince causes a flash of irritation to surge through me. She seemed to know him quite well last night as the two of them spoke together, but they are from the same land, so I shouldn't read anything into it. I also don't know why this bothers me so much.

"Perhaps if you're lucky, the master will sell you to him once the true *promessa* is found," Elia chimes in. The others give her sharp looks and she squawks, throwing her hands up in the air as if she doesn't know what she's done to deserve their ire. "What? She's not even from this land, so there's no chance she'll be the true *promessa*." Her eyes run over me, her disgust clear on her face before she turns back to her companion, pretending they are not listening to our conversation.

She's just trying to get under my skin, I know that, but her barbs hit their mark. Perhaps not in the way she thought though. She wants to be picked by the master, and for some reason she believes I want the same. I couldn't care less about being the *promessa* he chooses, but one word struck me more than the others.

Turning my accusing gaze on the females I'm sitting with, I try to keep my panic at bay. "What did she mean by that? That the master might sell me to the prince?"

Mia and Rayala flinch at my harsh tone, while Gail and Marella share a look, but none of them answer me. I wait a few seconds, my gaze boring into them. Still no answer. *Fine, I'll find my answers somewhere else.* I push up from the armchair, and the females stare up at me in surprise. Gathering my skirts in my hands, I give the *promessa* one last look and turn away, heading to the door.

"Wait, where are you going?" Gail calls, her annoyance clear, but as I twist back to face them, I see terror in her eyes. They fear the repercussions of my actions.

Not allowing that to weaken my resolve, I hold my ground. They have been friendly today, but they never once tried to help me while I've been beaten and held captive in the dungeon. They just continued to live their picturesque lives in their gilded prisons, preferring to turn a blind eye to the atrocities that happen here. "You have important information that will directly affect me, yet you refuse to tell me, so I'm going elsewhere." Raising my eyebrows, I make it clear that I don't think their behaviour is acceptable.

"Wait." Mia stands with a rustle of fabric, her expression apologetic. "Sit, please. We'll explain." Gesturing to the armchair I vacated, she gives me the smallest smile, which cracks my determination. Sighing, I return to the chair and perch on the edge, making it clear I'll just leave again if they don't give me the answers I need.

Mia's smile widens and she sits, glancing at her three companions who all wear uncomfortable expressions. Taking a moment to think, she hums to herself, and her smile drops slightly. "As you know, we all have to attend these sessions which are designed to determine which of us is the true *promessa*. They are also preparing us for after."

I blink. *After?* After what? The way she says it makes goosebumps appear on my arms. The idea that I'm being 'prepared' for anything without my knowledge is disconcerting. I want to ask more questions and demand she explains, but I see she isn't done yet.

"Although we've all been chosen, only one of us can be the 'one.'" She smiles at me, as if this is something we should be happy about. "That's partially what all of the balls are for. It gives nobles from other territories an opportunity to see us and place bids on us."

Horrified, I lean back, staring at them in disbelief. "You mean he truly means to sell us? Like we're property?" My anger builds and twists in my gut like a living creature. "And you're happy with this?" I demand, not believing that these females are pleased to be bid on and sold like they are livestock. I assumed that whoever wasn't chosen would be able to go back to their homes, but that apparently isn't the case.

They all appear uncomfortable at my questions, glancing anxiously towards the door as I raise my voice. Even Elia and Ave have stopped their conversation and are watching me.

"The master may offer some of you a place to stay if you please him enough," Elia purrs, but I see through her act. This bothers her too.

I'm about to retort that I would rather die, but a scaled hand lands on my arm.

"Please, if you cause a fuss, the guards will come in, and that will be bad news for all of us," Marella hisses, her unusual eyes flaring as she glances from the open door back to me.

They are right. Biting back my anger, I take a deep breath and glance down at my lap as I try to calm myself. They are victims just as I am. The only real difference between us is that they have accepted their fate. They obviously fear the guards despite how unconcerned they act in this room, but I seem to have stirred everything up. If I get punished for my actions or words, so be it. I won't bend or give myself over to the master. However, I don't want to make things worse for the other *promessa*, no matter how much I disagree with them.

Letting out a weary sigh, I look up at the others and settle back in my chair. "How do they know we're promised?" I ask, moving on.

This is something I've wondered since I was first

captured, and as I glance at the others, I notice that none of us share any physical traits, so it can't be based on our appearance. Only, that doesn't fit quite right, as I remember the look Elijah gave me the first time we met when I turned around and he saw me properly. His eyes had seemed to be drawn to something on my forehead, but I've since looked in mirrors several times, and I've seen nothing different. Only smooth, unblemished pale skin.

The *promessa* seem to relax now that I'm not threatening to march from the room, and Mia leans forward once more. "It's due to our circumstances. We all risked our lives for someone else and the gods blessed us. Those with higher power are able to see a mark that appears on our foreheads, but it doesn't last for long." She smiles widely, her eyes glistening. "You were very lucky Elijah was there to find you when your mark appeared."

My mind reels at this overload of information. I was simply in the wrong place at the wrong time. If I hadn't risked my life to save that human and left when I first heard the screaming, I might never have been 'blessed,' and they might never have found me. Yet I can't find it in myself to regret saving that man's life—or trying, at least. I've become many things over the years, but I couldn't turn a blind eye when someone needed my help.

Who are these gods she speaks of? In Morrowmer, we serve the Great Mother, our goddess, the one who offered me the choice to return when I was dying. *I cannot enter the realm your body has been taken to.* The words whisper through my mind as I remember our conversation. For some reason, my goddess cannot enter this realm. Is that because of these other gods Mia speaks of?

A familiar tug on my bond distracts me from asking

Mia any more questions, and I'm already turning in my seat as Elijah strides into the room. "Morning, *promessa*." His teasing gaze moves around the space, winking at the females until they are all giggling and swooning like adolescents. Rolling my eyes, I attempt to push down my annoyance at his flirting. *It's just a mask*, I tell myself. *Just a really good one.* As if sensing my irritation, he finally glances at me, humour glinting in his eyes.

"Let's begin."

At his words, the females jump up and form a line facing him, leaving me frowning and confused. Just what sort of 'sessions' are these?

Chapter 15

"You too, Annalise." Elijah gestures for me to join the line with the other *promessa* when I don't follow the others.

I slowly make my way over, standing next to a smiling Mia as I face my mate. Not that anyone would know, what with his flirting with the others and all. We wait in silence, the other *promessa* standing tall with their hands clasped behind their backs. Even Elijah seems to be waiting for someone, glancing back towards the doorway. Following his gaze, I see a slender female entering the room with an elegant walking cane in one hand. Oddly enough, her gait is smooth and graceful. In fact, she doesn't seem to put any weight on her cane, so I assume it's just for aesthetic purposes. She shares the same cat-like features as Elia, and as I glance down the line at the *promessa*, I see her smiling at the newcomer.

Her face is pinched, like she just stepped in something unpleasant, and her ears twitch upon her greying hair as she studies us. The nervous energy filling the room concerns me, especially when Elijah drops into a deep bow. Just who is this female? As if hearing my comment, her head snaps to me, her whiskers twitching as her eyes narrow.

"Is this the new one from across the mountains?" Disgust coats her every word as she walks towards me, looking me up and down. When she finally reaches my face, it's obvious she finds me somewhat lacking.

"Yes, madame, this is Annalise," he supplies, walking at the female's side until they stop just before me.

"I do not care what her name is," the woman barks. "Bring her up to speed. I don't have time to waste on beginners."

"Yes, madame." Dipping his head, he turns back to me and guides me away from the others. The look he flashes me tells me to keep my mouth shut, so I bide my time and follow until we're far enough away.

Now out of earshot, he spins so his back is to everyone else, his eyes only for me. "Are you okay after last night?"

He'd been there most of the evening, and he was the last one to see me before I was led away by Tarren, so what could have happened between then and now? His eyes flick to my lips as he waits for my response, and I realise he's worried about the kiss we shared, believing he may have upset me.

"I'm fine," I assure him. The low murmurs of the *promessa* reach me, and I know I can't risk saying what I want to out loud, so instead I reach for our connection. Closing my eyes briefly, I think about how I felt when he had me pressed against the pillar and the sensations that flooded my body when his lips moved against mine. His grunt of surprise indicates it worked, and I struggle to keep the smile off my lips as I open my eyes. His expression makes my lips fall, however, as his pupils have narrowed to pinpricks and a look of hunger is etched across his features. A cheeky grin appears slowly on his face, and I see his hands clench and unclench a few times as he fights the urge to leap forward and pull me against his chest. Taking a deep inhale, he closes his eyes as he attempts to control himself. I know this is exactly what he should be doing, we don't want anyone else to know about our connection, yet I can't help but be disappointed. Against his chest is *exactly* where I want to be.

"Not helping," he mutters under his breath, his lips twitching.

An uneasy thought hits me. "Can you read my mind?"

Blowing out a long, steadying breath, he opens his eyes and meets my gaze. His pupils have returned to normal now, and he seems to be in control of himself. Shaking his head, he glances around to ensure no one is within hearing range. "No. Even when the bond is complete, that won't be possible, but you're practically shouting your thoughts at me right now."

"Oh." Taken aback, I pull away from the bond, focusing on building a wall in my mind. The last thing I want to do is send all of my thoughts to Elijah. We may be mates, and I know he won't hurt me, but he still works for my enemy. I can feel him observing me closely, as if he can feel me pulling away from the bond. Needing to change the subject, I glance over his shoulder to the *promessa*. "What's happening here anyway? Who is she?"

Turning so he can see where I'm looking, he gives me a knowing smile. "That is Madame Klawr."

His smile tells me more than his words do, and from my earlier interaction with her, I'm guessing she's not going to be my favourite person. I give him a look as I process what he said. Madame Claw, seriously? He pronounces it with a harder 'K' sound at the beginning and extends the letters at the end of her name, yet it still just sounds like claw to me... for a fae that shares the features of a cat.

"I know." He tries to hold back his amusement at my incredulous expression. "Most address her by her title." Waving it off, he shifts his weight from foot to foot, his mood changing abruptly. "Do you know why you're here?"

His quick switch from joking to serious puts me on alert, reminding me where I am and that I can't let my guard down. The urge to reach out to him for comfort fills me, and I have to wrap my arms around myself to stop the foolish action. I know he sees all of this, and I can feel his end of the bond reaching out to me, but I ignore it and nod.

"Promised one classes and making myself ready to be sold by the master once the real *promessa* makes herself known."

"I won't let that happen, Annalise." The anger and urgency in his voice takes me by surprise.

Jerking my gaze from the *promessa*, I look into the rich brown depths of his eyes. "Can you do anything to stop it?" My fear breaks through, making my voice waver. I hate looking weak in front of him, so I clear my throat and focus on my anger instead. "I thought you couldn't disobey the master."

It's not fair to take this out on him, but I feel trapped, cornered like a wild beast, and it's only a matter of time before I snap. My thoughts are a constant whirling vortex of confusion when I should be concentrating on getting out of this alive. I'm experiencing emotions I've never felt before, and I feel like I'm being pulled in different directions.

A wave of different emotions fills me, and it takes me a few seconds to realise they are not my own—concern, fear, and desperation, but most of all, there's an overwhelming need to protect. In another world, I can imagine how this scene would play out. He would take me into his arms and whisper comforting words as he presses his cheek against the top of my head, stroking my back in a soothing motion. Only, we're not in another world, and all he can offer me is a hand on my shoulder.

"For you, Annalise, I would find a way."

His earnest words move something within me. I truly believe what he says, and while I should find it comforting, it worries me. Breaking the master's rules will not be tolerated, and for someone in a position of power like Elijah, the master would want to make an example of him.

A sharp bark from the madame has us both moving. Despite it not being aimed at us, it's another reminder that we're not alone. Clearing his throat, Elijah straightens and clasps his hands behind his back. "Anyway, you weren't far off on the barb about promised one classes."

It takes me a few seconds to catch up, and I realise he's commenting on what I said earlier.

Elijah gestures towards the other females. "At the moment, you all have the potential to be the true *promessa*. These sessions are about trying to unlock the abilities of the promised one."

This makes sense. I wondered how the master was going to pick his true *promessa*. If it were down to choice,

I'm sure he'd choose Elia. She's from this land, so it would strengthen his hold and power base, not to mention she's obviously aiming for the position. From her disgusting display last night, I'd say they were a good match.

Nodding my understanding, I think over what he just told me. "Abilities, what abilities?"

He tries to speak but makes a noise of frustration as no words leave his mouth, obviously bound by the master's orders. Sighing, I turn my focus back to the females. The *promessa* have all been split into pairs. Holding hands, they face each other with their eyes closed. Some of them are frowning in concentration, but others look serene. Other than that, they don't appear to be doing much. The madame walks up and down the line, observing them with a shrewd glare.

"What are they doing?" My voice is hushed, as if I may disturb them.

Elijah is quiet for a few seconds. "Can you feel it?" he asks finally, his tone casual. There's something off about him, and as I look up, his expression is odd, like he's trying not to give away his thoughts.

"Feel what?" I ask, opening my senses to try and feel what he's talking about. I don't notice anything, and I'm about to ask if he's feeling okay when I feel a strange buzzing sensation. I wouldn't have noticed it if I wasn't paying attention. It's not the same as when Elijah or the master use their powers, but more like short bursts of electrical activity fizzing through the air. "Wait, what is that?" I murmur more to myself than anything as I continue to 'listen' to the unusual energy moving through the air. Elijah lets out a strange noise, but I've already closed my eyes, trying to work out where the sensation is coming from. Whatever the source of energy, it's originating from this room. My eyes fly open as comprehension hits me. "It's the *promessa!*"

I spin to face Elijah, but he just nods, his expression thoughtful as he watches me closely. He's staring at me like he's never seen me before, and although he's trying to hide it, I can feel his awe and dread through our connection.

My excitement quickly fizzles out and is replaced by uncertainty. "Should I not be able to feel it?"

"Only a very powerful fae can detect the passing of energy."

Elijah was surprised when he first realised I was able to feel people drawing and using energy, so I don't understand why me feeling the *promessa* using their powers is any different. There's more to this than what he's telling me. His comment about powerful fae makes me purse my lips. "But I'm not powerful, and what do you mean by the passing of energy?"

"I believe you are much stronger than you think, Annalise, and what you believe you lack in power, you more than make up for in every other way. Never let anyone tell you otherwise." Although he's speaking in a low voice so as not to be overheard, there's fire in his tone. I've never had anyone talk to me like this before, and I'm unsure how to react, my cheeks flushing.

Most of my life I've been told I'm good for nothing but serving others, having my choices and options taken from me and my power suppressed until there was next to nothing left. Compared to many high elves in Morrowmer, I have very little power, as I never had the chance to nurture and develop it like most.

Sensing my discomfort, Elijah clears his throat. "The *promessa* and a few of the strongest fae can transfer some of their power to another. That's what they are practicing," he explains, changing the subject.

I try to sense their power again. It's easier now that I know what I'm looking for, but after a few seconds, I frown and glance at Elijah. "They don't feel very strong..."

Without pulling his gaze from the *promessa*, he nods in agreement. "They are not. Most of the fae in this land don't have very strong powers or the ability to use it. The lords, kings, masters, and their offspring have more, hence why they are in positions of power, but for most, their animalistic traits are stronger. That these females can even share what little they have just proves that they are *promessa*."

I'm silent as I digest what I've learned. It's another sign that they are promised. That should mean that this is something I'm able to do as well. I think back to all those times when I was with Elijah and had been filled with power, but somehow, I get the feeling that has to do with our bond rather than this particular gift of sharing energy. At some point, I'll ask him, but it doesn't feel appropriate here.

I still don't know why we're so important, and I know there's more that's being kept from me. While watching the *promessa* practicing, I can't help but wonder what the point of all of this is. Why would the true *promessa* need to share energy? A thought strikes me. "This is what the master wants us for? To transfer our power to him?"

Elijah opens his mouth to comment, his expression grim, when a shout comes from the other side of the room, followed by the banging of a cane on the marble floor.

"You, from across the mountains, come here," the

madame demands, her tone not allowing for any arguments.

Elijah makes a quiet noise of frustration in the back of his throat but gestures for me to do as she orders. I'm glad to see he dislikes her as much as I do, despite the smirk plastered on his face. Walking over with him at my side, I come to a stop a few paces from the other females.

The madame looks me up and down, tutting. Her whiskers twitch with disapproval. "Elijah told you why you're here?"

I fear that if I open my mouth, I'll say something I'll live to regret. There's something about this fae that puts me on edge, not to mention the behaviour of the other females around her. I don't bother to answer her aloud, simply nodding my head. "Good, partner up with Elia. She is the only one who pays attention to instructions around here." The other *promessa* seem to flinch at her scathing words but continue with their practice. Ave steps back to allow me to take up position across from the feline fae, but I continue to stand by Elijah's side.

Elia is practically preening at the praise, but that look soon evaporates when the madame appears at her side, slapping Elia's calves sharply with her cane. My mouth drops open in surprise, and as I spin to Elijah, he just shakes his head slightly, and I know what he's saying. *Not here, not now.*

"Stand up straight, Elia. Slouching is for peasants," Madame barks, and to my complete surprise, Elia instantly does as she's told without a trace of shock on her usually expressive face.

I suppose this answers my question about what the cane is for. Disbelief and outrage rise within me, but no one looks surprised, and I suspect it's a regular occurrence here.

Gesturing for me to come closer, I'm directed into place opposite the cat-like *promessa*, her smug expression long gone. She takes my hands in hers and immediately closes her eyes.

"Good. Elia will now send you her power, be open to receive it," the Madame instructs. It's clear she doesn't expect much from me.

Closing my eyes, I feel tingles covering my hands almost immediately. Reaching inside myself to my power, I open my senses and start to draw on the energy Elia sends to me.

"Good!" Madame seems surprised but pleased, her voice close. "Not too fast or you'll drain her, just allow it to flow into you."

I do as I'm told, and when the power stops, I open my eyes to see the madame watching me with an appraising look. Turning to the others, she slams her cane down on the floor again, making them flinch. "That is how you do it. This is her first time, and she makes you all look like children in comparison."

Everyone has stopped to watch me, and a mixture of expressions are aimed my way, from jealousy to surprise. Elia looks pale and a little unsteady on her feet, but she still manages to sneer at me. "Well, if I had Elijah spoon-feeding everything to me, I'd be an expert too." Her comment doesn't even make sense, yet she somehow manages to try and insult me and flirt with Elijah at the same time.

"Enough of that, girl. Jealousy is an ugly trait," the madame snaps and then turns her attention to me. "*Promessa*, transfer the energy back to Elia."

I'm surprised she addressed me as such. I suppose I'm in her good books now... How quickly her approval changes. That may not last long, however, considering I have no idea how to send energy.

Taking a deep breath, I close my eyes and focus on my power. I can see Elia's energy added to my own, and it feels different. Extending my senses, I focus on the physical, like the feel of her hands in mine. Pushing at the unusual power, I try to force it from me, but it only seems to bounce back, like there's a barrier around it.

"Open that place within you where your power resides. Just a tiny gap in your natural defence is needed to allow the power to flow out. Like a trickle, not a flood." The madame's words are soft as she guides me, almost as if she can sense my current dilemma.

Nodding, I focus on my power in a way I've never done before. The size, colour, and feel of it, even how it smells. I take it all in. In my mind, I see it as a glowing ball of energy within me, the strands waving in a phantom breeze like the ocean plants flow to and fro as the waves move above them. Extending outwards from the source of power, I come across an almost invisible layer covering the whole area. There *is* some sort of barrier surrounding my power and keeping it contained within me, which is what's stopping me from sending it to Elia. Concentrating on that barrier, I work on creating a hole in it, like the madame instructed. It takes a few attempts, but I manage it. As soon as the gap is there, my energy seems eager to flow from me, so I use the physical connection between myself and my fellow *promessa* and guide it across.

Elia gasps as her power returns to her in a rush. I hear the madame crowing with praise and the other *promessa* crowding around us. I've never felt so powerful before. It's like touching this raw ball of power has energised me, and I can feel everything—the power of everyone in the room, how close they are to me, and their fear, excitement, and resentment that I can do what they can't. I feel it all despite my eyes being closed. Elia's meagre power has left my body, and my own now pours into her.

"That's enough now," the madame murmurs, her hand landing on my arm, but she immediately jerks away with a shocked cry. "Stop, you're sending her too much!" Her usually strict voice seems to waver.

I'm too busy extending my senses through the castle to notice. Internally, I watch each fae I come in contact with, my power briefly touching them. Some notice, turning around and looking for someone as if it were a physical touch, while others continue on. The ball of energy within me extends even more, moving deeper through the castle. I have no control over where it advances, and it almost seems to be searching, looking for something. Down and down it goes until we reach the dungeon, and I realise it's not a something, but a someone that we're looking for.

As soon as my power has descended, Alric's head whips up. He glances around, frowning. "Annalise?" he calls quietly, like he can't quite believe what he's feeling.

My power instantly reacts and wraps around him. Where most might shy away from an immense, unknown wave of energy, he opens his arms and welcomes me. I can't seem to settle on him, though, continuously bouncing off of him, and I realise he's surrounded by magic. How this is possible when he's locked in the cells that nullify our power, I don't know.

"I don't know what's happening, Annalise, but you're expending a huge amount of power. You need to go back.

I'm safe, and I'll explain everything when you return. I promise," he says earnestly, talking aloud. I'm unsure how I can hear him, seeing as I'm not physically there, but I believe him. Focusing on myself, I give an almighty *yank*, pulling my power back to me. It returns like a physical blow, slamming into me and bowing my back.

Someone moves to my side, and I know it's Elijah, our bond humming at his closeness.

"Annalise, her body can't contain that much energy." Although he sounds calm, like he's just advising one of the *promessa*, I feel his apprehension through our bond.

I hear Elia's pained groan, but I can't seem to stop. Now that my power has been freed, it wants out. Fear fills me as I struggle to control it, desperately trying to break the connection with her. My body reacts to my panic, and the power builds even more.

"Annalise, you're going to kill her, you need to stop," Elijah snaps, and I hear the worried whispers of the others in the room.

I try to do as he says. Even though I don't like the female, the last thing I want to do is kill her. My body feels like it's burning up, and my breathing comes in great, unsteady gasps. Elia shouts out in pain, which only makes things worse. Panicking, I rip myself away from the *promessa* and open my eyes in time to see her fly across the room with a final blast of my power. Ave and Gail hurry over to her, kneeling by her slumped form.

That should be it, but now that my power doesn't have another vessel to escape to, it's leaking within me, filling my every pore. Glancing down at my hands, I see that I'm glowing, the pain building within me. Vaguely, I'm aware that the madame is directing the others away from me, their expressions fearful. Me, they are afraid of me. Thundering footsteps fill the room, and I hear Elijah shout at everyone to stay away from me. The room heats as my body continues to burn.

If I can't control this, I will die, that much is clear. I don't understand what's happening. I was barely able to create a shield around myself back in Morrowmer, so where has this power come from? I don't know how to stop this.

Suddenly, Elijah appears in front of me, wincing against the force of my power. He tries to hide it, but I catch his fear and pain.

"No, get away," I yell, reaching out to try and push him away. He hisses, and I remove my hand to find a hand-shaped burn mark on his chest. I did that, I hurt him. A mournful cry leaves me. My body gives out, and I fall to my knees.

Elijah kneels with me, so close that I see his brow glistening with sweat, the heat radiating from my body intense. "Annalise, I'll help you."

Unable to speak, I shake my head and try to move away, but I can't.

"Let me help you," he pleads, and I see panic in his eyes. He knows as well as I do that I'm going to die if I can't control this, and he doesn't care if anyone discovers what we are to each other. "I can't lose you." His whispered words break me, and a sob tears from my chest.

I hate hurting him, but I nod as the power builds once more. Without wasting another second, he quickly closes the distance between us and wraps himself around me, covering me with his body. I'm surrounded by his scent as he blocks me from the rest of the world. I hear his grunt of pain, but he doesn't complain, if anything, he just holds me tighter. Silent tears roll down my face, evaporating instantly.

"Focus on your breathing. Slowly, in and out," he instructs, and I concentrate on his voice, following his directions. Each breath feels like a dagger in my throat, but I do as I'm told. As my breathing slows, my mind becomes less foggy, and although I'm still scared, it's no longer controlling me.

"Reach for our bond and use it to ground you. You are safe, I'll keep you safe." He repeats the words over and over, not caring who might hear. His touch, his presence, and his bond anchor me to this world. "That's it. Pull your power back in and build a wall around it."

I imagine building a solid wall around my power brick by brick, and slowly, the pain and the heat fade. Our bond glows within me, but a tug in my chest tells me of things to come. Once the final brick has been placed, I open my swollen eyelids. The first thing I see is Elijah's concerned face staring down at me.

"Hi," I croak awkwardly, and he breaks out into a huge smile before burying his face against my neck and inhaling deeply. I wish I could stay here in his arms forever, but I become aware of the many eyes watching us. Clearing my throat, I gently untangle myself from him, wincing at his singed clothing. I feel sick, and I still don't understand what just happened.

With a deep breath, I face the now silent room. To my shock and horror, everyone is down on one knee with their heads bowed. Finally, the madame stands up and gives me a reverent smile, dipping her head. No one else stands, and the madame opens her mouth to speak before tilting her head to one side, her ears twitching as she hears something I've not registered yet.

Now I hear it, the heavy steps of someone running and getting closer by the second. Facing the door, I turn just as the master comes into view. I've never seen him so dishevelled or out of breath before, and his eyes widen as they land on me before scanning the other *promessa* who are still kneeling.

"*Ma promessa*, you finally made yourself known." The master stumbles towards me in awe. His smile is that of a youth getting everything they have always wanted. I watch him warily, my heart pounding in my chest. To my surprise and dread, the master kneels before me, his beatific smile wide. "I felt your call, *ma promessa*, and I came. Welcome home."

Chapter 16

"No." Shaking my head and backing away, I fight against my rising nausea. "It's not me, it can't be."

The master slowly stands, holding his hands out to the sides as if he's trying not to scare a startled animal. He gives me what I think is supposed to be a soft, encouraging smile, but with his snout and sharp fangs, it does nothing to calm me. "You have the power that's been gifted by the gods. It is you, *ma promessa*."

I just lost control of my power and almost killed myself and Elia, yet they are all acting like I'm a walking goddess. I don't care what they say their gods have gifted me with, they have got the wrong fae. "Stop calling me that!" Power flares around me, reacting to my panic as it starts to work its way through my carefully crafted wall. Closing my eyes, I look inside myself and see that cracks have begun to appear around my barrier, and my power is looking for a way out.

"Annalise," Elijah calls softly, moving nearer and

placing his hand on my shoulder. His closeness helps soothe me, and he smiles softly as our eyes meet.

Growling, the master balls his hands at his sides, his wicked claws gleaming. "Step away from her, Elijah." The order is clear, and I see many of the still kneeling fae flinch against the force of the demand, yet Elijah doesn't move.

"She's frightened, my presence helps settle her."

He's right, but seeing the master's possessive expression, I know Elijah won't be allowed to stay with me. Pain ripples through my body, and I'm forced to my knees again as the energy tries to push its way out. Movement flashes in the corner of my eye, and I feel Elijah kneel by my side, however this only angers the master even further.

"She belongs to *me*, and you will do as I order," he roars, the windows rattling with the force of the sound. Gritting his teeth, he glares down at his second-in-command. "Back away."

Elijah stands and steps directly in front of me, as if to protect me, not once following the master's orders.

My body begins to shake. "Elijah, what's happening?" Glancing at his back, I see him gazing down at me sympathetically, but he doesn't move from his defensive position. Looking around the room, I recognise a familiar face by the door. "Tarren?" I call out, reaching a hand towards her. Surely she'll help me. Her face twists, and I see her try to take a step forward, only to be met by some sort of barrier. Her claws slide out as she bares her teeth at the master, her body growing as she fights against her protective instincts.

Despair hits me. He's going to take away the only people that mean anything to me, all except Alric. However, now that he's convinced I'm the true *promessa*, is he ever going to let me out of his sight again? I'd be surprised if he sent me back to the cells. I may never see Alric again. The thought of being isolated from the three fae who have helped me since I've been here causes another surge of power to slam against my walls.

The master tries to step around Elijah. "*Ma promessa*, I need you to calm down."

"I said stop calling me that!" The shout rips from me, and I watch as he's pushed back by a wave of pure energy. Interestingly, Elijah is spared from this and stays firmly in front of me, but I don't have time to process this.

The master frowns, his expression becoming severe as he loses his patience with me. Gesturing a couple of his guards forward, he nods at me. "Bind her and take her down to the cells. The spell on the doors will contain even her power."

I was wrong, the master *would* send me to the cells. It's another way to control me. He's not going to risk losing me now. What will happen to this raging ball of energy once I'm locked away? It won't be able to escape, and sure, the spell on the cells will contain it, but will the power continue to eat away at me from the inside, or will it be truly nullified?

Three large apanthe guards start making their way towards me, a pair of stone cuffs in the leader's hands. I recognise those cuffs. They are the ones that were used on Elijah to contain his power.

Elijah must notice, because he snarls and lowers into a defensive stance, his own power radiating around us. "Don't come any closer," he snarls at the guards. Seeing how close he is to going feral, the apanthe do as he says. Confident that they are not going to move, Elijah's head whips around to the master. "Ajax, this is barbaric! You can't—"

The master moves across the space in the blink of an eye, appearing in front of Elijah. His body seems to expand in size as he bears down on Elijah, snarling. Waves of alpha energy pour from him, causing my mate to grunt as he forces himself to stay upright under the onslaught of power. "You forget whom you speak to, Elijah," the master growls, only just making his words understandable. "I've been lenient on you, perhaps too much."

The threat of violence on his face twists something within me, and my power reacts, immediately retreating. At the threat to Elijah, my mate, it would pull back, but only for now. It's still writhing within me like a predator prowling in the dark, waiting until the perfect moment to pounce.

Staggering to my feet, I hold up my shaking hands. "Stop! I'm calm, I won't use my power. Just don't hurt him."

This makes the master pause. He tilts his head to one side as if he's listening to something, and I realise he's feeling for my power. The guards use my distraction to hurry forward. One of them grips both of my wrists in his huge hands while the other binds them with the stone cuffs. Instantly, the link between myself and my power disappears. I breathe a sigh of relief, and I see many others in the room do the same. I probably shouldn't be so glad that I have no access to my power while in my enemy's clutches, but this sudden boost and what just transpired has scared me. I slump as exhaustion hits me like a physical blow. I feel Elijah reach through our bond, but he's locked in place by the master's order, his hands trembling at his sides as he tries to break free.

Humming, the master finally nods his head. "Fine. Keep the cuffs on and take her to my rooms." I'm about to protest, but Elijah roars out in anger, struggling against the alpha power binding him.

Ignoring him completely, the master prowls towards me and lowers his head as if to tell me a secret, his amber eyes boring into mine. "If you don't comply, then Elijah will be the one to suffer."

This was what we feared, that the master would use one of us against the other, but there's nothing we can do about it now. Of course I'm going to follow his orders if it means Elijah will remain safe.

"Okay."

The master smiles a toothy grin, nodding to the guards at my side. They lead me from the room. I would love to walk out with my head held high like none of this bothers me, but I'm so weak I practically have to be dragged. Elijah's roar follows me from the room, and I squeeze my eyes shut against the tears that threaten to fall as the harrowing sound follows us.

The master's suite is exactly as I expected it. Everything is opulent and over the top.

As soon as the guards brought me inside, I was left alone. I was so tired I only managed a cursory check to make sure that I truly was by myself before finding somewhere to curl up and nap. One of the rooms had a huge, four-poster bed with bright blue velvet curtains that could hide the occupant within. Seeing it caused shudders to run down my spine. There was no way I was sleeping somewhere the master sleeps. If he were to walk in and find me curled up in his bed, he would only take that as an invitation and a sign of victory.

Instead, I returned to the first room, which had a comfortable window seat surrounded by plush pillows. I'd fallen asleep as soon as I curled up, the sunlight warming my back through the glass.

Awake now, I glance around the room once more. The sun is beginning to set, so I know several hours must have passed, yet no one has disturbed me. Years of captivity made me a light sleeper, therefore I'm sure no one's entered the room. I'm surprised the master hasn't come to brag over his victory, as he obviously believes I'm the true *promessa*. A twinge of worry fills me at this. Did he carry through on his threat with Elijah?

Sighing, I push away those toxic thoughts and stand from the window seat. Time to explore. Comprised of several huge interconnecting rooms, everything in the suite is gilded or furnished in thick velvets and rich fabrics. This room seems to be some sort of reception area with shelves of books, a large fireplace, and several deep red armchairs positioned to face it. There are two doorways in addition to the exit. The smaller door to the left leads to a relatively small room in comparison to the others.

A large desk, a huge window, which allows in plenty of natural light, and more bookshelves indicate this room is a study. There is an additional door on the other side of the room, but it's locked. Turning to the desk, I check all the drawers, which, to my surprise, are all unlocked, but any paperwork I find is written in strange letters I don't understand, so none of it is of any use to me. Humming in disappointment, I leave the room, shut the door behind me, and walk to the other doorway. I know from my previous exploration that this is his bedroom, and I really don't want to think about what happens in here, but I inspect it anyway. Another window seat is built before another massive window. Examining the glass, I find that, like the others, the window is locked and too thick for me to break through.

On the other side of the bedroom is an additional door, which leads to the bathroom. As I walk in to fully inspect it, I whistle at what I find. A huge, walk-in bathtub is sunk into the floor, looking more like a small swimming pool. There are no windows in this room, just lanterns built into the walls. The domed ceiling and candlelight make the space feel cosy. I would love nothing more than to soak in there, but there's no chance I'm going to remove my clothes and make myself vulnerable to the master in that way. Besides, with my hands still bound by the cuffs, I'm more likely to drown myself than actually get clean.

Returning to the reception room, I sit on the window seat and watch the coming and goings outside of the castle.

I almost killed Elia today. Remembering the force of the power within me makes me shudder. It's never felt like that before. No, that's not true, I felt something similar when I protected Elijah from the whip in the throne room. It was just for a moment, and I was so focused on shielding him that it bent to my will. With Elia, it was like it was desperate to leave me now that it was finally free. Is it this land? A remnant of the block the queen put on me back in Morrowmer? Or could it be that this is additional power granted to me by their gods?

I continue to play the scene over and over in my mind, as if I'm going to discover an explanation, but I only succeed in making myself feel worse.

A knock on the door startles me from my musings. Jumping to my feet, I step into the middle of the room and stare at the door with a frown. Should I open it? The guards outside the door have obviously let the fae past, and if it were the master, he wouldn't be knocking on his own door.

"*Ma promessa?*" a steady female voice calls from the other side. "It's Paela, your maid. May I come in?"

This confuses me, but I nod until I realise that she can't see me. Releasing an irritated breath, I clear my throat and try again. "Yes."

The door opens, and an unfamiliar female bustles in, her arms full of bundles of brightly coloured fabric. Seeing me, she drops into a wobbly curtsy before striding past me and into the master's bedroom. Raising an eyebrow, I hesitantly follow, pausing in the doorway as I watch her spread out the bundles which are actually dresses.

"You're not one of my usual maids." I try not to sound accusing, but it doesn't quite work. Thankfully, she doesn't appear to be offended as she turns from her task.

"You are the true *promessa* now, and I've been assigned to you," she replies with a dip of her head before returning to the dresses. "The master requires you to attend dinner with him this evening, and I'm here to help you prepare."

I freeze as horror surges through me. "Just the master and I?"

My tone must give away my feelings on the matter

because I see her stiffen, but she doesn't lift her gaze, continuing to arrange the skirts. "I believe so, *promessa*."

Her answer was exactly what I feared. "No. I will not dress up for that beast." I back away, instinctively pulling against the cuffs as if I can break free from them. I know it's impossible, but I'm not thinking clearly right now.

She looks around nervously as if worried someone might have overheard. "I would be careful with what you say if I were you," she warns, tapping her pointed ears as she finally meets my gaze, and I realise what she's saying. We're being listened to. "You might have more protection now that you've made yourself known as the true *promessa*, but there are still ways you can be punished."

She's right. There's Elijah. Not to mention Alric and Tarren. He doesn't even have to threaten to hurt me and he knows it. He's realised that I'd much rather take the beating myself than put someone else at risk. Mother above, even if he threatened to harm one of the other *promessa* I would probably cave to his desires. I seem to be unable to walk away when someone is in danger, especially if it's because of me. I suppose that's why I'm in this situation in the first place.

Fine. If he wants to have supper with me, then I'll attend his dinner. It may be an opportunity to glean some answers. I just have to get through the evening without vomiting at the prospect of us being alone. Taking a deep breath, I dip my head in begrudging agreement, not missing how the maid releases her own relieved sigh.

Stepping into the room, I look down at the selection of dresses she brought with her. I'm beginning to get tired of this constant dressing up. Why can't I just wear the smart day dress I'm currently wearing? Biting my tongue, I choose not to say anything, knowing it won't get me anywhere. All three of the dresses are designed to show off the female body, the necklines low and revealing, cinching in tightly at the waist. The rich fabrics are beautiful, but none of these are what I would choose for myself. Sighing, I run my hand over them. One is a deep blue, the master's colour. No, I won't be wearing that one. The next is a rich red wine colour, but it is the most revealing of the three, with a deep, plunging neckline that would display most of my small bust. The final dress makes me pause. A steely storm grey, the fabric almost glistens in the light and reflects my turbulent mood. It's sleeveless, and the sweetheart neckline is the most conservative of the selection. The bodice is heavily beaded down to the waist, where the beads fade away, adding an additional shimmer and depth. I reach out and touch the fabric.

"A good choice, *ma promessa*," Paela remarks, removing the other dresses and hanging them in the large wardrobe on the other side of the room. Returning to my side, she gently guides me to the middle of the room, her fingers working quickly on the buttons at the back of my dress. I'm so used to maids dressing me now that I don't even flinch.

While she helps me get ready, I take the time to examine my new maid. She's around my height but doesn't have the same feline features the others do. No, that's not right, she has the slanted, almond-shaped amber eyes and thin, almost invisible whiskers like those who live here. Her dark hair is pulled back into a bun, exposing her pointed ears. They are more similar to mine rather than the cat-like ears.

"You're different than the others." I didn't mean to say this out loud, and I realise it could sound offensive. My cheeks flush red, and I open my mouth to apologise, but she places a hand on my shoulder, letting me know she doesn't mind the question.

"Yes, my mother was from Arpathe and my father from Vipos. I inherited my father's scales and ears," she explains as she helps me undress.

This isn't easy with my hands bound, but we manage, my mind caught on this new information. I realise that in certain light, her creamy skin glistens with tiny iridescent scales. I remember what I'd been told about half breeds, but I'd never expected to see one here. It's still something I struggle to get my head around. They all seem so separate and proud of their animalistic traits that it just hadn't occurred to me that they might mix. The fact that her parents had overcome these barriers gives me hope that this land isn't as cutthroat and brutal as it first appears. There seems to be an air of sadness surrounding her, however, so perhaps her parents' coupling wasn't as happy as I'd hoped.

"Do the three of you live here?" I keep my tone light, unable to stop myself from asking.

I wish I hadn't when she shakes her head. "No, my parents are dead," she says in a matter-of-fact way, holding open my new dress for me to step into. "The master offered me shelter here, and I've worked in the castle ever since."

Guilt gnaws at me, but I don't say anything for fear of saying something that might upset her. I don't know why I'm so chatty this evening. Usually when I'm nervous, I retreat into myself, falling back on silence as my shield. Perhaps it's because of all the changes today and the small talk helps me take my mind off it. Whatever the reason, I stamp down on the desire to ask any more questions and stay quiet as she dresses me.

Paela seems happy to work in silence, and soon enough, I'm dressed and my hair has been brushed until it's glistening. A delicate crown of flowers is placed atop my head, and I have to bite my lip again. It's very pretty, but it makes me look... well, like the other *promessa*. A red gloss is applied to my lips, but I don't require any further makeup. Flat silver shoes complete the look, and my maid leads me through the master's rooms and into the study.

"Enjoy your evening. If you have need of me, just speak to the guards outside."

I turn to find that she's not followed me into the room, instead standing in the doorway with her hands clasped before her.

"Wait," I blurt, nerves making me jittery. I knew I'd be spending the evening with the master, but now that the time has come, I find my earlier resolve is crumbling. "We're eating in here?" Although it's a genuine question, I'm asking more to keep her around longer, not wanting to be left alone.

"You'll be eating in the dining room through there." She gestures to the door that had previously been locked. Taking pity on me, she smiles slightly, patting me on the arm. "The master will come for you soon."

That's a terrifying statement, I think as she turns, beginning to pull the door closed behind her.

"Thank you," I call out.

She pauses, a look of surprise crossing her features at my gratitude. Cheeks flushing, she ducks her head and hurries from the room, shutting the door as she departs. She obviously isn't used to her work being appreciated, which doesn't surprise me.

Now alone, with only my thoughts for company, I pace the room. I'm going to go mad if I'm left waiting long, knowing I'm going to imagine all the worst-case scenarios about this evening. Nausea rises, and I have to take a deep breath. I doubt vomiting all over the master will help my situation. Or perhaps it would put him off and he would let me go. I want to laugh out loud at the wishful notion. I doubt he's ever going to let me go now.

A door slams open somewhere, bouncing against a wall, and the sound makes my heart pound in my chest. I hear a low rumble next, which I recognise as the master's growl. I'm confused for a moment as I glance around. I'm still alone. But then I realise he's in the dining room. With only the door between us, I'm able to hear him storming around the space. He's not in a good mood tonight. A second set of footsteps enters the dining room, and before I can speculate, the master is growling again. Whoever it is, I wouldn't want to be them right now.

"What is the meaning of this, Your Highness?" He sneers the last few words, insulting whichever royal has dared to bother him. The threat behind the tone is obvious. This fae has entered his castle uninvited, which I get the feeling is something the master isn't used to.

"I must see Annalise. I need to make sure she's okay," a male responds, clearly unperturbed by the unspoken threat.

My eyebrows shoot up as I recognise that voice. Prince Abel from Doerallia, the fae I danced with at the ball. What is he doing here? My heart flutters in my chest. He promised me he would get me out of this situation, that he would find a way, and here he is, demanding to see me. It's like the fairy tales my mother used to read to me when I was a youngling of damsels being rescued from monsters by handsome princes.

"I'm aware of your bid on her, Abel, but you're out of luck. She presented as the true *promessa* today," the master purrs as he lords this piece of information over the prince. "She's mine." The purr turns into a growl as his possessive side emerges.

There's a beat of silence as Abel takes this in. If I were merely another one of the other *promessa*, he could bid on me and take me away from here. But now that the master believes I'm the true *promessa*, he will never let me go, and the prince knows that.

I feel lightheaded and have to stumble back until I'm leaning against the edge of the desk. I hadn't truly believed he'd come back for me, but when I heard his voice, I briefly allowed myself to dream that he would get me out of here.

"I still need to see her," Abel insists. "I don't trust that you can keep her safe."

This was either a very brave or very stupid thing to say, and I find myself leaning forward so I can hear better. The master growls, and the sound of splintering wood startles me. His alpha power quickly follows but is rapidly quickly countered by an unfamiliar wave of energy. It reminds me of a fresh breeze, and I can almost smell pine trees. This must be Abel's power.

"I know about her care here. That you keep her in the dungeon and have her beaten. She almost died." The prince's voice becomes cold, and as he speaks, more of his power floods the room.

"That was something that should never have happened, but it was dealt with. All those involved are now dead. Elijah saw to that," the master concedes, and I can almost imagine him waving his hand at the irrelevance of the statement.

"That you keep that beast around her says enough about how you treat her. Is this how all the *promessa* are treated?" The prince holds his ground, and I remember Abel has been fighting for the release of the *promessa*.

"Things will change now. The true *promessa* will be treated like a goddess."

Nausea rolls through me again at the easy tone the master has now adopted. He doesn't consider the prince a threat and has calmed considerably.

"Is that what she wants? Have you even asked her?" the prince challenges, pushing him and not letting the subject drop.

"Why don't we ask her now?" the master purrs, and I can picture his smug expression. "Annalise, join us."

Caught off guard, I freeze at the demand. I guess if I was able to hear their conversation, then it wasn't a far stretch to assume he would be able to hear me too.

"I know you're listening behind that door. You can't hide from me."

There's a warning in his voice, and I know if I don't go out there, he'll come and get me. Wanting to maintain my dignity, I take a steadying breath and stride over to the door, twisting the now unlocked handle. As it swings open, my eyes go immediately to the biggest threat—the master. He's watching me like a predator, his pupils narrowing into slits as his eyes roam my body. Despite the prince invading his evening, the master's stance is casual, but I won't take that for granted. I've seen how quickly he can move. However, I don't think he's going to hurt me, not while the prince is here at least.

Certain he's not going to pounce, I turn my attention

to the prince. He's staring at me like I'm the sun, bringing life-giving light. His gaze is locked on me as he steps closer. He doesn't bother trying to hide his awe, and as he reaches me, he bows his head in respect.

"Annalise, you look beautiful." Scanning my body, he frowns slightly as his eyes settle on my face. "You are well?"

No doubt he sees the grey circles beneath my eyes and the exhaustion that makes my entire body feel heavy. Pondering his question, I deliberate how to answer. I obviously can't tell him the truth, and when I glance over at the master, I see his warning look. No, I can't risk him hurting Elijah because I have a loose tongue. However, I also don't want to lie to the prince.

"A lot has changed since last night," I hedge, knowing he's going to read around my words. "I am happy to see you again though, Your Highness." My admission brings a small smile to my face, and I attempt to drop into a curtsy to hide it, but he steps towards me until only a large chair separates us. He places a hand on my shoulder to stop me.

"You never have to genuflect to me." His expression is intense, and I know he wants to say more, but a humming noise breaks us apart.

"How lovely," the master croons.

Turning my attention back to him, I ensure my annoyance is clear on my face. Of course the master ignores it and gestures towards Abel. "The prince thinks I'm treating you badly. In fact, he demanded to see you." The lilt in his voice makes it sound like the suggestion is preposterous. He's enjoying making the prince uncomfortable as he makes his claim over me obvious. Smiling wide, the master places a hand on his chair. "Why don't you join us for supper, Your Highness?"

Abel wants to say no, in fact, I'm sure he wants to get as far away from the master as possible. However, I can tell he wants to truly make sure I'm okay, so he reluctantly pulls out the chair opposite the master and sits down. The master does the same with a satisfied smile. They both turn their attention to me. Swallowing against the lump in the back of my throat, I take my seat.

Now sitting, I take in the room around me. Wooden panels stretch from the floor to halfway up the walls, the rest painted a deep red. It's not a huge room like I expected, but large enough to fit the immense oak table and six ornate chairs. There are no windows and two doors—one to the study and the other to the rest of the castle, or so I assume. Compared to the ballroom, this is tiny, intimate. The thought that I would have been alone in here with the master makes my skin crawl.

Something catches my eye, and I drag my gaze down. There, on the table, are five deep gouges in the wood, exactly in the location of the master's claws. I suppose that explains the splintering noise I heard whilst I was in the other room.

With my bound hands resting in my lap, I watch as servants hurry in and set another place for the prince, bringing in plates and cutlery. Another servant arrives with three goblets of what I assume is red wine. The master instantly grabs his and starts to drink. I'm very aware of the prince watching my every move. My throat is parched, and I far would have preferred water, but I won't protest. I've learned that I have to take what I can get here as I never seem to be able to finish a meal before being dragged away somewhere. I reach for the wine, the task made difficult with my hands bound together as they are.

The prince makes a noise of disgust and pushes away

from the table, standing to his full height. His face is twisted in rage, and his magnificent horns look dangerous as he stares down at the master. "You have her in cuffs."

His sudden outrage makes sense. He must not have seen them before, the chair between us blocking his view. A wave of his power fills the room as his anger intensifies.

"How can you tell me that you treat her like a goddess when she is bound like a prisoner?" Voice raised, the prince plants his hands on the table and leans forward. "You've been throwing your weight around for too long, taking our territory and our females. I won't allow this to continue."

The master's hands ball up, his claws scraping across the tabletop, but he doesn't bother to stand. In his arrogance, he believes he's stronger and is showing it by refusing to react to the prince's display of power. "Be careful what you say, Prince. Remember what the consequences of defying me are."

Snorting, Abel shakes his head and pulls back from the table. "I'm returning to Doerallia. The king will be interested to hear what I've witnessed here." The warning is clear. Abel is not going to sit by any longer, and with the backing of his king... the consequences could be dire. Turning back to me, he kneels at the side of my chair, taking my bound hands in his. "Annalise, I will return and find a way to free you. I promise," he declares in earnest, bending to place a kiss on the back of my hand.

Standing, the prince strides to the door, which the servants entered through, and exits without glancing at the master, leaving us in silence.

I stare at the door, as if he's going to change his mind and come back. What just happened? Did the prince really threaten the master over me? No, I won't have them going to war because of me. Panic whirls in my mind. I need to stop him, but to do that I need to break free, which isn't going to happen.

The master breaks my internal alarm by taking a deep drink of his wine then placing it back on the table with exaggerated gentleness. I expected him to react badly to what just happened, to lash out—I've certainly seen him do it for smaller slights than this.

"That's a shame," he murmurs with a sigh, glancing over at me with a glint in his eye. "I was hoping I wouldn't have to kill the prince, for I was quite fond of him."

I knew he was going to retaliate in some way, but to *kill* the prince of another faction? My heart seems to freeze in my chest. No, I must not have heard him right. "What?"

Leaning back in his chair, he places his elbows on the armrest and steeples his fingers as if contemplating something. "He's become troublesome, defiant. That can't be allowed." Although he sounds disappointed at this outcome, I see the corners of his mouth twitch up, and there's a cruel hunger in his eyes.

Something sparks within me, like my power is stirring to life despite the cuffs that are supposed to nullify them. I reach for that power, for anything, but it slips away from me. Anger and rage I've buried deep down suddenly emerge thanks to my dread. Banging my fists on the table, I lean towards the master. "No. You can't kill him!"

"Hmm. Attached to the stag, are we?" He's smiling fully now, and I know I've just given him the ammunition he wanted. "What would you do to stop me from killing him?"

I freeze. I hadn't expected him to offer me a trade, but I suppose this is a perk of being the true *promessa*. He needs me, but for what, I still don't know, yet he can't risk pushing me away completely. What would I give him, or more accurately, how far would I go to stop him from killing the prince? Mouth suddenly dry, I reach out and take a small sip of wine, using my bound hands to cradle the goblet. I slam it down with more force than necessary and meet his eyes once more. "What do you want?" I wish I felt as confident as I sound, but inside I'm shaking like a newborn foal.

His face splits with a satisfied grin as he leans towards me. "Submit to me."

So that's what he was after and why he suppressed his anger with the prince. He knew if he threatened him that I would try to make a trade. However, this is something I cannot, *will* not give up. Praying to the Mother that the prince is swift and can protect himself, I slowly get to my feet. "I will never submit to someone like you."

Each word is enunciated slowly and with precision so he can't misunderstand me. The calm mask he wears finally falls as he roars and flips the table with a single, powerful move. Gasping, I jump back, stumbling against the wall as I watch him rage. He looks exactly like the beast I know him to be. He lifts his chair, hollering as he throws it, and splinters of wood scatter through the air, cutting my cheek. Making a stifled pained noise, I press my hand against the small wound. Somehow, the master hears this and spins to face me.

He snarls at what he sees. "I've waited this long for the true *promessa*, I can wait a little longer." His beastly nature has overtaken him, so his words are barely understandable. Guards run into the room behind the master, scanning the damage to the space, but none of them move towards us.

"I will break you, *Annalise*," he sneers, the threatening promise making me shudder. Glancing over his shoulder, he sees the guards and points at me. "Guards, take her back to the cells."

The apanthe guards hurry forward. Two of them grab me and start pulling me away. Stumbling, and with no other options, I follow as they take me back through the study. Hearing an almighty smash, I glance over my shoulder and just catch sight of the master grabbing the chair I'd been sitting on before tearing it apart with his bare hands.

Horrified by the whole evening, I go into a state of numbness as I'm led towards the cells. One thought replays through my mind, and it will haunt me all night. By rejecting the master, have I just sealed the prince's death?

Chapter 17

I don't know where Tarren is, but the male apanthe don't even acknowledge me as they march me down to the dungeon. I feel numb, and pure fatigue, both mentally and physically, threaten to overwhelm me, so I focus on putting one foot in front of the other. I stumble down the steps, and the only reason I don't fall is thanks to the guards holding me up. The prison door swings open, and I'm taken to my cell.

One of the guards enters after me, and fear pierces through my numbness. Eyes wide, I stagger back to put space between us.

"*Ma promessa*, give me your arms." He doesn't wait for me to respond, grabbing the cuffs. Before I realise what's happening, my wrists are free and the guard is backing from the cell, the door slamming shut behind him.

Left alone, I glance to my left where Alric's kept, needing to see a familiar face, but to my surprise the cell's empty. A crushing weight falls upon me. Stumbling over to my cot, I drop onto it, curling into a ball. I'm unable to keep my sobs at bay, and I'm sure this will be reported back to the master, but I don't care. Everything that happened today has finally hit me, and it's too much. My heart feels like it's breaking—for Elijah, for what might happen to Prince Abel, and even for Alric, wherever he's been taken to—but ultimately, I cry for myself. I was so sure that once I killed the elf queen and freed myself in Morrowmer that I would make a life for myself. When I was still her captive, I would dream of what I'd do with my freedom and promised myself that if I ever managed to get away, I wouldn't let a single day go to waste. Perhaps that is all it will ever be, a dream.

Several sets of footsteps move through the room, followed by the slamming of metal bars, but I don't bother to look up. The comings and goings of the guards and prisoners is fairly regular, so it's nothing important to pay attention to. The footsteps move away, and silence fills the room again.

"Annalise," a raspy voice calls.

My head snaps up, and I look straight into the neighbouring cell where Alric is kneeling on his side of the bars. I sit up, taking a deep breath to try to calm my tears, and wipe my face with the back of my hand. Standing on wobbly feet, I make my way over to him. I half kneel, half fall to the ground. Now that he's back, it's like a weight has been lifted. It still feels like I'm carrying the world on my back, but I can breathe a little now that I've seen him. After my altercation with the master, I feared he was going to take everything from me. He did promise to break me, after all, and what better way than to take away the familiar? The guards must have reported that I've become friendly with one of the prisoners, no matter how careful we've been to speak in whispers when no one's looking. An image of him standing by his cell door screaming at the guards to help me flashes in my mind. *Perhaps we weren't so careful after all.*

I scan his weathered face, getting stuck on his eyes, the crystal-clear blue so at odds with his elderly body. I realise he's doing the same with me, examining me from head to toe, taking in my evening gown and the tear tracks on my face.

"What happened today, Annalise? I felt..." He trails off, confusion creasing the skin around his eyes. Glancing over my shoulder, he ensures no one's listening before leaning closer. "I could have sworn I felt your power touch me today."

So that did happen. While I was aware of what was occurring, I wasn't in control of my power when it released during the class with the *promessa*, so I wasn't completely sure if the moment I had with Alric was real or not. As I think back on what happened to me, my face crumples and the tears roll down my cheeks once more. I'm too broken to be embarrassed at the state I'm in, and I wrap my arms around myself as if it will hold me together.

"Oh, Annalise, come here."

Hearing the concern in his voice shatters what little control I possess, and great, rasping sobs escape my chest. Crawling forward, I press my forehead against the bars separating us, my shoulders slumped as the weight of my decisions and actions finally crushes me.

A pair of arms surround me, and as soon as he touches me, my burden feels lighter. He presses his face to the bars next to me, and I can hear his steady breathing as his hands rub up and down my back. He doesn't say anything for a long time, letting me sob against him, knowing this is what I need in this moment. It's like a pressure valve within me has released and the events of the last couple of weeks flow out of me. Eventually, when I'm too exhausted to cry any longer, I let out a shuddering sigh, leaning against Alric like I'm in the middle of the ocean and he's my life raft.

"Whatever has happened, you are stronger," Alric whispers, his voice full of surety and far stronger than I've ever heard it before.

Pulling back from the bars, I examine his face. How can he be so certain? I've failed at so much and have lived most of my life as a prisoner. My doubt must show in my expression, because his hands move to my shoulders and grip them tightly.

"You *will* get through this, Annalise, I promise you." His face seems to light up as he speaks, like he's talking from his heart. "I also promise that when it gets to be too much, I will be there to help carry your burdens."

The declaration should surprise me more than it does. After all, we hardly know each other and have only become friends over our shared circumstances. Had I been placed in a cell on the other side of the dungeon, I wouldn't have seen him. I don't even know the basics about him, like where he's from or why he's locked away down here. There's also the fact that we have no idea what our future holds, so it seems like a pointless promise to make, one that's impossible to keep. However, none of that seems to matter anymore. For some reason, I believe him, and something in my gut tells me to trust him.

We continue to stare at each other, and my tears dry as I take comfort from his presence. "Thank you," I rasp, my words heartfelt.

He nods in response. Something about him changes,

his body stiff and his eyes flinty. I'm about to ask him what's wrong, but he cuts me off.

"Did anyone hurt you?"

Ah, so that's what the change in the atmosphere was about. If I'm honest with myself, I'm not sure how to answer him. Not all harm is physical, and I've learned the hard way just how scarring emotional abuse is. Physically, I'm unscathed, but mentally? Well, he just saw for himself the mess I'm in. Taking a deep breath, I shake my head. "No one touched me."

He looks at me closely, his eyes narrowing as he reads between my words. "They will all suffer for what they have done to you."

A shudder travels down my spine at the coldness in his voice, his body almost flashing before my eyes. Blinking, I take him in again, but he still looks like the same fae I've gotten to know. His face twists into a pained wince, and I frown as I reach out to touch his shoulder.

"What happened? Are you okay?" Something occurs to me as I remember he wasn't in his cell when I arrived here. The sound of the guards dragging someone to a cell must have been him, but I'd been so lost in my despair that I hadn't noticed. "Where did they take you?"

"They interrogate me every now and again." Shrugging like it is no big deal, he shifts his weight and attempts to hide the pain this action causes. "When I didn't give them the answer they wanted, they lost their temper." He winces again, but his eyes glitter with mirth. That look promises violence, and I feel sorry for the guards who harmed him if he ever does get free. I feel guilty that I didn't think to ask him before if he was alright, but he must see it in my expression since he wags a finger at me. "No, don't. Distract me, tell me what happened today."

I know I can't put it off any longer. Sighing, I shift from my knees so I'm sitting on the hard floor, then I explain the events of the day. I tell him everything, from what I learned from Elijah to what happened with Elia and my apparent emergence as the true *promessa*. He hisses with anger as I tell him about the cuffs they bound my power with before taking me to the master's rooms. I reassure him once again that no one touched me, as I can see him making assumptions on what happened in those rooms. Finally, I tell him about the prince and the master's demands, as well as my fear that I've doomed Abel.

Alric blows out a breath, his eyebrows raised. "You've had a busy day," he teases, trying to coax a smile from me, and surprisingly, it works. It's a tiny, fragile smile, but the one he gives me in return is bright enough to light the room. We fall silent as he examines me, and I wait anxiously for his verdict. Will he condemn me for my choices, or act differently around me now that I'm the true *promessa*?

He makes a noise in the back of his throat, and I glance up to see him watching me carefully. "So, should I start calling you the promised one now?"

Snorting, I shake my head adamantly. "Please don't."

He grins at my reaction, but it's soon replaced by a thoughtful expression. "It was your power I felt earlier." He seems to be talking more to himself than to me, so I stay silent as he works through the information I gave him. "Your power feels different now, you know, so much greater. I can almost feel you through the block on the cells, it's just begging to be free. What I don't understand is how it's so much stronger now." He scans my body as if he can see inside me to where my power resides. "I've heard of fae having blocks put on their power source, but I've never seen it. It's your power though, so I don't know why it would react so violently when it was finally released. Power of any strength is rare here, and the only fae who get overwhelmed with it are those who never learned to develop it. I suppose if a block had been in place for a long period of time and released suddenly..." He trails off at my expression, and horror flashes in his eyes before he shakes his head. "No, that can't be right, no one could survive for so long without their power, especially someone as strong as you," he argues, as if he can't cope with the idea of me being cut off from my power for so long.

Both of the scenarios he posed apply to me. I did have a block on my power when I was a captive of the elf queen, but that disappeared when she died. Is it possible I had an additional block stopping me from accessing the deep well of power that now glows brightly within me? I was taken when I was young, so I never had the chance to fully develop my power and abilities, and then I was in captivity for over a century. Is this how strong I would have been if my circumstances had been different? Is my power so volatile because of my lack of knowledge and ability to grow due to the blocks placed on me? There's still the fact that I had an additional block in place, but I can't begin to dissect that now, not after the day I've had.

"How did you know the power was mine?" I ask, needing to steer the conversation away from blocks to wipe the sad expression from Alric's face.

Sighing, he rubs a hand across his forehead. "It felt like you, and I could almost smell your sweet scent. It was like you were in the room with me, but I just couldn't see you."

His words stir something inside me, and I want to say something, but his exhaustion and reluctance to say anything more stops me. Grimacing, he shifts his weight once more, and I'm suddenly reminded that he's injured. Feeling like an idiot, I kneel and gesture towards his bedding. "Sit on the cot, Alric, you need to rest."

He snorts, those blue eyes sparkling again like they contain a secret. "Really, I'm fine, don't fuss."

Despite his words, he does as I say. Alric stands slowly, wobbles towards the cot, and lowers himself with gritted teeth. Watching him carefully, I wait until he's settled before getting to my feet and walking to my own. I perch on the end closest to him. With us both sitting like this, our arms brush through the bars, something I take comfort from.

We watch the comings and goings of the dungeon in companionable silence. Eventually, I can't hold my tongue any longer. Glancing over, I see his eyes are closed, but I know he's not actually asleep. I pretend to watch the prisoners on the other side of the room, turning my face away to hide my shame.

"Do you think the prince will be okay?" I whisper so as not to attract the attention of the guards, but I also can't bear saying the words any louder. My guilt is almost a living thing inside me, twisting around and squeezing until I can't breathe with the strength of it.

I feel Alric's gaze on me, but I don't turn to face him, not wanting to see any condemnation on his face.

"The master could have been bluffing," he responds. "Killing the heir to Doerallia would be an act of war. Although, with the information the prince had, it might have resulted in that anyway. Doerallia has been the most vocal about the treatment of the *promessa*."

My stomach clenches as he speaks, but I nod my head to indicate I'm listening as I stare at the door to the guardroom.

"Their *promessa* is the king's niece, I believe, so they don't risk doing anything that might cause the master to harm her, but they are constantly pushing the rules," he continues. Something lands on my leg, and I glance down to see his hand. I look up, and our gazes lock. "The prince is clever. He would have known that his display would put a target on his back. He'll expect the master to lash out."

I absorb the information, nodding my head. Everything he says makes sense. The prince wouldn't have got very far in life if he wasn't able to protect himself. If only this erased the nagging guilt I have in the back of my mind. Taking a deep breath, I process everything he told me, and something snags my attention.

"How do you know all of this?"

For an old fae who's been locked away in the dungeon, he seems to know an awful lot about the political nature of the factions. Is this just common knowledge in the fae lands, or does he know more than he should?

That mischievous twinkle in his eyes reappears, and the corner of his mouth twitches up into a half-smile. "There's so much more to me than what you see."

Frustration rises, momentarily erasing my other worries. Alric is a mystery I'm determined to uncover, yet I get a strange premonition that I'm not going to have much longer to work it out. "You have said that before." Twisting on my cot so I'm facing him, I demand, "Alric, who are you?"

He opens his mouth but pauses, tilting his head to one

side as if listening for something. What is he doing? His eyes suddenly shoot to mine.

"Get down," he orders, and without hesitation, I throw myself down onto the cot, my arms instinctively covering my head.

A great roaring boom echoes throughout the castle. The very walls themselves seem to rumble and shake around us. After such a loud noise, there's a moment of silence. Dust rains down from the ceiling, making me cough and shatter the quiet. Everything suddenly moves very quickly. Guards shout and race past the cells and up the staircase to the main castle. Inmates stand at their doors, their hands wrapped around the bars as they demand to know what's happening. Fear tinges the air as panic and mayhem ensues.

Lifting my head from the cot, I look around us. The dungeon is still intact, but given the amount of dust and the rumbling of the walls, I'd say we're in danger of the ceiling collapsing.

"Annalise."

At Alric's voice, I spin to face him, finding him standing at the bars. Climbing from my cot, I hurry over to him, my heart pounding in my chest.

"We don't have much time, and I'm sorry I have to tell you like this." His words are rushed as he looks over my shoulder, scanning the dungeon. Suddenly, his eyes lock on mine, and I get that strange feeling once more—everything is about to change.

"My name isn't Alric, and I don't usually look like this." He gestures to himself before he holds up a hand to stop my questions, obviously seeing the shock written on my face. "I'm a spy. I have the ability to change my appearance, and I got myself captured so I could get into the castle."

For a moment, I stare at him in astonishment. There is so much I want to know, but a rumble from above tells me we have limited time. All along, he'd been disguised as an old male. I feel stupid that I never worked it out and hurt that he lied to me, but at the end of the day, he didn't know who I was or if he could trust me, so I understand why he didn't. Trusting the wrong people could end up causing his death. There is a question I can't get my head around though...

"But the spell on the cells..." I trail off, watching the fae before me like I've never seen him before.

He sighs, as if knowing I won't trust him until I receive the answer. "Only the physical change requires my power. Once the change is made, I stay in that form until I will it otherwise, and only I can undo it," he explains. "I'd show you who I truly am, but in here, with my power bound, I'm stuck in this form." He flashes me a grin and a wink that doesn't fit with his current appearance.

Realisation hits me. "You. I met you at the ball, didn't I?" I accuse, remembering the fae I'd been convinced was related to Alric in some way. His comments make sense now, and I feel so stupid that I didn't figure it out sooner.

"You looked beautiful." He grins, confirming my suspicions.

I knew it. Anger, frustration, and betrayal are among the array of emotions I'm feeling, no matter how much the logical part of my brain is trying to justify his actions.

His smile drops as he watches me, sensing my sentiments with a grimace. "I wish I had more time to explain, but something is about to happen, and I need you to trust me."

Trusting him is the last thing I want to do right now, but as another boom rocks the castle, I know I'm out of other options. It's obvious he knows something about what's happening, and given the groans emanating from the ceiling above us, it's clear we're about to be in big trouble.

"What do you mean? What's about to happen?"

Shouting reaches us from the open door to the main castle, a roar making me flinch as the apanthe fight against whatever threat is upon us. Without realising it, I've turned my attention to the door, as if expecting someone to run through it, as if expecting *Elijah* to come, but Alric's hand shoots through the bars and grips my shoulder, his face stretched into a manic grin.

"We're breaking out of here."

Chapter 18

I gape at him. Has he gone mad? Did his latest interrogation session break him?

Rolling his eyes, he pushes away from the bars and moves over to his cell door. "Don't look at me like that, Annalise." Reaching into his pocket, he pulls out a smooth, flat stone. I watch in confusion as he reaches through and presses the stone against the lock.

Yup, he really has gone mad if he thinks he's going to unlock the door with a stone. These cell doors seem to be keyed to the touch of the guards and a few other fae like Elijah, so no piece of rock will ever—

The door to his cell swings open. *What in the Mother?* I curse internally, dumbstruck. Well, if he is who he says he is, then he must have had some way to escape his cell. But if he's had the means to escape all this time, why hasn't he helped me before? When I was being beaten and dying in the cell beside his, he could have let himself out and... No, that's not fair. He's here on a mission. If he casually let himself out in front of the guards, it would ruin everything. Besides, apparently I didn't know him at all.

Moving to stand in front of my cell, he raises the stone once more. "This is for us," he says, gesturing to the ceiling. I realise he means that whatever is transpiring above us is part of his plan. "Well, it's for you really. I was supposed to stay here longer and get some more intel, but everything changed when you showed up." His blue eyes flick up to mine. "I knew you were special for a while, I could feel it, so it's no surprise you are the true *promessa*."

The door swings open, and he holds his hand out for me to take. I'm about to step forward when I feel a ripple of his power, and in the blink of an eye, I'm no longer staring at Alric, but the handsome fae from the ball. His golden-brown hair falls in waves to his shoulders, and his caramel skin looks young and healthy. He doesn't have any animalistic features like most of the fae here seem to possess. Gone is the male I'd gotten to know and trust, and in his place stands a stranger.

"Don't look at me like that, Annalise." He winces, glancing around quickly to ensure there aren't any guards present before looking back at me and holding his hand out once more. "I wanted to tell you, I almost did at the ball, but—"

Another boom rocks the stone structure, and the screeching of the wooden beams above us is the only warning I have before the ceiling collapses.

"Annalise!" the stranger with Alric's eyes shouts, covering me with his body as stone falls around us.

My breath comes in fast pants, the sound so loud it blocks out everything else. I pray to the Great Mother for protection as the world seems to collapse around us. When the noise finally fades, I glance up to find Alric staring down at me with sweat on his brow as he braces himself above me. With a grunt, he moves to the side to let me out. Scrambling up, I gasp at what I see.

Half of the dungeon is demolished. The room above has collapsed down into the space where the guardroom and far cells had been. Alric grunts again, and I turn to see him standing with a wince. He's covered in dust, and from the rubble lining the floor, I assume he's been hit by several pieces. We were lucky and missed the worst of it; if I'd been another two cells down, I would have been buried.

Listening carefully, I try to hear if any of the prisoners who were in the far cells are still alive. Other than the slight shifting of rubble, there's no other noise.

Alric strides from the cell and stares at the huge pile of stones. Cursing, he turns back to me, concern lining his features. "The collapse has blocked our way out. We're going to have to go through the castle."

I realise with a twist of my gut that he's right. If we are going to get out of here, the easiest route would have been through the guardroom and the door that leads outside. Going through the castle is far riskier, since we're bound to come across guards.

"Annalise, come on, we need to go." He holds his hand out to me again, his tone urgent.

Do I trust him? I don't want to stay here any longer, but how do I know that if I leave with him, I'm not just going to walk into another bad situation? I don't really know him or who he's working for. What if I leave and end up in a worse place than here? A sense of peace settles over me, and I get the urge to take his hand. Meeting his deep blue eyes, Alric's eyes, I decide to risk it.

Trying to calm my racing heart, I hurry forward and

clutch his hand. As soon as I step outside the cell, my power slams into me so fiercely that it bows my back. It takes my breath away, and fear makes my body shake. Am I going to lose control again like I did with Elia?

"Annalise, listen to me. It's your power, and you control it. Build a wall around it," he instructs, his voice soothing, and I close my eyes and focus on the well of power within me. "I promise I will help you control this, but we have to leave *now*."

Nodding, I start to build that wall around my power once more, just like I did under Elijah's coaching. Alric is right, this is *my* power, I control it, not the other way around. As I work, I can't help noticing that it feels different now. It's still wild and wanting to escape, but it doesn't feel as overwhelming as before. Slowing my breathing, I work on settling it, soothing it, all the while building that wall brick by brick.

Now in control, I open my eyes and find Alric watching me carefully. "Are you okay?" he asks, and I know he doesn't just mean with my power.

Honestly, I don't know how to answer that question. I'm excited and exhilarated that I may finally be free, but I'm also frightened. There are so many unknowns, and I'm having to trust someone I don't really know. My overzealous power is just the tip of the iceberg, so instead, I just nod.

Running his eyes over me again as if he's not sure he believes me, he jerks his head towards the door closest to us which leads up to the castle. When the guards had run from the dungeon and up the staircase, they'd left the door open, so we don't have to worry about locks here. Hand in hand, we tread carefully over the scattered remains of the ceiling and exit through the door, taking the stairs two at a time as we make our way up.

"Do I get to know your real name?" I whisper. I know it's not the best time to be asking questions, but I'm running away with someone whose name I don't even know.

"It's Fabien." Glancing over his shoulder at me, he flashes me a grin. "Nice to meet you."

Fabien. That's going to take some getting used to.

We reach the top of the staircase and pause as he turns to face me, his brow pinched with worry. "We might have to fight our way out of here. Stay behind me and I'll protect you." His eyes bore into me as if seeing into my soul, and I know he will do everything in his power to get me out of here, including risking his life. I don't know how I know, but that surety in my chest tells me this is still the same Alric I trusted before, just with a facelift.

"If we get separated, run to the front of the castle and use whatever power you need to. Find Caldor, he'll be wearing a golden set of armour and has eagle wings. He stands out, so you shouldn't have a problem locating him," he continues, and it's obvious he doesn't even want to think about us getting separated, but we have to be realistic about this. There is a castle full of apanthe we have to get past, and we have no weapons other than our powers.

Not waiting for my reply, he places a finger to his lips, his other hand still gripping mine tightly. Entering the servants' corridors, we hurry through the passages, pausing every now and then at the sound of heavy boots running past. My heart is beating so loudly that I'm sure someone's going to hear it and come looking for us. It's a risk using these corridors. Sure, they are less busy and we're more likely to be seen in the main hallways, but if the guards were to find us here, there's no room to fight, and we could easily be trapped. Fabien obviously has the same thought, because when we reach the next doorway that leads into the castle proper, he peers out, checking for guards.

When he steps back, he seems tense, but he tries to use that half-smile once more, gesturing for me to follow him. Taking a deep breath, I squeeze his hand and we step out into the main hallway. We're alone, but I don't recognise where we are. All the hallways look the same to me, and I've only ever been taken to certain rooms, pretty much always using the servants' corridors. Thankfully, Fabien seems to know where he's going as he turns right and starts jogging, gently tugging me into action.

The tingle of power fills the air, and I realise it's coming from Fabien. I'm not sure what he's using it for, since I can't see anything, but now is not the time to ask. We round a corner and are halfway down the corridor when someone shouts. Spinning, I see a group of five apanthe guards hurtling towards us. Fabien pulls me behind him, throwing his hands up, and he sends a blast of power towards the guards. It slows them down, knocking a few of them off their feet, but it doesn't stop them. Growls fill the air, and I go to shout as one of them leaps towards us, only to bounce off an invisible wall. So that's what Fabien was using his power for. The scent of burnt fur reaches me, and I notice the apanthe who leapt at us is smoking from being burnt by the shield. The other guards are bearing down on us now, and Fabien grunts as they start pounding at the shield.

Perhaps I could help. I reach towards my walled off power. *If I could transfer some of my power to him...*

"Annalise, run." His grunted order breaks my train of thought.

He couldn't have said what I thought he did. I know he gave me instructions before, but I hadn't truly believed we'd be separated. "What? No, we need to leave together," I insist, my voice stronger than I feel. Really, I'm terrified of doing this alone. I will do it if I have to, I've always been good at surviving, but that was before I had anyone I cared about.

"I'll be fine. I can't fight them if I'm worried about you, and my shield won't last much longer," he explains, trying to keep his voice even, but I can hear the strain as he works to keep them away from us. "Run, find Caldor, and I'll be right behind you." Even he doesn't sound convinced by his own comment.

Shaking my head, I try again. "I could transfer you my—"

"Run!" he roars, ripping his hand from mine as he focuses on the guards.

Startled, I stare at him for a moment. He's right, he can't fight and be worried about me, I'd only be a liability. Taking a deep breath, I spin on my heel and run, leaving him behind. The growls of the apanthe get louder, and I feel Fabien's power swell as he uses it against them, but I don't turn back. I have no idea where I'm going, but a tug in my chest guides me. I run through the maze of corridors, following that feeling within me, and when I round a corner and slam into a hard body, I instantly know who it is.

"Annalise." Elijah pulls me against him as he buries his face in my neck, inhaling my scent. Closing my eyes, I embrace him back as something within me relaxes. I want to cry with relief. I'd been so worried that the master was going to punish him or try to keep him from me.

"The castle has been attacked." He pulls back and runs his eyes over me to check for injuries. "I tried to find you in the dungeon, but you were already gone." There's a question in his tone, but mostly relief that I'm alive and okay.

Nodding, I return his regard, checking him over. We must have passed each other at some point if he was searching for me. Perhaps Fabien's shield was able to hide our presence as well as protect us. "One of the prisoners was a spy, he's helping me escape."

"Annalise—"

I cut him off before he can try to convince me this is a bad idea. "I can't stay here, Elijah. You've seen how the master treated me, and now that I'm the true *promessa*, he's determined to own me." Eyes wide, I beg him to understand why I *must* do this. "I refuse to be his, and the longer I stay here, the more danger I'm in." I've not missed the looks the master would give the *promessa*, and I know that to be at his side would include being in his bed. Eventually, he would lose patience with me and take what he believes is rightfully his. I won't sit around and wait for it to happen.

Sensing my distress, he grips my shoulders, and his face pinches as if he's in pain. "I know you need to go, but a selfish part of me wants you to stay, to be here with me. At least I'd get to spend stolen moments with you, which is better than nothing at all, but I would be the worst mate in the world if I didn't let you go when a chance to escape arose."

The pain in my chest at the thought of leaving without him takes my breath away. "Elijah..." Shouting and sounds of fighting cut off whatever I was going to say. We only have moments before we're found. "Come with me."

He stills, his surprise and elation that I asked echoing through our connection. "The rebels would never accept me." His response is slow, and I can tell he's genuinely considering coming with me.

"They would if I explain who you are to me," I insist, my words breathless and rushed. I can't guarantee any of this, but I don't believe Fabien would hurt him. He already knows Elijah is my mate, after all.

Slowly, Elijah shakes his head. "I don't know if I can leave, the power the master has over me—"

I place my hands on top of his where they rest on my shoulders. "I'll help you," I promise, my voice cracking with emotion. "Come with me, please."

The look on his face breaks my heart, like he's taking me in for the last time. He cups my cheeks, and my hands drop to rest on his waist. Making a desperate noise in the back of his throat, he pulls me forward and kisses me like it's the last thing he's ever going to do. I melt against him despite the chaos in the castle, and all other sounds fall away as our lips move against each other. When he pulls back, the sadness in his eyes is enough to make me cry. He takes my hand in his.

"Come on, let's go," he urges, tugging me gently.

The fighting is getting closer now, yet I can't help but notice how he never actually agreed to come with me. I'm too afraid to voice my suspicion in case I'm right. We hurry through the hallways until I see a large staircase, the space glowing with the orange hue of the sunset. As we get closer, I realise the light isn't shining through windows like I expected. Half of the wall is missing. Gasping at the destruction, I glance up at Elijah, but he's already making his way down the stairs, picking his way over the rubble.

We're lucky the stairs don't collapse as we hurry down them, the creaking sound making me move faster. When we reach the bottom, all I see is chaos. *Mother above*, I curse, not knowing where to look. Apanthe are fighting fae of all shapes and sizes. The power zipping through the room makes the air seem electric, and I realise how unprotected I am. Reaching inside myself, I take a deep breath and slowly release a tiny amount of power, moulding it into a shield around me. Once it's strong enough, I shut down my connection and brick it back up.

We're in the entrance of the castle, the grand doors smashed open, and beyond, I can see a figure with a large set of wings arching over his shoulders. That must be Caldor, and somehow, I have to get to him. When I look up at Elijah, I see his face has gone pale, and he's wearing an expression of horror.

"Annalise, the master is coming. You have to go *now*," he orders in a rush, pushing me towards the doors.

Holding my ground, I shake my head vehemently. "Not without you."

A flash of pain crosses his face for a second, but it's quickly replaced by resolve. "When he gets here, he will force me to try and stop you. You need to leave."

A loud roar like that of a lion rips through the room, briefly stopping the battle as everyone turns to watch the master stride forward. The fighting quickly resumes, but I keep my eyes locked on the threat prowling towards us.

"*Ma promessa*, just where do you think you're going?" he purrs, anger in his eyes. The fact I'm so close to freedom, that he almost lost me, infuriates him.

"I'm sorry," Elijah whispers to me, wrapping me in his

arms tightly before pushing me away and turning to face the master. I feel him reaching for his power, the strength of it monumental as it builds around him. Whatever he has planned, it's going to be destructive, not just harming the master, but himself too.

No, he can't do this.

The master opens his mouth, his rage palpable, and I know he's going to order Elijah to stop—only the order never comes. Another blast rocks the castle, much closer this time, knocking me to the ground with the force of the blow. On my hands and knees, I look behind me to see the corridor smoking as dust falls from the ceiling. I know I should be running, but shock has set in, and I simply stare at the dark hole that had been a hallway only seconds ago. A figure appears in the smoke, and to my amazement, Fabien sprints to my side. He's covered in ash and cuts, but he isn't acting injured. In fact, he seems more concerned about checking me over.

"Annalise, come, we have to go," he orders, but I barely hear him over the ringing in my ears.

Looking back at Elijah, I see he's locked in a battle of wills with the master, his hands balled into fists at his sides.

"You have to leave him here."

I look up at Fabien, my eyes glistening with tears, but I hold them back. I know he's right. Now that the master's here, we've lost our window of opportunity. Stumbling to my feet, I lean against Fabien as he hurries through the entranceway, using his power to knock the guards back. When we reach the doors, we race down the stairs, and I breathe in the open air for the first time since I was brought here.

There are more rebels out here, and Caldor is waiting

by the front gates. As we hurry forward, I can feel the eagle fae's eyes on me, but I'm too focused on what's happening to the bond between Elijah and me. He's trying to anchor himself in the bond, and if our connection had been completed, it might have worked.

"Fabien, good to see you alive and causing a scene, as usual," a deep voice says sarcastically, and I look up to see that Caldor is jogging towards us. Tall with bronze skin, his golden armour glints all the more in the fading light.

The bond between Elijah and me suddenly becomes taut, making me gasp and stumble to the ground. Elijah lost whatever battle he was in with the master, and he's coming for us.

"Stop them! Do not let the *promessa* escape!" the master roars, and all attention turns to us.

Fabien kneels at my side, trying to pull me up and get me moving, but I'm watching the doorway where Elijah appears. His power rises once more, and with a wave of his hands, half of the rebels to our left fall to the ground, all crying out in pain. All emotion other than determination has been wiped from Elijah's face, but I can feel his horror as he tries to fight against the master's order. He won't hurt me, that much I'm sure of—our bond, whole or not, won't allow him to. That doesn't stop him from killing or maiming the rebels who are trying to help me escape though. Seeing him like this is painful, draining all the fight from me, and I realise I'll truly have to leave without him.

"Annalise," Fabien pleads, but he gives up when he realises I don't have the strength to stand. Grabbing my waist, he throws me over his shoulder, and the world bounces as he hurries to meet his friend.

"Is she okay?" the deep voice asks again, concern lacing his tone.

"Caldor, get her out of here," Fabien orders, passing me over to the other fae.

This wakes me up as I realise what's happening. Struggling against Caldor's iron hold, I look to Fabien in confusion. Over his shoulder, I can see Elijah getting closer with apanthe on his heels, cutting down any rebels in his path.

"Sorry about this," Caldor grumbles in my ear, holding me tighter and stretching his wings wide.

"No, wait!" I call out, reaching towards my mate, but it's too late. With one powerful beat of his wings, we're airborne, and Fabien and Elijah become smaller by the second.

Watching me being taken away seems to snap him from the master's control. Falling to his knees, Elijah reaches towards me. "Annalise!" he shouts, his voice breaking.

Heart shattering, I keep my eyes locked on him as I'm whisked into the sky, his broken bellow following us, and I don't bother to hide the tears that roll down my cheeks.

Epilogue

The beast rolls in the darkness with a wicked smile on his face as the feeling reaches him once more.

The promised one has awoken.

He has been locked in his prison for so long, he is but a whisper to those who walk the land, a scary tale to make young fae behave.

He will finally be free to roam the land once more, and when he does, no one will be safe.

The End

Pre-Order Now

A Spark of Promise: Book Two
www.books2read.com/SparkofPromise

Acknowledgements

This last year has been crazy. There have been immense lows, as I'm sure the rest of the world can agree with, but there have also been some amazing highs. In July last year I was able to become a full-time author. The fact I can do what I love everyday has been amazing, but of course I wouldn't have been able to do any of this without the support of the people behind me.

My husband and family, you help me through the bad days and celebrate with me on the good.

My PA team help keep me on track, I'd be useless without them. Of course, without my amazing editing team, none of these words would make sense. A huge thank you to Norma who stepped in at last minute to proofread for me. Kaila, my formatter- you're awesome. Thank you to Jodie who made my covers, I just love them.

My author tribe, you know who you are, I couldn't do this without the support and angry Gifs when I mess with a character you love.

Finally, as always, thank you to you, the reader. None of this would be possible without you.

Also By

The Shadowborn Series:

Hunted by Shadows

Lost in Shadow

Embraced by Shadows

The Shadowborn series- the boxset

Born From Shadows Series:

Demons do it Better

The War and Deceit Series:

Fires of Hatred

Fires of Treason

Fires of Ruin

Fires of War

Fires of the Fae:

A Lady of Embers

Erin O'Kane and K.A Knight

Her Freaks Series:

Circus Save Me
Taming the Ringmaster

The Wild Boys:

The Wild Interview
The Wild Tour
The Wild Finale
The Wild Boys Series- the boxset

Erin O'Kane and Loxley Savage:

Twisted Tides
Tides that Bind

About the Author

Erin lives in the UK with her husband and now works full time as an independent author. She started writing in 2018 when she published her first book, *Hunted by Shadows*. She specialises in writing fantasy and reverse harem paranormal romance.

She met K. A. Knight in 2018 when they became partners in crime and began writing together. In 2019, she became co-authors with Loxley Savage, writing fantasy reverse harem.

She's Disney obsessed, loves cookies and baking, and is always planning her next story.

Printed in Great Britain
by Amazon